TOO MUCH STUFF

TOO MUCH STUFF

A NOVEL

DON BRUNS

Oceanview Publishing

LONGBOAT KEY, FLORIDA

ISBN 978-1-60809-017-4

Published in the United States of America by Oceanview Publishing,
Longboat Key, Florida
www.oceanviewpub.com

2 4 6 8 10 9 7 5 3 1

PRINTED IN THE UNITED STATES OF AMERICA

To the souls who lost their lives in the Florida hurricane of 1935.

ACKNOWLEDGMENTS

Thanks to Kathy Ebert at the Islamorada, Florida Library. She was immensely helpful in digging up the facts I needed about the 1935 hurricane. Thanks also to Wendy Dewhurst and Bill Lodermeier who filled me in on a scuba diving segment.

A shout out to Kathy Salvatori at Pelican Cove Resort who has been a friend for many years, and to all of the bars and restaurants in Islamorada that play a part in my tale.

The cemetery at Cheeca Lodge really does exist, and if I took some liberties with other places and historical facts, remember, this is a work of fiction.

Thanks to Chris Combs from JW Fishers Manufacturing, who taught me about metal detectors, and to Charlie at Tuff Tie, makers of disposable handcuffs. Famed sculptor Mark Anderson explained sand sculpting to me. A special thanks to Bob and Pat who champion the writing, to Maryglenn McCombs who is my wonderful publicist, to the entire Oceanview team, and to my wife, Linda, who always reads the first pass.

The book *Too Much Stuff* was much inspired by Les Standiford's book, *Last Train to Paradise.* I highly recommend his story of Henry Flagler's railroad to Key West.

Finally, thank you to Mary Trueblood, Maria Sanko, Dr. Praveen Malhotra, Dr. James O'Neill, and Matthew Kriegel, who donated generously to nonprofit organizations so they could be characters in this novel.

Don Bruns, Sarasota, Florida

Once there was a railroad whose tracks went out to sea,
It chugged across the islands, stopping on each Key.
It slowed down on the bridges so passengers could see
The Florida East Coast Railroad really rumbling over the sea.

In '35 a hurricane blew away that train,
But on a quiet moonlit night it goes to sea again.
And if you listen carefully you'll hear a ghostly clack
As the Florida East Coast Railway goes rumbling down the track.

From a plaque in Islamorada, Florida

TOO MUCH STUFF

CHAPTER ONE

It took six years for Henry Flagler to build his railroad to Key West. It took two-hundred-mile-an-hour winds and an eighteen-foot tidal wave about sixty seconds to bring it down. Give or take a dozen or so people, five hundred souls were lost in that horrific storm. And even though James and I had studied that event in eighth grade Florida history, I'd never read about the Florida East Coast Railway finance director, Matthew Kriegel, and the ten crates of gold bullion that he supposedly loaded onto Old 447's baggage car that fateful September 2, 1935.

I'd learned about the treasure from Mary Trueblood, Kriegel's great-granddaughter, when my girlfriend Emily gave her one of my business cards, More or Less Investigations. And I also learned that the gold, $1.2 million worth back then, had never been found.

What Mary Trueblood failed to tell me at the time was that the last investigation team she hired to find the gold had disappeared and not been heard from in over six months. Of course, my partner James Lessor would have taken the job anyway. Even though we were simply offered expenses.

"Expenses, *and* a percentage, Skip. Do you know what that gold is worth today? Over thirty-four thousand ounces? More than forty-four million dollars, amigo. And she's willing to give us a half percent. That's two hundred and twenty thousand dollars, dude."

James pulled one of my beers from our tiny refrigerator, popped the top, and took a long swallow.

"She'll give us half a percent *if* we find this phantom gold. And who's to say it's hers to claim, James?" James always thinks we're going to strike it rich. A fortune is just around the corner.

"Listen, pally, the company doesn't exist anymore. Flagler's railway company went under after the hurricane. That means the gold is finder's keepers. Like Mel Fisher's shipwreck treasure."

I seemed to remember that the state of Florida claimed at least 25 percent of any treasure that was discovered. That was already diluting our find by fifty-five thousand dollars.

"What about our jobs?" This private investigating company wasn't exactly a full-time gig.

"Skip, my man, do we really care about these dead-end jobs?"

He had a point. As college grads we had bottomed out in grades *and* our job search. James was a line cook at a fast-food place called Cap'n Crab in Carol City, Florida, and I sold security systems to people in the same town—a town where no one had any money, any prospects, or anything they needed to secure. We needed a change and the far-off chance of making one hundred sixty-five thousand dollars did sound tempting.

"So maybe we ask for leaves of absence." A couple of weeks to see if we could locate this fortune in lost gold. "At least we've got something to come back to."

James shook his head and took another swallow of my Yuengling beer. He was slouched on the stained sofa, feet propped up on the scarred coffee table in our tiny Carol City apartment.

"Jobs? We don't need no stinking jobs."

I smiled. James was a wiz with the movie quotes, but he had this one wrong.

"It's badges. We don't need no stinkin' *badges. The Treasure of the Sierra Madre.* Humphrey Bogart, nineteen forty-seven."

"Forty-eight, but it's kind of fitting don't you think?"

"I'll tell you what's fitting, my friend. It's another quote from that same movie."

"Give."

I concentrated for a few seconds. "Gold itself ain't good for nothing except—"

"Except what?"

"I'm working on it." I channeled the movie. "Gold itself ain't good for nothing except making jewelry with and gold teeth."

"Good one, mate." James was genuinely impressed.

I can't explain it. The two of us remember a lot of trivial, useless crap.

We both finished our beers and it got real quiet.

"Skip, this Mary Trueblood, she's got the treasure map."

"Well, she's got an idea of where this stuff may have gone."

"Dude, we'll get leaves of absence. We'll get some expense money up front and take two weeks off. If we find the gold, we're each rolling in it. If we don't, it's an adventure, right?"

Adventures with my best friend James have almost gotten us killed. Several times. I should remember that a lot more than I do.

CHAPTER TWO

The Chevy box truck was low on gas and two quarts low on oil as James pulled into the Exxon station. He shoved the prepaid credit card into the slot and was pumping fuel in fifteen seconds.

One thousand dollars. That's what Mrs. Trueblood had put on the card. If we needed more, all we had to do was ask her. If she thought we were being frugal with her funds, she would supply more. On the chance that I could make forty-four million dollars, I know that I would advance more.

"Take the card, buy a case of oil, and we should be set, amigo."

I studied the truck. The magnetic signs on the side were nothing but reminders to me that we'd had *one* investigating job. More or Less Investigations. Yes, we were licensed by the state of Florida. But that didn't mean that everyone who needed a PI firm called us.

It didn't mean that anyone called us. I'd started a Facebook page for More or Less Investigations, and the only response I got was from kids who graduated from our high school. They were laughing at our endeavor, letting us know that if we were the same two guys they remembered from six years ago, we weren't qualified to be dogcatchers.

I'm not sure that they were wrong.

I started a Twitter account, but only heard from people who wanted to know where our next "gig" was. I didn't get that. And LinkedIn tended to be people who wanted business advice or wanted to sell something.

The business advice I had for them was: You need a private investigating firm. And for those who wanted to sell me something, I had no money to buy it.

So much for social networking. Mark Zuckerberg made billions by inventing Facebook. I was making squat.

I walked out with the case of oil and James drained two quarts into the engine. That process would be repeated many times during our trip.

"We could buy a brand-new truck if this deal comes through, Skip."

"We could." It was more of a mutter than a solid statement.

The drive into the Keys is not this adventurous, Third World country experience that some people imagine. They picture a jungle-like atmosphere, with thick mangrove trees and flocks of ospreys, forgotten outposts scattered by the water on each side of what is laughingly called a highway, and mysterious waterfront bars with Edward G. Robinson and Humphrey Bogart drinking rum, smoking cigars, and planning nefarious deeds.

No, it's nothing like that. It's two lanes of traffic, occasionally broken by the excitement of four lanes for fifteen seconds where everyone floors the gas pedal to pass all the really slow drivers.

And when your Chevy box truck only goes fifty-eight miles per hour at its top end, you really can't make up a lot of time. I had to face it. *We* were one of the really slow drivers.

Nonetheless, James kept on course. There is no other solution. If you want to get to Islamorada, you just keep it pointing south.

Occasionally, there are some breaks, like a diver's supply shop that put up a billboard, LAST CHANCE FOR ALCOHOL, 34 MILES. People certainly didn't want to drive to the Keys sober.

And in the middle of scrub pine and scrawny bushes, on this narrow strip of land that extends to Key West, there's a sign saying: 7 ACRES. $175,000. What would you do with it? Put up a liquor store and sell alcohol?

"Remember D. B. Cooper?" James was smoking a cigarette, blowing most of his product out the window at some cheap shell shops and a roadside cigar store.

"The guy hijacked a plane, right?"

He nodded. "Nineteen seventy-one, Portland to Seattle, this mysterious stranger grabs a flight attendant and tells her he has a bomb in his briefcase. When they land in Seattle, he asks for two hundred thousand dollars and a couple of parachutes."

The story was that D.B. jumped somewhere over Washington State and was never found. Five or six thousand dollars were recovered years later by some hikers, and the FBI figure to this day that he died in the jump, but it's the only unsolved airline hijacking case in history.

"I know the story, James."

"Never found the money, Tonto. Never found the body."

"And your point is?"

"Well, we need to do some research on the Kriegel guy. He had the gold, and when the hurricane hit, he could have used that as an excuse to split and take the bullion with him."

I shook my head. "Do you know how much that stuff would have weighed? You don't just *split* with ten cases of gold. That would be—"

"Over two thousand pounds of the yellow stuff. I figured it out."

James kept his eyes on the road, and we passed a place called the Caribbean Club. A big billboard there announced that this was where the movie *Key Largo* was filmed. So there *were* some bars where Bogey and Edward G. Robinson had hung out.

The faded letters also announced that the Caribbean Club featured karaoke every Wednesday. Too bad it was Thursday.

"Are you thieves or what?" James glanced at me with a sly grin on his face. "You want money, is this a robbery?"

We'd spent too many hours watching the old movies during college, when we should have been studying, and this one with Bogart and Edward G. was a classic. I knew the answer.

"Yeah, Pop, we're gonna steal all your towels."

And then we passed Craig's, with an even bigger sign that touted: HOME OF THE WORLD-FAMOUS FISH SANDWICH. We were "crackers." Florida natives. You'd think we would have heard of this. It being world famous and all.

Suddenly all the brake lights in front of us lit up at once. Red as far as the eye could see.

"Shit. Probably some accident up ahead."

The Keys were legendary for traffic jams that could last all day. Or, in some cases, days.

"We've got four cases of beer."

My roommate nodded. "Two big jars of peanut butter, a couple of jars of strawberry jam, and four loaves of bread." We did. In the back of the truck. Just in case the money ran out.

"So, if there's a traffic stop, we're good for—"

"Oh, hell, at least two days."

CHAPTER THREE

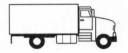

We met Mary Trueblood at Pelican Cove. The place is a neat little waterside resort very close to where the train went off the track. You can rent a motel-type room that can be expanded to have a kitchenette, or expanded further to a two- or three-bedroom suite with living room, Jacuzzi, and kitchen if you had the keys to open the proper connecting doors. Heck, you could own the entire place. If you had enough money. We had all kinds of money. Expense money. If we could prove that we needed that money. To be honest, we'd already spent four hundred dollars on a laptop computer. That and the fill-up and a case of oil. And the beer and peanut butter. So we were already watching our pennies. We had to have a computer with us, didn't we?

As we stared at the sparkling water from her balcony, Mrs. T. passed out margaritas. "Boys, there's a fortune out there. Are you up to finding it?"

I had a coach in high school who pushed the cross-country team the same way. "Boys, are you ready for an adventure? Are you up to running hundreds of miles each and every week?"

I wasn't and I quit the team four days into the season.

Glory and honor do not compare to thousands of dollars, so in this case I put up with Mrs. Trueblood's little speech.

"Matthew Kriegel had ten containers of gold on that train."

"Why?"

Who loads ten crates of gold onto a train?

"Fair question," she responded. "The Flagler enterprise, by now called the Florida East Coast Railway, consisted of railroads, hotels, restaurants, whorehouses, gambling casinos—"

"Slow down." She had James's attention.

"Did I say something that you didn't understand?"

"Whorehouses?" He gulped at his drink.

She gave him a stern, schoolmarm look.

"Whorehouses." She pointed back to where the two-lane highway ran. "Brothels. There had been thousands of people out there working on the railroad. Thousands. Almost one hundred percent of those people were men."

"And?"

"Do I have to spell it out for you? The men worked better— more productively—if they had some release. Mr. Flagler was against it. Very much opposed to the floating party boats, the gambling, the girls, and the booze, but his company quietly funded some of those more seamy ventures."

"Ah." James absorbed it.

"And even after Henry Flagler died, the enterprise kept producing. There were always camps of men working on maintaining the railroad. There was property that needed to be purchased. The federal highway construction crews were building a road to paradise and there were existing Flagler businesses that needed cash infusions."

"Lots of places to spend money." I got it. I assumed that James did too.

"There had to be places to go if the railroad was to get riders. There had to be destinations."

The lady sipped her margarita and gazed outside at the azure-blue water where two lodgers kayaked in bright yellow skiffs. Inside, Mrs. T. had the bright kitchenette, the seductive Jacuzzi, and all the other amenities. We had one room and a bath.

I noticed James checking her out in her black one-piece. She'd been on the beach sunning herself and she'd come directly to her suite. This lady probably could have been James's mother, but it didn't stop him from looking. Dark hair, great figure, a smooth tan. I had to admit, for an older lady she was hot.

"So the assumption is that they needed the gold to support activities in the Keys. Gold was used a lot back then."

"But this was a rescue train. They threw it together at the last minute, didn't they? I thought its purpose was strictly to bring camps of highway workers back up to Miami. I mean, these guys were going to be in the middle of this hurricane and they were housed in tents." I remembered the story well.

She smiled, standing up and stretching herself. James never took his eyes off of her body. "Boys, no one had a clue how strong that storm would be. My great-grandfather was going to leave for Islamorada the next day and his boss decided to send him down early. It's as simple as that. The Flagler system wanted him to spend the gold on the various enterprises that the system owned and enterprises they *wanted* to own.

"He and a security guard were going to be dropped off, with the gold, and spend a week in Islamorada and points south. They had a car waiting for him, a driver, a room that was reserved at the Coral Belle Hotel, but there is no record of exactly what the expenditures would be used for. There was speculation that he was going to purchase another hotel, and possibly a fishing camp located nearby. He would purchase more places for tourists to travel when they took the train."

I swallowed the sour drink and absorbed the information. That's what good PIs do. They absorb information.

"The Florida East Coast Railway looked at this last train ride more as goodwill than as a means to divert a catastrophe. I believe the managers and the owners thought this hurricane was going to pass them by, but they would look like heroes coming down on a white horse and saving these six hundred fifty plus workers."

"And this money, this gold, was going to be used to buy property and support whorehouses and casinos throughout the Keys?"

James couldn't leave that alone.

I got off the edge of my chair and approached the lady.

"I apologize for my friend. As you've noticed, he can be a little immature."

"But I'm charming, Skip. I've got my charm going for me."

Mary Trueblood smiled. "Gentlemen, Florida was born with graft, corruption, whorehouses, and gambling saloons. Like the Old West, this was cattle country and railroad country. Cowboys and construction workers are the same wherever you go."

"So the gold was never found."

"It disappeared. There were those who thought it washed out to sea, but I would think that the sheer weight of it would have prevented that."

I had a vision of James and me diving for sunken treasure, swimming back up with a gold bar clutched in my hand.

"And your great-grandfather?" I already knew the answer.

"His body was never recovered. Neither was the security guy's."

"But," James stated, "most of those bodies weren't ever identified. You told us that they burned hundreds of them before the rotting corpses started an epidemic."

"That's true. Apparently some of the workers wore gas masks. The stench was terrible and when they burned them in funeral pyre-style, it was even worse."

11

"Must have been a very nasty experience."

"I've seen pictures," she said. "Heads torn off bodies, tree limbs buried in people's chests, bloated bodies twenty feet up in the trees."

Information overload.

"So," I walked to the balcony edge and drained my drink, hoping she'd offer another, "you think you know where the gold is."

"I have some direction."

"If they never identified his body and never found the gold, then how would you have a clue?" James just blurted it right out.

Mary Trueblood smiled, a thin-lipped smirk. "Because my great-grandmother got a letter."

"Okay."

"I found it in an old jewelry box when we cleaned out my mother's home after she died. There was no signature and the whole thing was very cryptic."

I glanced at my partner and saw that gleam in his eye. "Who was it from?"

I added, "So what did it say?"

"Oh, I'll go you one better." She walked inside to her open suitcase that was sitting on a bench and pulled out an envelope. "It was from Matthew Kriegel to his wife, my great-grandmother, and I made a copy. This is for you."

CHAPTER FOUR

The letter was two paragraphs long. Short and sweet, the flow of the dark blue ink was like a work of art. Thick, luxurious swirls of letters that are lost in today's computerized world. I mean, why would you?

> *My Dear Mary,*
> *Upon receiving this, you can assume that something has happened to me. By following our aforementioned guidelines, I leave you with this.*

From that point on it was a jumble of letters spelling words I couldn't even pronounce.

> *Sohdvh frph wr lvodprdgd dqg—*

We both stared at the letter. Code. The only thing close to code I'd ever used was lemon juice. As kids, James and I, along with a handful of neighborhood buddies, would write messages using citric acid. When it dried on the paper, it was invisible. When you held it up to a candle or a hot lightbulb, the message would materialize. Of course our messages were not quite as important as the location of forty-four million dollars worth of gold. We wrote things like, "Meet you at my house after school."

"Do you want us to figure this out? Is that part of the job?"

Mary Trueblood smiled, then licked salt from the rim of her glass. "No. I've already figured out the code."

"So? What does it say?"

"It's what it doesn't say."

By definition, a code is cryptic. The Trueblood lady had solved the code and now *she* was being cryptic.

"So," I tried to bring some common sense into the conversation, "what doesn't it say?"

Holding the copy she pointed to the jumble of letters.

"Every letter is three letters off in the alphabet."

James stood up and walked over to her, taking the paper from her. She touched his arm and gave him a very sweet look.

"So if the letter is *A*, it's really *D*?"

"Exactly, James."

I interrupted the intimate moment. "Mary—Mrs. Trueblood—excuse me, but what is the message?"

"Obviously it's from my great-grandfather. Written to his wife, as I said. He says, in a very short message, that he has survived the storm."

"That's it? Why did he write in code? Was this something they did for fun?" It made no sense to me.

"As to why the code, I have no idea. And as to the content of the letter, of course there is more," her voice stern like a schoolteacher's. "He describes the location of a hotel that had been blown off of its foundation. The Coral Belle. The two-story inn had been owned by the railroad, and, as I said, this was where Matthew Kriegel was to stay the night of the hurricane."

"Why would he describe someplace that didn't exist anymore?"

"First of all, there were sixty-three buildings in Islamorada before the hurricane. Sixty-one of them were blown apart. But," she pointed her finger at James, "the foundation of the inn remained. It was made from actual poured concrete."

"And?" I hated people who dragged out a story. James, on the other hand, was like a puppy dog, hanging on her every word.

"And, he said that if she did not hear from him in four weeks, she should find her way from Miami to Islamorada and dig under the southeast corner of the stone and concrete slab."

James was practically salivating. "How cool. He buried the gold. Oh, man, buried treasure."

She shook her head. "The letter alludes to the fact that there would be instructions for her there. To bury that much gold he'd need more than the corner of a slab of concrete. This was ten crates of gold, each weighing two hundred pounds."

A telephone rang from inside the suite and she went to answer it.

"Pard, this could be very cool. I mean if no one ever found the instructions it could mean that—"

"And I'm certain that the slab under the Coral Belle is still right where it was, seventy-five years later." Give me a break.

He was quiet for a moment. "There's always that."

"James, it sounds like a wild-goose chase. We were crazy for coming here. You know it, I know it."

"Dude, she's investing some money in this venture. She believes the gold is here, and the lady is no dummy."

She walked back onto the balcony, a thin cover-up thrown over her bathing suit and I noticed the look of disappointment on my friend's face.

"We may have a little problem."

It was so unusual for James and me to have any problems. Only about every ten minutes.

15

"What is it? Something we can take care of?"

She shook her head. "I don't know. Someone called the resort office and asked if I'd registered here."

"A friend? Relative?"

"No." She walked to the edge of the balcony, gripping the rail with one hand and looking out at the water.

"Who?"

"I didn't tell anyone where I was going. No one. You two are the only people who knew where I was going and where I was staying."

"Wow." James was impressed to be in select company.

"And I told you not to say a word to anyone."

"I didn't." I hadn't even told Emily, my girlfriend, and I tell her almost everything. That is, when we're speaking.

"Skip?" She had this disapproving look in her eyes. "Your girlfriend Emily is the one who gave me your business card. She's the reason I hired you. Are you positive you didn't tell her where you were going?"

"To the Keys. That's all I said."

She swung her gaze to James.

He shook his head back and forth.

"You're sure?"

James turned to me. "Well, I might have just mentioned it to the manager at Cap'n Crab. Julie wanted to know why I was taking two weeks off work."

"You mentioned this specific spot?"

"Oh, maybe I mentioned something," his voice faded away.

"Someone knows I'm here. My guess is they also know why."

"This thing happened over seventy-five years ago. I mean who would know? Who would care?"

"Who would care? Let me tell you something. Something I didn't share with you before."

A cold chill went down my spine.

"I hired another detective agency to look into this."

James's eyes got wider. "So there's someone else down here?"

"I don't know."

"But you just said—"

"I said I hired an agency."

James frowned. "Did they find this information buried somewhere under the old Coral Belle?"

She hesitated, then spun around and looked at both of us.

"I don't know. I don't think so. They came down here, and I hadn't yet given them all the details that they needed."

"That means?"

"I hadn't translated the letter."

The lady liked to give half the story. You had to pull the rest out of her.

"So what happened to them? Did they find anything or not?"

"Six months ago, they vanished."

"Vanished?"

"Vanished."

A very descriptive term. Disappeared. You'd think maybe they got lost in the fog. But vanished. That was the ultimate disappearance. Without a trace.

"No sign of them, no calls?"

"Nothing."

"What do you think happened?"

She shook her pretty head, the hair moving softly around her face.

"I have no idea. Their phone in Fort Lauderdale has been disconnected, letters have been returned, and their website has been taken down."

Letters and websites. Old school. "You've tried texting, Facebook, Twitter?"

"Nothing."

That chill went down my spine again.

17

"That's why I'm here this time. I don't want something happening to you guys."

More like, *I'm not sure I can trust anyone.*

"So our job is to find the information, or map, or whatever it is that's there?"

James jumped in. "We do *not* follow maps to buried treasure, and *X never, ever* marks the spot."

I had to think for a moment. *Indiana Jones and the Last Crusade.* It was a line Harrison Ford throws out to his students.

"Just a movie quote," I said to her.

The lady looked puzzled. "Well, in this case he may be right. I'm not sure we'll find a map, and I'm not certain that we'll find the *X*, or the exact location of the old hotel."

She walked to her door, both of us following like puppy dogs.

"There's one more job that we have to do."

"Yeah?"

"Yeah. We've got to find Todd Markim and Jim Weezle."

"Weezle?" It was all James could do not to laugh out loud.

"The investigators who came down here. Their company is—was—AAAce Investigations."

Trying to be first in the Yellow Pages. AAA. I had to give them credit.

"And why do you want to find them?"

She opened the door, and waved her hand. She wanted us out of the room, no question about that.

"Two things could have happened to them. One, somehow they found the information, and maybe the gold. In that case they are buying their vanishing act. They've taken off with the treasure and we'll never hear from them again."

"And number two?"

"They were killed by someone who wanted to have the gold for themselves."

TOO MUCH STUFF

She closed the door, leaving us on the outside walkway, looking at each other, and wondering what we'd gotten ourselves into.

CHAPTER FIVE

There was another hurricane where stolen gold was involved. In 1733 a hurricane grounded a Spanish ship loaded with treasure on what is now Islamorada. Wreckers, land pirates who went out and looted wrecked ships, made off with all of the loot. Historians believe they took it down to Key West and as a result, Key West became the richest city in the country. The richest city in the entire United States.

The state of Florida was, by Mary Trueblood's definition, a land of cattle barons and railroad magnates. But my impression of my home state was a country of pirates. Surrounded by water on three sides, Florida was ripe for the seafaring trade and those who preyed on that trade.

We'd taken the magnetic MORE OR LESS INVESTIGATIONS signs off the truck and put them in our room. James replaced them with SMITH BROTHERS PLUMBING signs.

"We're basically undercover, amigo. May as well disguise the truck."

I thought it was a dumb idea. It had gotten us in trouble before, with people mistaking us for real plumbers.

"Why don't you just leave the truck naked, James? No signs. We don't have to be anything."

He dismissed the idea with the wave of his hand.

As my best friend drove the oil-burning vehicle south, he puffed on a small cigar.

"You know, amigo, somebody stole a gold bar from Mel Fisher's sunken treasure museum in Key West a couple of years ago. Thing was worth ninety-nine thou. All kinds of security, and these two guys just waltzed in and lifted it."

"Your point is?"

"I think this Kriegel stole the gold. I think he saw his chance and took it. Think about it, dude. The ultimate heist. Everybody thinks you're dead and that the gold has washed out to sea."

I seemed to remember that the state of Florida claimed at least twenty-five percent of the treasure when Mel Fisher found the wreck of the *Atocha*, the Spanish galleon that sank back in the sixteen hundreds off the coast of Key West. Twenty-five percent. That was already diluting our take of fifty-five thousand dollars.

"And where did he take it?"

"Key West."

"Back then, you could get lost in Key West."

Some vehicle with a loud engine was behind us, and I caught the driver coming around on James's side of the truck. It was a black Harley-Davidson motorcycle with a shiny gold fender. The driver wore a dark helmet with the Plexiglas face guard pulled down. The bike screamed by with its trademark roar and James flashed him the finger.

"Damn, these lanes are narrow enough."

We watched the bike disappear in the distance, then James got a grin on his face.

"Ooooh. I know. Cuba. Damn, you could sail to Cuba back then. Rum drinks, sexy women, gambling. I think back then a guy could get lost in Cuba and have a very good life for a million-plus dollars in gold."

"Well, if he took the gold to Cuba, we sure aren't going to find it here."

"Point well taken." He was silent for a moment. "So officially I don't think he went to Cuba. The gold is here in Islamorada, and we're going to find it."

I had to smile. "We've got a clue. A real clue with that letter."

James glanced over at me, both hands on the wheel. "Another clue. Which will lead to another clue, which will lead to another clue. That's all there will ever be—another clue."

I knew it, but couldn't place it.

"You're slipping, partner. *National Treasure*. Nicolas Cage."

We were on our own for lunch and it was an expense. So, on the card. We decided on The Green Turtle.

"According to the Internet report you Googled, this was one of the two places that survived the hurricane."

I nodded. The Rustic Inn, as it was called in 1935, was the only structure that suffered almost no damage. There was a hotel that had been hit pretty hard, and the Rustic Inn. That was all that remained.

"I don't think this is the original building, but this is the spot where the survivors met."

The story we'd read was that the Rustic turned out to be the meeting place for all the survivors. Not many of them were left, but if you showed up after the storm, at least you were alive. There were families with, like fifty members who lost all but ten. The more I read about the hurricane, the more I heard stories, the worse it seemed. Almost no one had lived in Islamorada before the storm. You subtract five hundred from almost no one and what do you have? Not much.

We passed Cheeca Lodge, the location of a resort that had

been thriving during the '30s. Vicks Chemical Corporation or some other big business had built a resort on the property in the early 1900s, and alongside of it was Millionaire's Row. Some of the hotshot northerners who owned big companies built vacation mansions on that row. Those homes were blown away by the '35 hurricane, and I would bet that most of the priveledged owners were up north when it happened. As I pointed out, only two businesses survived the big wind and tidal wave. Only two.

James pulled into the parking lot of the Turtle and we got out of the truck.

"Damn!"

James was staring at his side of the truck, his fists clenched and his face screwed up in a frown.

I walked around the vehicle, and checked out what he was looking at. Spattered across the side of the truck was what appeared to be black paint.

"Who would do that?"

I shrugged my shoulders.

"And why?"

"We'll get some rags and—"

"What? Smear it?" He banged his fist on the back of the box truck. "No, we'll get some solvent and do it right, back at the resort."

In spite of the paint, in spite of the mess, I smiled. And James smiled. Resort. We'd never stayed at a resort in our lives. A poolside bar, waterfront, an ocean view. This wasn't bad at all.

"Let's grab some lunch, pard."

And with that we walked into The Green Turtle. Could have been the best move we made the entire trip, because we met Maria. But as it turned out, it wasn't.

CHAPTER SIX

At The Green Turtle there's a room out back with a sunporch feeling. Wicker chairs, windows, and a cheery, open-air atmosphere. Plus, James could smoke. And of course, I had to cater to James's worst habits. So, that's where we sat. Our laptop was in the bag next to my seat.

"If we're going to figure this out, we have to find out where the Coral Belle was located. Our primary job is finding that gold. If it still exists." I assumed that this was the primary objective. Under the Coral Belle foundation was some clue regarding the treasure.

"Let's explore the other end of this." James sipped his beer.

"I thought finding the gold was the end."

"Skip," he took a drag on his cigarette, "there could be a good deal of work involved in this investigation. We've got a very limited amount of time to spend on it. Am I right?"

"You are."

"Okay, follow me. We need to see if we can find AAAce Investigations."

I stared at him for a moment. "What the hell are you talking about?" I swallowed a quarter of the bottle of my beer, thinking we should have had some breakfast.

"The lady said find Markim and Weezle." A broad smile now on his face. "Wouldn't you change your name if it was Weezle. Weezle, for God's sake." Then he broke out in a muted chuckle. "Weezle!"

"James, that's a sidebar adventure. We're here to find the gold."

"And Skip, what if our boys, our crackerjack investigators Markim and Weezle already have the information? What then?"

"I've lost you, dude."

"Pay attention. These guys come down here and get lucky. They find a diary, a map, a letter."

"And?"

"We'd be better off to find *them*. They've done all the work. Now all we have to do is just get the information from *them*."

James had a point. It came from his lazy nature, but he had a point.

"So, Mrs. Trueblood says that their website is down. Their phone has been disconnected."

"And?"

"Pull out our computer, my friend."

I took it from the bag.

"Check it out." He pointed to a small sign on the wall. "Free Wi-Fi."

"James," the guy seemed oblivious to the facts, "they've vanished. These two detectives no longer exist."

"Google Yellow Pages."

I did.

"Now, in the search box, type in AAAce Investigations."

I did.

"So, what did you find?"

"A site."

"Ah, grasshopper, but not a personal website. They've taken that one down. But, they probably didn't take down sites from some reviewers. Am I right? Tell me I'm right."

"Yeah, of course. You're always right, James." He wasn't. But in this case—

"Click on the one that says photos."

I studied the options.

"How the hell did you know there would be—"

"Click it."

I did.

"Pictures, right?"

There were. I nodded. It was a Yellow Page ad that was still posted.

"Ah, I knew it. Ego guys. What do *we* have in our Yellow Page ad, pard?"

"*We* don't have a Yellow Page ad."

"Do you see? No ego." He drained his bottle, banging it on the table.

No money. That's what it boiled down to. James had ego. Trust me. If we'd had the money, James would be front and center in all the Yellow Page ads. Oh, my friend James had ego.

"Can we print this? Get a feeling for who these guys are? I want to know it when we run into them."

"We can print it back at the," I hesitated as the word made both of us smile, "resort."

We laughed out loud.

"Resort. Okay. Let's view the enemy. Hopefully we'll recognize them."

They stared at us from our computer screen, names under their photographs. Two guys not much older than we were. Weezle had a stubble of beard and a *Miami Vice* sort of wardrobe. T-shirt, jacket, and slacks. Markim, while not black like Tubbs,

26

was dressed like him in a suit with a tie and a very cocky look on his face. James and I didn't even own a tie. Between us.

The body copy in the photo ad read as follows.

AAAce Investigations. We succeed where others fail.
Undercover investigations
Photo service
Surveillance
Multiple vehicle surveillance—car, truck, boat, motorcycle
Discreet video and audio work
Wiretapping where legal

"It doesn't say where they are, James."

"No, but we know who they are."

I studied the faces. Two guys who had enough money to buy a Yellow Page ad. It was impressive. We didn't have a boat. We didn't have a—

"Skip, look at that ad again."

"I just did. We've got a car. Mine. It may not be worth much, but we've got a car."

"We've got a truck." James nodded his head.

"But we don't have a boat."

"No," James agreed, "and we don't have a motorcycle."

"But—"

"But, amigo, somebody ripped by us today on a motorcycle. And I've been thinking ever since that—"

"Yeah. That the guy on the motorcycle spattered the paint on the truck. Same thought, James."

"Excuse me." She came out of nowhere.

We both looked up and were surprised at the attractive woman approaching our table. She didn't appear to be a waitress.

"What can we do for you?" Charming James.

She smiled. She beamed. An almost flirtatious look on her

lovely face. "Do you own the truck outside? The white box truck with the splash of black paint on it?"

James frowned. "Yeah. What about it?"

She pulled up a chair and sat down. Maybe thirty-five, and very interesting. Very expressive eyes, dark, probably Italian, but you could never tell and—

"I'm Maria Sanko. I'm a realtor."

We both nodded. Women inviting themselves to our table was not something that happened on a regular basis.

"I was having lunch in the other room," she pointed to the main dining room, "and I got a text."

I could tell from James's puzzled look that neither of us had a clue where this was going.

"I manage a number of rental properties in the Islamorada area, and occasionally I get an emergency."

"Okay." I was impatient. The lady dragged the story on, just like Mary Trueblood.

"There's a major leak at one of my apartments, and I saw your truck—"

Shit. The Smith Brothers Plumbing sign.

"We don't . . . we can't . . ." James was stumbling. He'd turned pale, and I was concerned he was going to trip over his tongue.

"It's not far from here, and my tenant is really concerned. If you two could just follow me to—"

"I am sorry. What my friend is trying to tell you is that we're on vacation."

"Really, it won't take long. And I'll pay you whatever you say. I really need some help, guys."

"No, no. We left our tools back in Miami. There is nothing we could do. The truck is empty."

James's color returned. "Yeah. Tools are back in Miami. We're sorry."

The lady gave us a suspicious look, as she probably should have.

"Okay." She reached into her purse, pulling out a white business card. "If you are ever interested in moving down here, call me. I could use a good plumber. Not just now, but about every other day. And the guys down here, the guys who call themselves plumbers, they're working on island time."

"Next time, for sure. It's just that right now, we're not prepared." James flashed her a shaky lady-killer smile.

She stood up and walked away.

"You didn't want people to know we were investigators so you had the plumbing signs made."

"Yeah?"

"We could be called Smith Brothers Hauling. We could do that. Haul stuff. Or, like I told you, you could have just gone signless. Now, we stick out like a sore thumb. I mean, a plumbing truck with no tools and no plumbers."

"Yeah. I get your point."

"You know, James, sometimes your answer to a problem just causes more problems."

Little did I know how prophetic that statement would be.

CHAPTER SEVEN

James drove back to Pelican Cove, the magnetic Smith Brothers Plumbing signs now thrown in the back of the truck.

"Now we're just a white box truck with a splash of black paint on the side."

He was upset that our humble transportation now bore a scar. I didn't care so much about the scar, but I was happy we weren't plumbers any longer.

"Now no one will ask us to do them any favors." I breathed a sigh of relief. Signs? We didn't need no stinkin' signs.

"Dude, I wonder how much she would have paid us."

A question that had no answer. We had no talents in plumbing. Hell, we had no talents, period. I'm reminded of that from time to time.

"I think we could have made some serious jack, you know? She said to charge whatever we wanted. Who knows? Maybe we could have made enough on the side to get two rooms instead of one."

Oftentimes, I couldn't believe what came out of his mouth.

"James, it makes no difference." Sometimes I seriously think he's clueless. "Neither of us knows the first thing about plumbing."

"I can use a toilet plunger."

I didn't say anything.

"I thought of something you said back at the Turtle. Something you said about the gold and it got me thinking."

"Yeah?"

"You said finding the gold was the most important thing."

"I did." But I'd agreed that if we found the missing detectives, it could mean our job was a whole lot easier.

"First of all, I still think we need to find those two detectives. Their disappearance is way too strange."

I nodded my head in agreement.

"But you said finding the gold was the first priority. I already told you, I think if we find these two Miami hotshots we find the gold, but— "

"But what?"

"The lady. Maria Sanko."

"What about her? She's got a leaky pipe and no one to help her." It actually sounded dirty.

James chuckled. "Skip, she's a real estate lady."

"Yeah?"

"She knows about property and stuff."

James was doing the same thing, dragging the story on, like I was supposed to pick up on every—

"Ah." It hit me. "A real estate person just might know where older properties were located. Right?"

"Right, amigo. This lady might be able to tell us where the Coral Belle hotel used to be."

Sometimes he hit a home run. Not that often, but—

"James, that's a great idea. You've got her card. Let's call her."

He reached into his pants pocket and pulled out the card. He flipped it to me as he drove north.

I dialed the number on my cell phone, worrying about how many minutes this would eat up. She answered on the second ring.

"Maria Sanko, Sanko Properties. How can I help you?"

"Miss, Mrs.—"

"Please, call me Maria."

"Okay. Maria, this is Skip Moore. You approached my friend and me in The Green Turtle about a plumbing problem?"

"Oh, thank you for calling. You're too late though. I found Jimmy Sheldon at home and he—"

"No, no. It's not about that. James, my partner, well, the two of us wondered how much you know about the history of property here in Islamorada. You know, where buildings were back in the thirties? Stuff like that."

"I've lived here all my life. Of course, I wasn't around in the thirties—"

"No, ma'am, I didn't mean to infer that you were old or—"

She laughed. "I'm older than you are, but not *that* old."

If the lady was over thirty-five, I'd be very surprised.

"Well, we have some questions and wondered if you'd agree to sit down with us and maybe fill us in a little bit?"

"Sure."

Just like that.

"Well, would there be a charge?"

"Are you thinking about coming down here? On a permanent basis?"

I could detect amusement in her voice.

"Do you mean like setting up shop here in the Keys?"

I thought James was going to run off the road.

"Sure. We're considering it."

I watched him mouth the words, "Are you crazy?"

"Then I'd be giving you some history of the Key in a professional sense. Giving you reasons to move your plumbing business down here."

"Yeah. You would."

"Plumbing is your business, right?"

Clearing my throat, I stared out the window at the collection of stucco strip malls running by the ocean. My business was selling security systems to people who didn't have anything to secure. James's business was being a line cook at a fast-food restaurant. We were pretenders, pure and simple. As detectives and most certainly as plumbers. What were we thinking?

"Sure. That's our business." I wasn't sure *what* our business was anymore. And I suppose we were as well equipped to be plumbers as we were to be private investigators. What she didn't know, couldn't hurt us. Could it?

"Okay, where do you want to meet?"

"We're staying at Pelican Cove Resort."

"I know exactly where that is. Right next to Holiday Isle. And Holiday Isle has three great bars."

Our kind of lady.

"Well, why don't we meet at the pool bar at Pelican Cove? We can start there and see if—"

"And who knows," she picked up the theme, "we may move the party next door later on."

Sounded good to me.

"Half an hour?"

"I'll be there. Skip, was it?"

"Yes, ma'am, and James is my partner."

"Please, don't ma'am me. It's Maria, okay?"

"Okay, Maria."

I hung up the phone and looked out the window, catching the sideview mirror in my peripheral vision.

"James, there's a motorcycle back about two vehicles."

I could feel him staring at me.

"Eyes back on the road, James."

The last thing I wanted was to have an accident in a strange town. We had a job to do and, as bad as the truck was, it was crucial to our transportation.

He looked out the windshield. "There are thousands of motorcycles on the roads down here. What the hell makes this one so special?"

"It's a black Harley with a gold fender, and the rider has a dark helmet, facemask pulled down."

"Could be a coincidence."

"No."

My partner was quiet the rest of the trip, and we never lost sight of the Harley.

CHAPTER EIGHT

Bobbie was at the pool bar, entertaining a man and woman who seemed to know her. They were laughing as she served them frozen drinks.

"Hey, Bobbie."

The eighty-five-degree temperature and humidity smothered me as the frizzy-haired barmaid glanced my way, a puzzled expression on her face.

"The usual," I said.

"Who are you?"

So much for the previous five-dollar tip and three Yuenglings I'd had earlier in the day. I thought that resort bartenders catered to the tourists and got to know everyone by their first name and their drink. Of course, I could have been wrong.

James came down from the room a couple of minutes later, winking at Bobbie. I glanced at her and she was winking back.

"Hey, James," she shouted, "cold Yuengling draft and some pretzels, right?"

"Sure."

Hell, he didn't even know her name.

"Maria should be here in a couple. Let's figure out what we want from her." He acted as if the last twenty seconds had never happened.

"What we want, James, is the location of the Coral Belle hotel. We need to know where it was located."

"What else?"

"That would give us a great start." I could think of nothing else. Unless she knew the location of the gold. And that would have been impossible.

"Busy, Bobbie?" he asked her as she put down the bottle of beer and the paper basket of pretzels. James gave her that personal smile, and she melted. Bobbie. At least he knew who she was.

"With you here?" A smile plastered over her face. "Well, now I am seriously busy."

He smiled back. She was called to the other side of the bar and he looked at me. Now James was all business.

"Skip, there are two agendas. First of all, we find those two slimeball detectives. I think they've got answers."

"And second, we find the Coral Belle Hotel foundation."

He turned and stared out at the ocean. "Man, we weren't alive when that hurricane hit."

"Duh."

"Well, it was a long time ago. I mean, if you were, what, ten years old, and you were a survivor—"

"There weren't many of them, James."

"Yeah, but if you'd made it through the storm, well, you'd have vivid memories of that catastrophe."

"What's your point?"

"Kids remember the strangest things. Maybe someone saw people moving those crates with the gold in them. Maybe one of their parents was paid to help bury the wooden boxes. I mean—"

I caught her approach from the corner of my eye. My peripheral vision had kicked in, and she looked as good as she had at the restaurant.

"Hi, boys. You said you needed some advice? Some information?" Maria Sanko had even gone home to change. Tight jeans and an orange tank top. Wow!

James nodded at her. I could see the sparkle in his eyes.

He engaged me one more time, for just a few seconds.

"We need to find a survivor, Skip. That may be the answer."

She was on her second margarita, and we were on our third beer.

"The Coral Belle. It turns out it wasn't a hotel for the common person. There was another hotel that most people stayed at." She nodded at James. I was simply the guy at the end of the bar.

"The Matecumbe Hotel was partially destroyed, but it was one of two buildings still standing when the storm passed through. Tourists stayed there. Traveling salesmen stayed there. Prostitutes worked out of the Matecumbe. It was not the hotel for the upper class.

"Who stayed at the Coral Belle?"

"Rich folks. People who had five hundred thousand dollars in their portfolio. A million dollars. Railroad officials who were making investments in the Keys. A couple of presidents stayed there. I believe Woodrow Wilson was reported to have visited and maybe Warren Harding. And the authors Zane Grey and Ernest Hemingway spent time at the Coral Belle."

"Hemingway? Two presidents. Very fancy."

She looked back at James and pushed her hair back from her face. "James, there was supposedly a ballroom with a very expensive cut-glass chandelier. And when the Vicks Chemical Corporation had a party, they'd have chefs down from Miami, and fly in Cuban dancers and musicians. Teenage hookers from Cuba were also flown in for parties at the hotel. The Coral Belle was quite a place."

"How do you know all of this?"

Finally, she glanced at me. "My grandfather worked for the railroad in Miami the last five years it existed. He told my father some stories that were hard to believe. A lot of crazy things went on back then. By today's standards they would be, well, by today's standards they are still salacious."

James pushed back his stool.

"Gonna go up to the room and get a pen and tablet. I want to write some of this down. I'll be right back." He wobbled a bit when he stepped off the stool, and we watched him as he walked to the outside elevator.

"So, Maria, where was the Coral Belle?"

She pointed in the direction of the business district. The business district of Islamorada being the thin strip of shops, restaurants, and bars that ran up and down the Overseas Highway.

"A mile and a half down the road. There's a medical office on the property now. Some doctor who has a vein care center. I think he operates on varicose veins. An Indian name." She paused. "Malhotra. I think that's his name. He's got half of it. The other half is an orthopedic surgeon's office. Neal or O'Neill. Something like that. Their signs are out front."

And there it was. That simple. Although nothing in my life is that simple. Couldn't be. Never was. The property mentioned in the cryptic letter was one and a half miles down the road.

"This is a strange question, but was the foundation of the old hotel still intact when they built the medical office?"

She shook her pretty head. "I have no idea. I just know that that's where the hotel was."

She stared off into the blue ocean and I followed her gaze, watching colorful sailboats offshore with red, white, and blue canvas, two loud Jet Skis racing on the parallel, and two pelicans swooping down to capture unsuspecting fish in the clear blue water. For a couple of minutes there was a peaceful calm.

Then the thunder of a motorcycle split the afternoon and someone spit up a white cloud of dust in the parking lot as they headed toward the highway.

"Why are you so interested in the old hotel?"

"James is sort of a history buff."

She gave me a sideways look. "James? That James? Didn't seem to be the history type."

When it came to making money, James could be the history type.

"Skip! Get up here. Stat."

I looked up, and on the second-floor balcony stood James, pointing his finger directly at me.

"Should Maria come up too?"

"Get your butts up here. Now."

I nodded my head at Maria and we both hopped off our stools.

Halfway to the elevator, I heard the voice. "Hold it. I need to be paid for those drinks."

"Bill my room!"

And then I realized she had no idea who I was. As far as I was concerned, Bobbie could eat the bar tab.

I ignored her, and we both ran to the elevator.

CHAPTER NINE

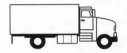

Pelican Cove, for all of its wonderful features, has very, very slow elevators. We should have taken the steps. But, no, I decided we would take the elevator.

When we finally got to the second floor, we raced down the walkway to our room. James was standing outside the door.

"Nobody should see what I'm going to show you guys." He closed his eyes and took a deep breath.

"James, what's this all about?"

Maria looked at James, then at me, then back at James, obviously confused.

"Honest to God, pally, this is not suitable for children."

"No kids here, James."

He slid his key into the slot and slowly opened the door to our small room.

Immediately I could see the bed, covers torn off. Not even a sheet on the mattress, which led me to believe that the maids had done a half-assed job.

Clothes were strewn around the room. We weren't the neatest guys in the world, but the room looked like a hurricane had hit it.

"James, somebody's tossed our room."

He was pale. With no comeback, my best friend was shaking his head.

"Over here, amigo."

He motioned to the far side of the bed.

I walked toward him.

James was pointing, looking at me as if he couldn't focus anywhere else, but still pointing.

Lying on the floor, faceup, was a man's body, the side of his head bashed in. Eyes wide open, he stared at me, dark blood soaking into the carpet.

"Oh, my God." Maria Sanko was frozen, her mouth hanging open, the color drained from her face.

"I checked." James swallowed hard. "There's no pulse. He's not breathing."

Grabbing the phone by the bed I dialed zero.

"We've got a dead body up here in three fifteen."

"A what?"

"Dead body. Guy with his head bashed in."

There was a long silence. Then, "What should I do?"

"Ma'am, somebody broke into our room, trashed it, and there's a dead body on the floor. You work here. Has anything like this ever—" Well, of course, nothing like this had happened before.

"I'm sorry, my manager isn't in and I—"

"Just call nine-one-one. They usually take care of everything."

Maria had regained her composure and was standing by the sliding glass door, looking out at the pool and the ocean. James was sitting on the bed watching me.

"If you can stand it, look again, Skip."

I walked back to the body. He was dressed in a green T-shirt and jeans. I forced myself to look up at the face, those glassy eyes staring through me. He had one of those three-day beards that I've tried to grow but it never worked.

"It looks like he bashed his head on this nightstand when he fell."

James nodded. "Fell or was pushed."

"Pretty nasty gash."

"Recognize him?"

And then I did. From the Yellow Pages. It was Jim Weezle from AAAce Investigations. We had found half of the vanished team.

CHAPTER TEN

Of course, all hell broke loose. We called Mrs. Trueblood, and wearing jeans and a Bon Jovi T-shirt, she came stomping down before the cops arrived, shaking her head, and muttering something about how "everybody in the damned world is now going to know about that damned gold."

It didn't seem to bother her that one of her former employees lay dead on our floor.

Some guy in a blue denim work shirt with thirty keys dangling from his belt came running in, assaying the damages. He quietly gazed at the body still oozing blood, went into the bathroom, loudly threw up, then walked out, nodding at us as if he'd taken care of things.

A young blonde lady with an official name tag pinned on her blouse stuck her head in, saw the commotion, and slowly backed out muttering, "Oh, my God. Oh, my God."

The four of us walked out onto the concrete walkway, waiting for the Monroe County Sheriff Department to arrive. I looked right out into the parking lot and could actually see some of the highway from there.

"Are you all right?" I noticed Maria hadn't said a thing and I figured I should check in with her.

"No."

I put my hand on her shoulder and she pushed it off.

"How did I get mixed up in something like this?" She walked to the railing and stared down at the broken-shell parking lot.

"You agreed to help us. I've got to be honest with you, this happens to people who hang around with us."

She actually smiled, then gave me a little laugh. The problem was, I was dead serious. *Dead* serious.

I saw the white car with green-and-black lettering pull in with its rooftop lights flashing as if they were going to pull someone over for speeding. The lettering on the side of the vehicle said it all.

SERVING THE FLORIDA KEYS
KEY LARGO TO KEY WEST

So these guys patrolled a one-hundred-mile stretch of highway, dealing with everything from speeders and drunks to, well, possible murder. Two officers stepped out of the car, looked up at us, and I waved. Lights on the car still flashing, they walked to the elevator. I should have told them it was slow. Really slow. Almost two minutes later they exited, a one-floor ride.

The red-and-white rescue unit pulled up thirty seconds later, preceded by its screaming siren. And then there was the second sheriff car, and a third, and the officers separated us while two men walked into our room and immediately put crime tape over the open doorway.

I don't know what all went on in that room, but cars kept coming and men and women were going in and out, lifting the yellow crime tape, then putting it back, and we were all herded downstairs where the police cleared the pool area. A mother and father with three small children were not very happy.

At the bar I saw Bobbie frowning at me as she slammed drinks down as fast as possible. Every seat was taken and the buzz was intense. Young people in bathing suits, older people with shorts and colorful shirts. There were two European couples, the corpulent girls in string bikinis and the two guys in what appeared to be colored jock straps. The assembled crowd watched us, pointed to the balcony above, and seemed to devour the excitement that only a gruesome murder can deliver.

The sheriff's deputies questioned us individually. We were spread out at the four corners of the fenced-in pool, and we each had our own officer. It was almost comical the way they handled it, but I suppose they couldn't rule us out as suspects. It did happen in our room, but we hadn't even been there.

"Mr. Moore, you were the one who found the body, right?"

"No. My roommate found the body."

"Mr. Lessor?"

"Yes."

"Were you with your roommate, Mr. Lessor, before he found the body?"

"I was with him maybe five minutes before."

"So he went to the room and five minutes later, he calls you and," he glanced at a paper in his hand, "a Miss Maria Sanko to come up and see the body?"

"I don't have a stopwatch. My guess is that—"

"Five minutes."

"I guess. I'm not a good judge of time, but—"

"So Mr. Lessor had at least five minutes by himself?"

It sounded for all the world like the first thing this guy wanted to do was accuse my partner. So I obviously thought the quickest solution to the problem was to start defending James.

"Mr. Lessor,"— I'd never called him mister in my life—"did not kill anyone. He was shocked. He didn't even know this guy."

And this deputy didn't know James. James hated cops. As an

accountant, his father had been arrested in their home for failing to pay withholding taxes from the company he worked for. Strict orders from the company's owner. But it was James's father who did the time.

Cops stormed into their home and cuffed his father in front of the family. His father was locked up and spent years in prison. James said they emasculated him. James hated cops.

The officer glanced back at where they were interviewing James. The look in his eyes told me there was going to be trouble.

"Just a moment."

He walked back to the far corner of the pool, conferred with that officer for a moment, then came back.

"Mr. Lessor did not know the victim, is that correct?"

"That's correct."

"Isn't it true that the victim was a private detective?"

How he'd already arrived at that conclusion I didn't know. Unless James had already told them.

"I don't know that for sure. I mean, we saw their pictures online and—" Online. Wrong word to use.

"And why were you looking them up online?" The line delivered like a B-movie actor. Intimidating. Threatening. "If you didn't know the victim, why were you searching for him online?"

"They were—"

"They? Was someone else killed too?"

I sensed it was not going well. This thing with James and a dead Weezle was a little more complicated than I'd imagined. And maybe Mary Trueblood was right. Now everyone was going to know about the gold. I was just worried about James.

"Mr. Moore, again I'm asking you, why were you and Mr. Lessor looking up the victim online? You claim neither you nor Mr. Lessor knew him."

And so it went. Everything pointed to James searching for the guy online and then finding the body. And the insinuation was that if James had five minutes before he called us up, he had time to kill the guy who broke in.

I know James. I've known him since we were in grade school. He's my best friend, and while he may be a good talker, he's not a fighter. He's terrible at confrontation. James couldn't kill anyone. And why would he? These guys, Weezle and Markim? We'd never heard about them until this morning.

I figured Maria was getting the same questions, and James was probably being grilled about what he did for those five minutes, bristling every second of the interview.

And Mary Trueblood, she was probably telling these officers that we were there to find forty-some million dollars worth of gold. At this moment I wished I'd listened to my inner voice back in Carol City. I should have put my foot down and said no. Anytime James thinks something is a good idea, it isn't.

"You can't account for those five minutes that Mr. Lessor was gone, correct?"

I must have told the cop at least five times that I could account for those five minutes. "The elevators here are very slow. Very slow."

CHAPTER ELEVEN

They took him away. Cuffed. I couldn't believe it. Honestly my mouth was hanging open. They handcuffed him, walked him to one of the squad cars, pushed his head down, and had him climb in the back of the car. He glared out the window, staring at me with a scowl on his face.

"Is he being arrested?" This was quickly turning into a nightmare.

"He refused to go voluntarily to the station. He was unco-operative."

James hated cops. He knew that sometimes when you leave with an officer, you don't come back. For years.

"He found a dead body. That's it. That is not a crime." I was screaming at the uniformed officer. They held me back as I tried to rush the car. What the hell? James was not a murderer.

"My God. We just stumbled on a corpse with his head bashed in. Give the guy a break."

The officer gave me a grim smile. This was Florida and things are a little different down here. I mean, we got our private investigator license from the Department of Agriculture. That's who licenses PIs. Seriously. I hesitated as I realized we might lose our brand-new license if I attempted anything that was illegal. Immoral. Or just not right.

"For God's sake, at least take the cuffs off of him." Neither of us had ever been handcuffed. Neither of us had ever been in a squad car. This was a first.

"Where are you taking him?"

"To the station."

"And where is the station?"

The officer rolled his eyes. "Behind Boardwalk Pizza."

"And that's where?" My tone was intense. I didn't know the area, and I needed geographical references.

"About two miles north of here on the highway."

"James, I'll pick you up as soon as this is over. Call me." I shouted as loud as I could.

Another uniform walked down the stairs, our laptop case in his hand.

"We'll need to take your computer. If it's clean, we'll get it back to you."

"I'm a private investigator. I have information on cases we're working on. You can't just take that and—"

"Yes. We can." He kept on walking.

We'd only owned it for three days. Other than the AAAce Yellow Page ad and James's new subscription to Match.com, there wasn't much stored on the machine. And I watched as my best friend was transported through the parking lot and down the side road that led to the Overseas Highway. Everything was a blur. We'd come down here to make a little side money and now he was being held on suspicion of murder.

I felt Maria Sanko's hand on my arm. I didn't brush it off.

"Skip, I'm sorry."

"He'll be out in an hour. He didn't kill that guy. They're just fishing."

She nodded. "I know two of the cops who were here. Dated one of them a while back. I'll make a call once they get back to the station and see what they plan on doing, okay?"

I nodded. I forgot we had a local on our side.

"Look, I'm still here to help you with your search."

And it suddenly occurred to me that whoever interviewed Maria didn't bring up the gold. And the officer who talked to me didn't mention gold. So everyone didn't know about the gold.

But there was one thing she did know. We weren't plumbers. That had become pretty evident.

I grabbed her elbow and steered her toward the bar. I didn't care what Bobbie thought of me, I needed a drink.

"So what did they ask you?"

She gave me a little-girl smirk. "They asked if I was intimate with James."

"Really?" Probably trying to establish relationships. Still, it was a rather leading question.

She cocked her pretty head. "I thought it was a strange question, but, well, he is kind of cute."

"What else?" Cute. They all thought he was cute. Every girl he met thought James was cute. It somehow pissed me off. I never had a girl tell me I was cute. But, then again, I'm interested in someone. James is interested in everyone. "They didn't ask if you and I—"

"That didn't come up, Skip."

"Anything else?"

"He wanted to know how long James was alone in the room upstairs."

Mary Trueblood walked up. "Damned police. Why can't they just accept that a couple of guys probably broke into your room and one of them killed the other one? Why couldn't they just accept that?"

"Mrs. Trueblood. What did they ask you?"

"Why I was here."

I studied her carefully. "And you told them what?"

"The truth. Of course." She gave a sideways glance to Maria. "I told them I'd hired you two to help me with the history of my great-grandfather who had been apparently killed in the nineteen thirty-five hurricane."

I saw Maria's eyes get even wider, and she looked at me with a sly grin.

"Glad I didn't hire you guys to fix my leaking pipe."

Mary Trueblood looked at both of us, shook her head as if confused, and walked away.

So no one knew about the gold. No one except James, Mary, me, and Ted Markim, now that Jim Weezle was dead.

CHAPTER TWELVE

They carried the body down on a stretcher, a blood-stained sheet covering him. Two guys from the rescue unit brought him down the stairs. They'd already figured that out. Not the elevator. The stairs.

Some new guy in a short-sleeved shirt and tie told me it would be at least a half hour before they would have our personal items packed. No one could go back into the room.

"This really sucks, doesn't it?" Maria frowned.

"You think so?" I didn't even have a room. Maria probably had a home somewhere. A fancy condo with a swimming pool. And James was in a cell somewhere behind a pizza joint.

"Actually," she pursed her lips and looked up at me, "this is the most excitement I've had since my divorce over a year ago. I may even make the news tonight."

"Well, I'm glad we could brighten your day." I'm not sure James would be so happy about it.

We strolled down to the beach where couples lounged on chairs and watched the ocean lap at the shore.

"You guys have been friends a while." She glanced at me, a look more as a friend than an inquisitor.

"We have. Since we were kids. And what I said before about getting into trouble—just hang around long enough and we do manage to attract our share of problems."

She laughed. "There's more to this expedition than just a search for history, isn't there?"

I didn't say anything.

"You know, Skip, people come down here to get away. They just want to get lost. I've watched it happen. For a week, a month, some people for their whole life. It's like in the middle Keys you can just disappear. But you're not down here to disappear, are you?"

"No."

"People come down to dive, to go deep-sea fishing," she pointed toward the ocean. "The deep-sea fishing here is the best in the country."

I nodded.

"They show up to tie one on for a couple of days. People come down here to have an affair, but no one comes down here to research dead relatives."

"And your point is?"

"I think you two are treasure hunters."

"What?" She couldn't possibly know. I'd just decided she knew nothing and she hit me with that.

"You want locations. You're trying to find the remnants of an old building, the Coral Belle Hotel. I don't think this has anything to do with somebody's great-grandfather. I think you're looking for gold."

I just kept walking.

"But, I could be wrong."

"You are."

"Listen, people come down here looking for wrecker camps. Is that it? You're trying to find a wrecker camp?"

"I don't even know what that is." I lied.

"Really? When ships would crash out on the reef or the rocks, wrecking crews would go out and salvage the boats. They'd take whatever was valuable and usually bury it at their campsite. There weren't any safes or banks around so they would bury it using landmarks as locators."

I breathed a sigh of relief. She really didn't have the right answer.

"Today, when a construction crew breaks ground, they'll sometimes stumble on an old wrecker camp. Lots of times they'll find silver and gold. I thought maybe you had a lead on one of the old camps."

She was just a little too close to the truth for comfort.

"Maria, do you know anyone down here who has a Harley-Davidson motorcycle with a gold fender?"

"Boy, you sure know how to change the subject."

"Do you?"

"No. Not off the top of my head."

And all of a sudden it hit me. I'd heard the distinct sound of a Harley in the parking lot just before James called us up to the room. Somebody had pulled out, leaving a cloud of dust.

"My ex-husband Drew had a Harley."

"He did?"

"Yeah." She smiled. "Had one."

"What happened to it?"

"I got it in the divorce."

It was my turn to smile. "Really? Did you sell it?"

"Sell it?" Her eyes got big. They were dark brown and very expressive. "How do you think I got here today?"

A biker babe. James and I had landed a biker babe with pretty brown eyes. I was impressed.

"Hey, do you think you could call your former boyfriend down at the sheriff's office? I'd really like to know what's happening with James."

She pulled an iPhone from her purse and punched in a couple of numbers. Here was a biker babe with the police department on speed dial. Cool. I need to know more about this girl.

"Officer Danny Mayfair, please."

A couple of seconds later her face lit up.

"Danny, it's Maria." She paused as the officer talked.

"No, no. I'm not still trying to sell you the condo. Although you passed on a very good deal. The prices are going up, Danny."

She sat down on one of the plastic chairs and looked up, giving me a very charming smile. The girl liked to flirt. Two guys at once. Officer Danny and me. If James was here she'd probably try to work him in too. He was cute.

"No. Danny, I'm with Skip—" She looked at me inquisitively.

"Moore," I said.

"Skip Moore. He's—yeah, you guys interviewed him. Along with me and the older lady."

Mary Trueblood would not be happy to know she was being referred to as "the older lady."

"Can you tell me the status of James?"

She nodded, rolled her eyes, and I couldn't tell if it was good news or bad news. I wanted to grab the phone out of her hand and just get to the heart of the matter.

Maria glanced up at me. "Danny says James has been hostile to all of them. Belligerent and what else, Danny? Noncommunicative." She frowned at me, shrugging her shoulders.

That was James. Described him to a *T*. He hated cops.

"The good thing is, they don't believe he had anything to do with the murder."

"And?"

"When are they going to release him, Danny?" She waited, waited, and waited. My fists clenched. I needed to know.

"They're going to release him in about an hour."

I breathed a deep sigh of relief. I couldn't wait to tell Mary Trueblood. And then I reconsidered. The lady hadn't shown any compassion at all about her former employee being knifed to death. She probably wouldn't care about James's incarceration.

"Can you ask him who the dead guy is?"

She nodded. "Danny, can you release the identity of the dead man?"

She giggled. "Of course I'm not going to call the press. It's between you and me."

Standing up, she kept a distant look in her eyes, like she was focusing on someone who wasn't here. Maybe this Danny character.

"Okay. I'll keep it very quiet." She nodded emphatically as if the person on the other end of the phone could see her.

"I still love you, big D."

She stuffed the black phone back in her pocket.

"Big D?"

She blushed. "Well, he's kind of big."

Then I blushed. "Did he tell you who the dead guy is?"

"He did."

Big D. An ex-boyfriend.

"And?"

"Well, you heard me, I promised not to tell."

"Maria."

"But I'll tell you, okay."

"Please. Who was the victim?"

"A guy named Peter Stiffle."

"Stiffle?"

"Stiffle. Peter."

"You're sure? Peter Stiffle?"

"I'm not sure. Danny is sure."

Big D was sure the cadaver had previously been a living, breathing Peter Stiffle.

Things just got weirder and weirder.

CHAPTER THIRTEEN

One hour was still one hour. There was time to do a little investigating and I took advantage of it. Maria offered to drive, handed me an extra helmet, and with a throaty roar from the engine she shot out of the parking lot like a bullet, full speed ahead toward Dr. Malhotra's Vein Care Center. It took all of about fifteen seconds for me to realize I should have stayed at Pelican Cove.

The lady raced through traffic, moving at breakneck speeds as I hung on tight, dangerously close to touching off-limit areas of her body. She'd lean to the left, lean to the right, slipping between cars, and there were two or three times I thought we were going to lose it altogether.

As we pulled into the parking lot, I'd felt the hot stinging Florida sun burning my wind-whipped face. When we stopped, the roaring from the Harley engine still rang in my ears.

"You're sure this is where the old hotel was located?" I shouted. I couldn't hear anything.

A white stucco building fronted the narrow highway, three dark windows and a door the only breaks in the plain vanilla surface. Two signs hung on a rusted metal post planted in the parking lot. The first was a weather-beaten wooden sign that simply said VEIN CARE CENTER. Below that hung a much larger plastic sign with raised letters.

JAMES O'NEILL ORTHOPEDIC SURGERY
SPECIALIZING IN TOTAL JOINT REPLACEMENT SURGERY

"I've always been told that this was where the Coral Belle was located."

I checked my watch. James would be free in about fifty minutes. I could go inside, ask a few questions, and I'd still make it back to pick him up when they released him. I knew James didn't want to spend any more time than he had to at a sheriff's office.

"I'm going to go in. See what they know."

She lifted her denim-clad leg, dismounted, and smiled at me, still flirting. If I was about five to ten years older—

"You're still not going to tell me what you're looking for, are you?"

"I will. Right now. I will tell you exactly what we're looking for. But, I don't think you're going to like it."

"Really?" Excitement in her voice.

We'd already lied to her about the plumbing business. And we hadn't been entirely truthful about our search.

A noisy truck rolled by about twenty feet from us, followed by an old Chevy with a really loud muffler. I could smell the exhaust.

Give her the partial truth. It was the best I could offer. "Mary Trueblood asked us to find out what we could about her great-grandfather. One of the last places she can trace him to is right here, at the site of the Coral Belle Hotel."

"And you were pretending to be plumbers in disguise? Why? Because you were looking for family history? I don't think so." She put her hand on my arm, a plea for the truth. "Because you were looking for a great-grandfather? Was that the reason you lied to me?" She folded her arms over her ample chest and smiled at me. "Skip, don't insult me, please. I'm already deeper into this thing than I want to be, and I don't even know what this thing is."

She had me.

"Seriously, Skip—"

I shrugged my shoulders as I walked up to the door and entered, not bothering to hold it open for her. I didn't tell lies well.

The doorway opened into a spacious waiting area, with a sparkling white ceramic floor and a desk that would have been worthy in a brand-new Holiday Inn. At least a Holiday Inn.

A curt voice asked, "Can I help you?"

An Asian girl in a white smock and shoulder-length coal-black hair sat behind the reception desk, never looking up, working her keyboard at 120 words per minute.

"Do you have any history on this building?"

She looked up, disdain apparent on her face.

"History? I've been here six months. Does that qualify as history?"

It honestly didn't. "Is there someone here who can take me back to nineteen thirty-five?"

Maria Sanko appeared beside me, punching her elbows into my rib cage. She obviously wasn't happy that I'd shut the door in her face. And that I wasn't sharing the entire story with her.

"Doctor Malhotra would probably know the history of the property."

"Can I talk to him?"

"I'm sort of busy here." Evidently not happy with my request, she looked back at her computer screen, and I gazed around the empty waiting area. She didn't seem that busy to me.

"Ma'am, I've driven quite a ways. I'm searching for the history of a relative. I would sure appreciate it if—"

"Oh, all right. I'll see if he has any time." She waved her arm at us. "I suppose you can have a seat."

We did.

Dr. Malhotra walked out about five minutes later, a distinguished Indian-American guy with brushed back salt-and-pepper hair, a neatly trimmed graying beard and mustache, a dark complexion, and a white doctor's coat.

"Hello." A slight accent.

He studied us with a stern look on his face. "How can I help you? Veronica said you wanted some history on this building?"

"Yeah. I'm looking for the history of a relative back in the thirties and I think this property may play a part in that history."

"I started this practice in 1999. But the building has been in my wife's family since maybe the late forties, early fifties."

I glanced around at the opulent interior with expensive-looking chairs and sofas, ornate wooden coffee tables, and elite magazines like *Forbes* and *Island Life* lying around. The vein business and orthopedic surgery must be very lucrative.

"Doctor," Maria smiled at him, "I'm Maria Sanko. I'm a realtor here in Islamorada."

He nodded.

"Is this the property where the Coral Belle Hotel used to sit?"

He folded his hands in front of him.

"You're the third person to ask that in the last month."

"Really?" We both said it together.

"Really."

"Is it?" I needed the answer.

"No."

"Oh." I knew I sounded disappointed. This would have been so easy. The hotel foundation would be here, we bring a shovel at night and—

"Do you know where the Coral Belle was?" Maria kept digging.

He nodded his head. "It was on the water. The property right behind this building, right across the old highway. Next to the Ocean Air Motel."

"What's on that property now?"

"Nothing."

Waterfront property with no development?

"There's a boat dock there. That's it. You can see that from the water or the beach at the Ocean Air."

"So we can walk back there and—"

"It's fenced and locked."

"The empty property, right?"

Again he nodded his head yes.

"Well, do you know who owns it?"

"I do." He'd folded his arms across his chest, staring at me.

"Great. If you could just give us a name—"

"I own it, my friend. Now, unless you'd like to make a medical appointment with Veronica, I'm going to ask you to leave."

With that he spun around and walked back into the offices.

Maria gave me a questioning look.

"Well. That went well."

CHAPTER FOURTEEN

James was waiting in front of the station when I pulled up in the truck. He got in the on passenger side and didn't say a word.

"We're going to take a trip down to a motel on the beach. There's a property there you're going to find interesting, James."

He was biting his lower lip, staring straight ahead.

"Want to tell me what happened?"

"No."

"Hey, bright side. You're free and we're still employed. I checked with the front desk. They're comping us a second room. We both get a room and one's got a kitchenette. Pretty cool."

He didn't smile.

"We're moving up in the world, James."

Turning left just before The Vein Care Center clinic, we crossed Old Highway and pulled in at the Ocean Air. Motel apparently wasn't the appropriate word. The sign said Ocean Air Suites. A forty-something guy with short hair and an earring stood on the white porch, watching us get out of the truck. Slowly walking to the oil-guzzling truck, he approached me.

"We were thinking of maybe staying here sometime in the next couple of months. Thought we might check the place out."

He kept staring at us.

"So, I wondered if we could just maybe take a quick look at the beach down there? Just a quick look."

He nodded. "You understand it's for guests only?"

"Just going to look. We'll be right back."

"Okay, then." He didn't sound happy about it. "You see it, then you come right back, you hear?"

James and I walked down the shell-covered path, heading toward the ocean. In the distance I could make out several wooden deck chairs and a tiki hut with a grass roof.

"So what are we going to see?"

I pointed to my right, where a tall metal fence ran the entire length from the road to the water. Trees, orange-flowering bougainvillea, and high grass blocked any view of the property next door.

"We're hopefully going to get a view of that property."

"And why are we doing this?"

"We might want to come back some night this week and bring a shovel."

James's eyes opened a little wider. "So, you found it already."

"I did."

"Pard, that's great." He punched me on the shoulder.

"Property is owned by a doctor on the Overseas Highway. Not a very pleasant guy. He keeps it under lock and key."

"What's so valuable?"

"Don't know."

We reached the beach, a little point of sand that stuck out into the water. An older, heavyset couple was sprawled out on two chairs, lathered in lotion, their tiny suits covering far too little. She was bright pink and the guy with socks and sandals was pasty white. European, for sure. I'd seen it before. The sun was bright, and I figured the guy's white skin would be red soon. Except for his feet.

Walking farther to the edge, we could look back into the fenced-off grassy ground.

"Dude, there's nothing there."

A wooden boat dock reached into the water. Other than that, there was grass. Grass and more grass. The lot was vacant, fenced in on all four sides. Three sides were covered in trees and lush flowering plants, the waterside free of vegetation, but the fence ran all the way to the water's edge.

"Why do you keep a vacant property locked up?"

I stared out at the sky-blue water, then back at the empty land. There was no boat at the dock.

"Picnickers? Kids? I mean this would be a great place to drink a six-pack, make out with your girlfriend—"

"Maybe go skinny dipping?"

"So you put up a sign that says private property. No need to put up a major security fence." It seemed to make no sense.

"A sign would be a lot cheaper than this fence, that's for sure."

"Time to vacate the premises, boys."

I spun around and there was the guy with the earring, perched on a white electric golf cart. Electric. A silent approach.

"I told you, we were just looking."

Glancing down at the seat beside him I saw a nickel-plated revolver. Just lying on the white vinyl. A subtle threat, or else he was going to do some target practice with the dolphins.

"Move it. Guests here pay for this privilege. Understand?"

It was a spit of land, with no ambiance, no personality. Hardly worth the price.

The golf cart guy sat there, waiting for us to make our move.

"No problem. I don't think we'll be making reservations today. Okay?"

"We have no problem with gays, but you two are an exception." He paused for a moment and just as I got ready to say something, he said, "Okay?" We walked back toward the truck, James kicking the occasional big piece of shell.

"Gays?"

"Everybody is trying to push your buttons today, James. Just settle down."

"Sons of bitches seriously thought I might have had something to do with that Weezle guy. They thought that I would have killed someone. I mean what kind of a person would just automatically assume that—"

"James, you were not cooperating."

"You think? When the first question out of their mouths was, 'Did you kill the man in your room?'"

I hadn't realized they would be that blunt.

"Hey, you're free. They couldn't make that connection because it didn't exist. And by the way, that's another thing I found out."

"What?"

"The dead guy. It wasn't Jim Weezle."

"What? There's no question, is there? We both recognized him from the Yellow Page ad online, right?"

Flipping the keys to James, I opened the passenger door and climbed up into the white beast.

"I thought so. But the name with the body is Peter Stiffle."

"Stiffle?"

"That's what Big D says."

"Big D?"

James started the engine and it coughed several times before catching. Glancing in my side mirror I saw the cloud of oily smoke as James pulled away.

"Big D is—was—Maria's boyfriend. He's one of the cops who was at the Cove."

He backed up, and we headed back to the highway.

"You know, I was gone one hour. I watched my time very carefully."

"And?"

"In that time, in one hour, you learned that Maria has an ex-boyfriend named Big D, you learned that the dead guy was Peter Stiffle, you met a doctor you're not too fond of, and you found the location of the old Coral Belle Hotel."

"I did."

"Why do you need me along, pard? You're a one-man detecting machine."

I smiled, looked out the window, and that's when I saw the red flashing light in the side mirror.

"Did you cut somebody off? Change lanes with—"

"There are no lanes. Damn it, Skip. These guys aren't going to leave me alone."

CHAPTER FIFTEEN

"We knew who you were, because you had that black paint spatter on your truck. Easy to identify."

James said nothing through the rolled down window. The dark look on his face and his rhythmic heavy breathing gave it all away.

"We have a question for you," the officer said. "Something you weren't asked during our previous interrogation."

James turned to me with a pleading look on his face. I would have to take the questions because if James said what was in his heart, they'd take him back to jail, toss him in, and throw away the keys.

"That question is?" I leaned over and shouted out James's window. He absolutely wasn't going to cooperate. I knew that.

"Somebody saw a Harley-Davidson pull out of the parking lot at Pelican Cove, about the same time that the resort reported the dead body."

I'd heard that Harley. Wondered about it as well.

"The driver had a helmet on, face guard pulled down, and he . . ." the officer hesitated, looking back at his partner, "he, or possibly she, rode a black cycle with a gold fender." Taking a deep breath, the officer continued. "Does any of that sound familiar? Do you know anyone who owns that cycle?"

"No." I shouted out the answer to his last question. We knew no one who owned that cycle. So technically I was telling the truth.

"Guys," the officer looked up at James, "we want to solve this homicide as soon as possible. Understand that with every minute that goes by, it gets harder to solve the crime. We just want to put it to bed by tonight." He looked back at his partner. "Is there any reason that the driver can't answer any of these questions?"

James gripped the wheel even tighter.

"If we have any information, we'll call you." I shouted it out. "Who should we call?"

"Danny Mayfair."

"Big D?"

He paused.

"Where did you hear that?"

"Not important. I just wanted to make sure you were the guy."

I leaned back and nodded to James. He took his foot off the brake and coasted out of the shell-filled parking lot. We crossed Old Highway and got back on the Overseas Highway. Both of these roads were definitely not highway status, but it made no difference. We would ride it back to our abode.

He drove in silence for a minute or two, stopping at a long red light. Finally, James turned to me and grinned.

"Dude. You smarted off to that police officer. The "Big D" thing."

"I did."

"You're the buttoned-up guy. My man who usually plays by the rules, doesn't want to ruffle feathers."

"I am that guy. Usually."

"Pard, I'm impressed."

A tandem semi pulled up behind us, the driver's air brakes screeching. For a moment the sinister-looking dude made eye contact, the man nodding at me as I checked my side mirror.

"You're not a murderer, James. You're my best friend. I don't hang around with killers. You know?"

Without missing a beat my best friend turned to me and said, "You killed Ferraro. How did it feel?"

His eyes were steady, turning back to the road as cars whipped by us in the southbound lane.

"A quote, but I have no idea from where."

"*His Kind of Woman*. Nineteen fifty-one. You had to love it. Robert Mitchum, Jane Russell, Vincent Price. Private yachts, planes, and mayhem."

"My God, James. Sixty years ago. Black-and-white for God's sake. I bow to your knowledge."

He nodded, a smile forming on his lips.

"I have a soul in the history of cinema, Skip." Tapping his fingers on the steering wheel, he said, "It may not be relevant to what's happening today, but—"

"*What's happening?*"

"Oh, come on, pard." He lifted his hands from the wheel. "Rerun. That's from *What's Happening*. But it's a TV show, so it only counts for half a point."

Damn. I'd been found out.

CHAPTER SIXTEEN

Mary Trueblood was waiting for us when we got back. She must have seen the truck pull in and she met us in the parking lot while James added oil to the engine.

"Boys, this is getting a lot messier than I thought it would. If you walked away right now I wouldn't blame you."

"Mrs. T., we found the Coral Belle."

Her eyes got big. "Any chance we can find the foundation?" No more thought of walking away.

"The property is empty. Some doctor has it all fenced off, but we can probably sneak in there tonight. We were thinking of maybe taking a couple of shovels and seeing if we can find any sign of a foundation."

"You want to stick it out?"

James nodded enthusiastically. "Look, we know where the hotel was. That's a real positive. And someone was killed while they were searching our room, leading us to believe people want to stop the investigation, so it seems we're on the right track."

"Okay." She still sounded skeptical. "What's your next step?"

"There's got to be a library in this town. Let's see if we can find pictures of the Coral Belle."

Every once in a while James comes up with a good idea.

Kathy Ebert, the library director, pointed us to files and files of newspaper stories, and we sorted them out on a large table.

"There was just one restaurant back then. Look at this." James pointed to a photograph of The Russell Café. The sign outside boasted Key lime pie and coconut cake.

"And here's the Matecumbe Hotel. After the storm. That windy sucker knocked one whole corner off the building."

"But it's still standing in that picture."

James studied one page, I studied another.

"There was a post office, a Methodist church, a school—"

I looked up from my page, "and pineapple docks. They imported a lot of pineapples from Cuba, then transported them by train up to Miami."

"I thought we got most of our pineapples from Hawaii."

"Check it out, James. Hawaii was thousands of miles away. According to this story, Islamorada imported cheap pineapples and limes from Cuba. Havana and Matanzas, Cuba."

"Cuba. Who would have thought. We're getting a history lesson here, brother."

"Yeah." History. We were investigating something that happened seventy-five years ago. Something we'd studied in the eighth grade.

"I guess you just loaded the fruit on a boat and brought it into Islamorada." James looked back at the old news article.

"Unload it at the docks here, load it onto Flagler's train, and take it to Miami."

"Looks like it was a big business," I said.

"And there was a Methodist cemetery." James pointed to another article.

"There still is," Kathy said. "The Methodists were insistent that it stay in the same place. They refused to give in to the Cheeca Lodge, so right there, by the swimming pool and the beach, is a home for dead people."

"It still exists?" I couldn't believe that people would tolerate a cemetery in the middle of a resort.

"It does. The Pioneer Cemetery."

My cell phone buzzed and I grabbed for it. Em.

"Hey, Em. I miss you."

"You miss me where?"

"In my heart?"

"No, silly, where are you that you miss me?"

"Well, we're somewhere in the Keys. Mrs. T. didn't want us to tell anyone about our mission and—"

"Skip, I got a letter today regarding Mary Trueblood and you."

"What? Me and Mrs. T.? She's a little old for me, Em. And besides, nobody gets letters anymore."

"I did, Skip, and it isn't funny. The letter is unsigned, and it scared me."

"What did it say?" I couldn't imagine someone writing Em and saying that I was having an affair with—

"It said that all the gold in Islamorada couldn't save you if you didn't abandon your treasure hunt. You, your partner, and Mary Trueblood would end up at the bottom of the ocean if you didn't go back home."

I was silent for a moment. James was poring over old papers, and Mary Trueblood was back at the resort. Was I the intended victim in the room at the Pelican Cove? Did the killer make a mistake and knock down the wrong person?

"Skip?"

"Yeah. I'm here."

"Someone wants to kill you. Did you hear me?"

73

"Maybe someone already tried."

"What do you mean?"

I walked outside the library and got into our truck for privacy. I told her about the murder, about the gold, and about the fenced-in property. I knew it was supposed to be a secret, but I end up telling Em almost everything. Almost. What I don't tell her, she usually finds out.

When I hung up, I looked across the street. There was the monument that had been built to commemorate the hurricane victims. Three hundred people's ashes were in that stone structure.

I walked back in, and James motioned me to the table.

"Check it out, amigo. Here's the Coral Belle. You can see the water about twenty, twenty-five feet from the porch."

"Yeah. And the southeast corner would be straight across from where we were on that little beach."

"Skip, if that information, in whatever form it is in, still exists, we seriously might be the first people to find it. Think what that could mean."

I felt his excitement. This property was vacant and maybe, just maybe, the foundation for that long-forgotten hotel still existed.

"Plan. We go buy a couple shovels, charge them to that dwindling debit card. Then we have dinner, we go over to Rumrunners—that bar at the Holiday Isle—have a few drinks."

"I like the dinner and drinks part. And charging it all."

"About three a.m. tomorrow morning we drive down to the vacant lot, scale the fence, and put our shovels in the ground."

"It sounds like what we should do."

"Then it's a plan."

"Good to go, James."

"Dude, when is she getting here?"

I gave him a blank stare.

"Come on, man. I heard part of the conversation. I saw the look in your eye. Em's coming down to give us a hand, am I right?"

"She got a note, James. Somebody wrote her and said if we didn't drop this project, all three of us were going to get killed."

"Jesus."

"Em has good ideas. You know she does."

He rolled his eyes. "Seriously? Someone wrote her and said they were going to kill us?"

"They did."

"What about Mary?"

"*What About Mary*, a movie staring Cameron Diaz, Ben Stiller—"

"Not this time, pally. I'm asking what you're going to tell our employer?"

"She knows Em. They work out at the same gym. Em's the reason we got this job."

"It's another mouth to feed, Skip. Are we going to have to share the wealth?"

"We'll worry about it later. Right now, we could use the help."

"Oh, it's all right. I get along so well with your girlfriend."

He didn't. But I was anxious to see her, and with two separate rooms back at our resort, this could be a good time.

It's just that I hadn't seriously planned on someone really trying to kill us.

CHAPTER SEVENTEEN

We picked up two shovels and a big flashlight at the Overseas Ace Hardware on Highway 1. The plump female at the register kiddingly asked if we were digging for treasure. We just laughed.

We headed down U.S. 1, James saying he was surprising me for our evening meal. He'd found a special place. James worked for Cap'n Crab, a fast-food restaurant in Carol City, so his culinary tastes should have been suspect, but he was a culinary major in college. The guy knew good food. He'd picked a restaurant where we ended up having a very expensive dinner.

"Dude, she's paying for it."

The restaurant was a place called Ziggie and Mad Dog's on the Overseas Highway. World famous by the way. Lots of things in the Keys were apparently world famous. Who knew?

"Why did you pick this place?" There were a lot of places cheaper than Ziggie and Mad Dog's.

"Did a little Internet research back at the library, Skip. Way back, when this was a saloon, they had casino games here. Al Capone even played cards in the back room. Now, one of the owners is Jim Mandich. This guy played for Michigan, then for the Dolphins. He played in two Super Bowls, seventy-one and seventy-two. When he was with the Dolphins they had a perfect season in seventy-two."

"This Mandich was Mad Dog?"

"Is."

"The nickname says—"

"He's a crazy man. On and off the field."

That made sense. James Lessor is a crazy man. He tends to gravitate to people like that.

"So we're eating here because?"

"We can tell people we did. It's world famous."

For James it was a magical evening. Apparently Jim Mandich occasionally came into his restaurant and pressed the flesh with the locals and tourists. We saw no signs of celebrity this evening.

I was not alive in seventy-one or seventy-two, and Mandich's history had no relevance to me. James, on the other hand, wanted to immerse himself in the experience.

Upon arriving back at Pelican Cove, James walked over to Rumrunners, a multilevel, tiki-style building with the main bar on the second level.

I waited for Em. She showed up half an hour later in her new black Porsche Carrera. Em worked for her father, a very wealthy contractor, and she lived on a different plane than I did. She'd offered to get me a job with Dad, but for some reason I couldn't bring myself to do it. And besides, who would look out for James?

"I missed you." She kissed me in the parking lot. Then kissed me again.

"It's only been two days."

"I missed you." She kissed me again, and I started to get interested. Em can be a very persuasive girl.

I hesitated to ask, but I did anyway. "What do you see in me? You've got so much going and—"

She threw her arms around my neck and pulled my mouth to hers. She kissed me again.

"Shut up and show me our suite. This could be fun."

With the threat of my demise, I questioned that comment, but the next forty minutes were unbelievable.

CHAPTER EIGHTEEN

"Skip, Em, this is Amy." He was shouting over the music.

We'd walked over to Rumrunners, hoping to run into James. It didn't surprise me that he'd made the acquaintance of a young, attractive lady. She had a brief white knit top on and a tan skirt that came up mid-thigh.

Smiling, she nodded at both of us.

"James has told me so much about you two." She smiled, like we were going to be best of friends.

It was as if James and Amy had a long-term relationship and Em and I were just catching up.

"He's never said a word about you." Em started on James immediately. The two of them just went for the throat.

He gave her that look that said: Don't be a smart-ass.

The same look she usually gave him.

The song ended and the crowd applauded the guitar player who introduced a Jimmy Buffett tune while working a rhythm machine. When he started the next song, his voice was slightly off-key. He was loud, and the voices at the crowded bar went up a decibel.

I always wondered why an entertainment establishment hired a talent who couldn't carry it off. They did it on a regular basis.

"Amy is from New York. She's a designer." James was practically shouting, a smug look on his face.

I nodded. Talking much louder I said, "Emily is from Miami. She manages a large construction firm."

"Well, Amy is a diver. She's taking a trip to the San Jose shipwreck tomorrow. She's a historian as well."

"Well," I turned and looked attentively at my attractive blonde girlfriend, "Em is an accountant, and tomorrow she is going to spend the day with me and only me, mostly in bed."

Em glared at me. I still wondered why she put up with our relationship. It never made any sense.

There was no conversation for sixty seconds. Finally, I motioned to James. "We need to talk."

He patted the brunette on her bare shoulder, picked up his bottle of Yuengling, and followed me up the stairs to another level of the bar. A couple was hanging on the railing, looking out at the evening ocean. When they turned and saw us, they walked down the steps.

"Em is coming with us tonight. She's going to be our lookout."

"We need a lookout?" He cocked his head. "Yeah, I guess we do. We don't know what we're getting into, do we?"

"James, it's about the letter. Listen, dude, I saw the letter. When you see that stuff in print—"

"Letter?"

"The one that Em got. Threatening our lives. What kind of letter do you think I'd talk about?"

"Oh, yeah. That letter. Pard, I don't think—"

"Whatever you think, someone has gone on record that you and I need to be dealt with. Are we going to take this seriously and go home or are we going to see this thing through?"

"Am I going to take this seriously? We're young, amigo. This is not the time to let someone squash our dreams."

"And our dreams are?"

"We're going to make a lot of money, Skip. We're going to be rich, famous philanthropists."

"Are we going to go through with this?"

Mr. Danger, James Lessor, took all of two seconds to respond.

"Come on, Skip. It's a joke. Maybe these two investigators, Weezle and Markim, sent a letter to throw us off the scent."

"The scent?"

"You know what I mean."

"One of those guys is dead, James. And maybe that body was supposed to be you or me."

"The name was Peter Stiffle. Remember? It wasn't Weezle or Markim. We were wrong with our identification."

"James, think about it. What happened to our plumbing company?"

He stepped back, eyeing me.

"I'm not exactly sure what you mean."

"You came up with this idea for a fake company. To throw people off the scent. Right?"

"I did."

"So these guys, Weezle and Markim, take it one step further. They have fake IDs made up. They don't want people to know that they are private investigators, right? And one of the fake IDs is for a Peter Stiffle."

"No."

"Dude, we both recognized the body from the online Yellow Page ad. It was one of the private detectives. You know it, I know it."

"We only saw an Internet picture, Skip. We could be wrong." He stared out at the water. "Okay, the dead guy was probably Weezle. And somebody just made a mistake in the identification process."

"That's what I'm thinking. And the cops will run fingerprints and eventually figure out the same thing."

"Skip, I really want to follow this through. I think it's all a bluff. But what happens if someone really wants us dead?"

"It's happened before, James. There are now three of us."

"Count Mrs. T. in there, and there are four of us who don't know anything about what's going on."

I couldn't believe that I was the one who was stoking the fire.

"James, I read the letter. I'm a little concerned. But, dude, we've never had a better opportunity. There's a lot of money at stake. If you're on board, let's find this gold. Okay?"

"We could up the ante." He took a long swallow of beer and peered off into the dark night.

I had no idea where he was going with that.

"Our lives have been threatened," he said.

"And?"

"We're worth more now, right? When your life is on the line, you are worth more than when it's not."

"I suppose." In a very strange way, it all made sense.

"So we want a share. Five percent of the gold."

"That's over two million dollars, James. You can't ask for—"

"She's getting over thirty, pard."

She was. Getting thirty-three million dollars.

We went back to the bar and found Em and Amy in a deep conversation.

"I've got plans tonight, Skip. I sincerely hope those two aren't going to suggest we hang out for the rest of the evening."

"No way."

TOO MUCH STUFF

Em smiled and beer in hand, she walked me to the exit.
"We've got a three a.m. meeting at some vacant property.
We'd better catch some sleep before we start our adventure."
She gave me a very seductive smile.
And I knew she had no intention of sleeping.

CHAPTER NINETEEN

At two thirty I heard the knock at my door. To be honest, we'd drifted off an hour ago. You can only be intimate for so long—or maybe it was just the two of us.

"Skip, you guys ready?"

"Give us ten minutes."

Watching her cute bare butt as she walked to the bathroom, I listened to her.

"You know Amy is married?"

"Amy?"

"James's newfound flame."

"She told you that?"

"Married. Then she met some other guy three years ago at a funeral. This guy is married too. Anyway, they hit it off, and they've been seeing each other four or five times a year at romantic locations like this."

"This guy wasn't her husband?"

She called from the bathroom, the water running.

"No. The guy she's been seeing left for his home yesterday and she was taking an extra two days to unwind."

"Unwind?"

"This boyfriend, her lover, wears her out. She said the sex was intense. Boring with the husband but intense with the lover."

"So she has intense sex with this longtime lover, he wears her out, then she picks up James and tonight they are—"

"We don't know yet, do we?"

"James seems to—"

"He's that kind of guy, Skip. He can have about whatever he wants."

I couldn't bring myself to ask the next question. Em didn't even like James. They had a history of animosity. And yet she was saying that—

"Everything?"

"It certainly seems that way." She was quiet for a moment then she turned the water off.

"Everything except me."

"Thank you."

Em walked out of the bathroom, and nudity aside, I realized just how much I loved this beautiful creature. I didn't want anybody else.

I marveled at her physical beauty as she dressed, and when she was done, she motioned to me to do the same.

Five minutes later I opened the door and James was standing there, holding the flashlight.

"Time to dig, guys."

I nodded. The shovels were in the truck, and we had a six-pack in the cab. It was two thirty in the morning and what could go wrong?

What indeed.

CHAPTER TWENTY

It was hot and I could taste the thick humidity in the air. The temperature was still in the eighties at three in the morning and the lingering odor of salt layered with the sweet smell of frangipani drifted across the early morning. My hands were sweating, either from the heat or my nervousness.

"Okay, Skip. Em stays on the perimeter. We scale the fence and approximate where the foundation would be."

I was scared to death, but I seriously had high hopes. I was thinking that this thing might be doable. And if we found the information, we were going back to Mrs. T. and asking her for two million dollars as our cut. Two million bucks. I couldn't even fathom that much money.

"Em, you're good with all of this?"

"I'm going to walk three sides. The street side of the fence, the Ocean Air side, and the other side that you've yet to explore."

James nodded in the dim light. "It doesn't appear that you can walk the waterside. The fence goes right to the water's edge. So, you'll monitor the three sides and simply yell if someone seems threatening."

"I can handle that, James." She had never cared for his condescending attitude.

"I hope so."

My biggest concern was keeping the two of them from killing each other until we had our information.

I walked to the fence, looked up, and told James to put his foot in my clasped hands. Once he did, I thrust him up and he was able to grab the top, pull himself up, and straddle the fence. It wasn't razor sharp, but if he slipped and his crotch landed on the fence top I shuddered to think of the consequences.

James dropped from sight.

"Em, clasp your hands."

She did, and I put my foot in the cup she made. Grabbing the metal fence weaving, I asked her to give me a boost.

I was up and straddling, lifting my leg and dropping into the vacant lot. James stood there, smiling.

"Don't aim for anyone, Emily." James had that taunt in his voice. "Just toss the shovels, dear."

"Here they come, Jim."

He hated being called Jim.

The first shovel landed inches from my best friend, the second much farther away. He said nothing.

We picked up the two spades and headed out to the southeast corner of the grassy property.

"There are two kinds of people in this world. Those with loaded guns and those who dig. You dig." James kept walking in the dim light.

"I've got it, James. *The Good, The Bad and The Ugly*. Eastwood."

"I'm proud of you, grasshopper."

We both pulled up at the same spot. It felt right. This entire mission felt right.

"I'll try it up here." James motioned to a plot of ground. "You, back maybe ten feet. What do you think?"

"If it's the southeast corner there's a lot of southeast."

"A lot of corner."

I stuck the shovel in the ground and felt sandy earth. The tip went deep. Pulling a chunk of sand from the ground I dug back in, wondering what the owner would think when he inspected his property in the next several days. Clumps of packed sand piled up as I kept digging.

"James, anything at all?"

"Nothing."

I forced the blade of the shovel deeper, hoping to find a solid base. Again, nothing.

Again and again. How much sand would have accumulated over almost eighty years? Inches, feet, yards? Still, I felt we were on the right track.

"We can change locations. Move in about two or three feet." James walked closer to the center.

"Everything okay, boys?"

Em was on the Ocean Air side. I could barely make out her soft voice.

"Nothing yet, Em."

Five feet and I planted the shovel in the ground. Again, the same old boring nothing. Once more and I felt the jarring in my hands and arms. I'd hit a stone. A rock. I moved the head of the shovel to go around the obstacle. I hit the same surface.

"James, I may have found something."

In the dim light I saw him jerk his head up.

"Oh, my God, Skip. Do you think it might be—"

At that very moment I saw the light. The bright beam from a boat coming straight at us.

"James. There's a boat heading for shore, right here. They're heading for the boat dock. We've got to get the hell out of here."

"Dude, you found a solid foundation."

"James, there's a frigging boat about one minute from docking."

In the warm silence I heard the clink of metal on metal. Then a creak of hinges.

"Friend, someone is opening a gate. Can't you hear it?" I loudly whispered my comment, aware of the clanking of metal.

"Let's get out of here."

And that's when I heard the dogs barking. Not just barking, but growling with a killer instinct.

I could barely see James as he ran across the property, his feet flying. He grabbed the fence on the Ocean Air side, and grasping at the metal grate he moved up the structure and reached the top, vaulting over.

I spun around and there they were. Two big, muscular, black dogs, lips peeled back, sharp teeth bared, and ready to rip human flesh. My human flesh.

CHAPTER TWENTY-ONE

Running like I'd never run before, I hit the closest fence, clawing my way up. The dogs sounded like they were moments away and I jammed my fingers into the metal web, pulling and pulling, and finally I was at the top and I perched up there before dropping down. I felt the jolt in my ankles and knees.

The hounds howled on the other side. My Em stood there, her mouth hanging open. I had the same reaction. I'd escaped. I really had.

"I never saw them coming, Skip. I was on the Ocean Air side." She sounded breathless, speaking in a soft voice. "I am so sorry."

And as I glanced around I saw that I'd landed on the side we'd never seen. Four small block houses ran down to the water on the other side of the street from the fence.

"I noticed a truck when I walked over there. Somebody must have gone in with the dogs, but from where?"

"Where is James?"

"He's safe. The dogs had to have gone in from the west gate. The Old Highway side. That's it. I don't see any other entrance."

James and I hadn't even noticed a gate. Once again, our

inexperience and lack of attention to detail was evident. I hoped we'd get a little better after we'd been at this for a while.

But this side was the side we'd never seen. Foliage was hiding most of the view, but there were several open spaces as I looked down the fence line. On the other side of the street were those block homes that had ocean access.

I motioned to Em and we crept down to one of the viewing points.

"You think James is safe?" I whispered.

"Doesn't he usually skate? Your friend gets away with just about everything. He's probably safe." There was a sigh.

I stood back from the fence, watching through a small clearing as the long boat bumped the dock. The moon had come out from a cloud cover and I saw somebody was already on the wooden planks. A deckhand tossed them a rope.

Em touched my shoulder and I jumped.

"You guys don't seem to have bothered them too much. It looks like they're ignoring the fact that the dogs chased you out."

I nodded. "They probably get kids who break in. James thinks it's a place for skinny dipping."

"Oooh. That would be interesting."

We kept our voices low. "So they're used to people being there. And getting run off. At least that's our theory."

The boat was tied tight and people started getting off. A lot of people were getting off.

"How big is that boat?"

I know nothing about boats, but I would have guessed forty-six to fifty-two feet long.

"Maybe fifty feet."

"So far I've counted thirty people."

Another five walked off before the parade ended.

I swatted at a mosquito and wiped sweat from my brow.

"What do you think? A dinner cruise?" The soft voice was

behind me and I jumped again. James had approached from the rear and was watching through our clearing.

"You scared the hell out of me."

"Maybe a hotel shuttle? Late night fishing trip?"

"They're carrying bags, James."

"We made it out with our limbs intact, pard."

"We did."

"Our surveillance team missed this one." He glanced in Em's direction.

"James, I am so sorry. I never saw it coming. You have my apology. I promise you I will be much more attentive when we do this again tomorrow night."

I shook my head in amazement. I had never heard Em apologize to James. Never. It was unheard of.

"Tomorrow?" James sounded surprised.

"Hey, you guys hit something out there."

"Skip did," he said. "You're right."

"Well, don't you want to see what it is?"

"Yeah." I did.

"Plus there's another reason you've got to go back."

"What's that?"

"Your shovels are lying on the ground."

It was a valid point. I could only hope that no one canvassed the property and confiscated our tools.

The parade of people was walking over to the Ocean Air side of the property. I saw them walk into the dense foliage that hid the fence and every one of them disappeared as if by magic.

James was staring at the far fence.

"Where the heck did they go?"

"It's like they fell off the edge."

We'd walked the fence on that side down to the pointy little beach. I hadn't seen any opening. No gate that I remembered.

"There was nothing there, amigo. Don't you think we would have noticed some kind of opening?"

"Apparently we didn't pay enough attention, James." We never paid enough attention, and it was coming back to haunt us.

James shot back, "She gave me a bunch of crap about me not listening to her or something. I don't know, I wasn't really paying attention."

I knew it right away. But before I could spit it out, Em said, "*Dumb and Dumber.* Jim Carrey and Jeff Daniels."

She'd nailed it.

"Sometimes when I'm with you two guys I feel like I'm in that movie."

CHAPTER TWENTY-TWO

Walking around the fence, we carefully crept by the Ocean Air Suites and down to the beach where I finally turned on the flashlight. Right at the end of the galvanized steel fence there was smooth sand. Someone had raked a path from the fence, across the beach and all the way to the first building.

"Different texture to the sand," James said. "Now why do you suppose that is? Why rake a path like that?"

I shone the light out farther toward the water. The sand was rough: footprints, seaweed, and sea debris marking its natural state.

"Turn it off, Skip." Em was waving at me. "Somebody's going to see that light and send the dogs again."

I nodded and pushed the switch. Someone could be watching. I had to start thinking a little more carefully.

Walking up to the fence, right where the raking started, I could see no sign of an opening.

"This has to be where those people disappeared."

"Maybe there's an underground something on the other side," James said.

"Like a cave?"

"Yeah. Or a tunnel. Maybe they went down a tunnel and ended up, you know, ended up—"

"Boys, there's an ocean right there. An ocean. A huge, deep body of water. In the Keys you don't have underground caves next to the ocean. Unless they're filled with water. You don't even have basements. In many cases, you bury bodies above ground. This is sea level. Cave? Tunnel? Underground something? I don't think so."

And, of course, she was right.

We silently walked back to the truck, wondering if there was any more to this adventure. We'd already been witnesses to a dead body, had the truck splashed with paint, dug for buried treasure, been chased by dogs, and watched thirty-five people mysteriously vanish into thin air. Pretty incredible.

"Lots of stuff happening today." I said it almost to myself.

"None compares to the threat on your life." Emily squeezed my hand as we walked. "That's the worst part of this."

"I think Weezle would disagree with you."

As we approached the truck, I heard him chuckle, then James snorted and laughed out loud.

"Weezle. My God. Weezle." And he kept laughing.

"James, a guy died today. Someone either caved his head in, or knocked him into the furniture, but someone—"

"It's not funny, amigo." He spit out a muffled laugh. "I know that." He was almost hysterical.

"James," I shook him by his shoulders.

"Skip, his name is Weezle. Wouldn't you change that name?" And he laughed uncontrollably.

It appeared that someone did change it.

To Peter Stiffle.

And I think that's a pretty funny name too. Peter Stiffle.

CHAPTER TWENTY-THREE

At nine a.m. there was a pounding at my door. Stumbling from the bed, I cracked the door open to see Mrs. T.

"I've got to come in and talk to you."

"Let me get some pants on," I said as I stood there in my boxer shorts. She spun around and walked away.

Closing the door, I turned and saw Em rubbing the sleep out of her eyes. She yawned and looked at me inquisitively.

"Not good."

"What's not good?"

"I didn't tell Mrs. Trueblood that you're here."

"Smooth move, Skip. Well, maybe you should go outside and explain the situation to the lady."

I pulled on a pair of cargo shorts and a polo shirt.

"Go hide in the bathroom for a second."

She frowned at me but got out of bed, wearing only my T-shirt, and walked into the bathroom.

Pulling open the door, I went out onto the walkway.

"What's up?"

"The police. The sheriff's department. It seems someone reported your truck with the black paint stain parked near the medical complex last night."

That damned black paint.

"We found the Coral Belle. It's not that easy to work during the day when your work involves digging up private property."

She nodded. "Well, apparently the guy who owns a motel down there, The Ocean Air, called and registered a complaint that you guys trespassed on his property."

"Wow. We got permission. From him. We really did." The first time.

"Listen, I want this to succeed." She leaned in, her warm breath on my face. "I want this to succeed more than you could possibly know. But you've got to be more careful. You're called private investigators, in part I presume because you're private. So far, it's a wonder that everyone on this entire Key doesn't know what's going on."

Her arms were folded across her chest and it was more than obvious that she didn't seem to be happy with our performance so far.

"This may not be the best time to bring this up, but number one, Emily got an anonymous note back in Miami, saying that if James and I didn't give up this project, we'd find ourselves dead."

"Really?"

"You were included."

She pursed her lips and looked out at the water.

"Second, Em is here. She came down to help. I know you said not to—"

Taking a deep breath, Mrs. Trueblood gave me a look like my mother did when she would call me Eugene.

"Look, we work better with her. She's a good balance."

"Was she with you last night?"

"Yes."

The frown stayed on her face. "Do you have any more good news to share with me this morning?"

Now I was the one taking the deep breath. The warm breeze, the tanginess in the salty air, it all gave me a little more energy. I should have waited for James to make the announcement, but he'd probably never bring himself to do it.

"Our lives have been threatened."

"I understand that."

"So, James and I were talking and we think we're worth a little more now. We have a little more value."

"How so?" She cocked her head and I knew she wasn't buying it.

"Well,"—it all sounded good when James had laid it out— "anything that is threatened with extinction is more valuable than it was before, you know?"

"And how much value do you think you have?" A stern tone in her voice. This was a lady not to be trifled with.

"We were thinking about two million."

She stepped back.

"An anonymous letter gives you that much value?" She stood back, her head slightly turned, staring at me. "My goodness, just think if that letter had been signed."

I didn't laugh.

"Look, we both think that whoever killed the guy in our room thought it was James or me."

"I'd considered that."

"Mrs. Trueblood, we both also think there's a real possibility that the gold might be here. In Islamorada. In today's value it's worth like forty-four million. We know that. If we're the ones who find it, we think we're worth one-twentieth."

"Okay."

"Okay? Really?" I swallowed a mouthful of air and almost choked.

"Okay, I'll think about it."

"Oh."

"In the meantime, I expect you to keep working on the project. We do have an agreement, even though you'd like to change it."

"We'll keep working on it."

"One thing you might consider is cleaning that black paint off your truck and changing the license plate."

"The plate?"

"It's a Miami plate. The cops, that motel owner at Ocean Air, and half of Islamorada now know that truck."

She finally unfolded her arms, shook her head in disgust, and walked away.

I was disgusted as well. We should have figured that out ourselves. We were marked and too lazy to do anything about it.

Walking back into the room, I saw Em had already dressed. Some cute red shorts and a collared blouse.

"James called."

"Yeah?"

"Said he and Amy were going to take some time getting to know each other this morning and he'd catch up with us this afternoon."

I grabbed the phone, dialed his room, and he picked up on the third ring.

"James?"

"Amigo. Em tell you that I called?"

"She did. Get your ass down here right now. You've got sixty seconds, *amigo.*"

It was about time we started treating this like a business and not a vacation.

CHAPTER TWENTY-FOUR

We scrubbed. The streak of black paint spread maybe a foot across the door and with paint thinner, rags, and some steel wool the three of us worked on that stain. James stood back to comment on the effort more than we did, to admire our work. But, to be honest, he put in some serious time.

"Wax on, wax off. Breathe in through nose, out the mouth."

Em gave him a scowl.

"*The Karate Kid*, nineteen eighty-four," I said. "Not the lame newer version with Will Smith's kid in it."

"That was lame."

"James," Em stared at him. "*Wax on*. This is your truck, remember?"

He put some serious work into it.

Once we had the black scrubbed to a dull gray, James pulled out the can of spray paint we'd picked up at the Ace Hardware in town. They were getting used to seeing our faces. No more cracks about digging for buried treasure. Shovels, a flashlight, screwdriver, WD-40, and some spray paint.

"All right, everyone, stand back."

He shook the can until the little steel ball was bouncing around inside, then aimed at the area and let go. The paint slowly covered the gray, running in tiny rivulets down the side.

"Get me a rag."

I handed him one and he blended the rivers of white into the body.

There was light applause from above and we looked up to see Amy, with a smile on her face, clapping.

"Now do you have time to come up and keep me company?"

"You don't." I said it very firmly.

"Skip, there's a time for—"

"I'll drive back to Miami with Em, and you can sit here and deal with Mrs. T. and this entire fiasco by yourself."

I was hoping he'd cave, because if she agreed to that two million this could be one really, really sweet deal.

James looked at Amy, then at Em, and never at me.

"Okay. What has to be done next?"

"We need new plates."

He looked up at Amy again, dressed in a very brief bikini, or else colorful underwear. I had to admit, she looked very sexy. If it had been me—

"Can't do it right now, Amy. I want to, but—" he spread his arms out as if overwhelmed by the entire situation.

I sincerely believe he was overwhelmed.

We found the truck behind a strip mall about two miles down the road. A white box truck very similar to ours. There are hundreds of them in the Keys. Delivery trucks, handyman trucks, plumbing trucks.

James kept a lookout on one side of the mall, Em on the other. They were both in my view, and I put the Ace Hardware screwdriver into the rear plate screw. It was frozen tight, so I sprayed some of the WD-40 onto the screw.

"Hurry up, man." James said it in a hoarse whisper.

Trying again, I could feel the screw turn slightly. I turned, pushing harder, and it rotated again.

I saw him before he saw me. The skinny guy in cutoffs and a ragged undershirt as he exited the rear of the building. He looked straight at me, obviously confused.

"What are you doing, man?"

"Putting a plate on my truck."

"That's my truck, you son of a—"

He was racing toward me, head bent low. As he reached me, I politely stepped aside and he plowed on through into a hedge of shrubs. Prickly shrubs, apparently, from the sound of his screams.

James and Em were nowhere in sight, but I knew our truck was—had been—in front of the building. I ran at top speed around the corner of the mini strip mall and saw them both in the vehicle, the engine running.

Leaping into the seat beside Em, I shouted out to James. "Were you going to leave without me?"

"Only if there was trouble, dude."

"Of course we weren't," Em spit out. "We were coming around to save you."

As it turned out, I didn't need any saving. But it was good to know that you can't necessarily trust your friends or lovers when you're in a dilemma like that.

CHAPTER TWENTY-FIVE

We finally found another truck behind Woody's. Woody's was a strip club not even two miles from Pelican Cove. The sign said: LIVE NUDE GIRLS.

"Do some clubs feature dead ones?" Em asked.

She'd never been inside a strip club. I made a mental note to take her to one. She'd probably refuse.

This time I had James do the dirty deed. I watched from the privacy of the truck as he struggled with the plate.

Twenty minutes later, we drove our truck onto the street with a new plate and a new paint job. Pretty cool. We were finally acting like real detectives. The thought that rankled me was that someone else had to tell me where we were going wrong. Our employer.

"Let's hope whoever owns that truck doesn't realize we switched the license plate."

"James, let's head over to the vacant property."

"In broad daylight?"

"We'll park the truck a couple of stores down from the

medical building, then one of us can walk back and see if the shovels are still there."

"You told me you met a realtor with a motorcycle." Em spoke up, wedged between us on the cracked vinyl bench seat.

"Yeah, we did."

"Give her a call and ask her to go to the property and check it out for you. For her it won't be a big deal."

"Why her?"

She turned to James. "Who has unlimited access to almost every property in the area and no one will question them?"

She was right. For a natural blonde, she was pretty sharp.

So I called Maria Sanko, and we all met for coffee at a seaside bar and restaurant called Lorelei.

The day was heating up, but the breeze from the gulf was perfect. Living in our crummy apartment in Carol City, I sometimes forget how great Florida can be.

"So, we want to be totally open with you." James could lie with the best of them.

A small boat puttered by, the engine stuttering.

"You're not looking for somebody's great-grandfather?"

"We are. Sort of."

A great egret landed on the railing just in front of us, and the big bird hopped to a vacant tabletop. I looked up and a shorthaired lady in a dirty apron was bringing a plate of scrambled eggs out from behind the bar.

She set the dish on the floor and the bird hopped down and started eating.

"A bird eating eggs," said James. "It doesn't seem right."

"Only scrambled. He only eats the scrambled ones." The woman watched the tall white bird for several seconds then disappeared behind the bar.

"Actually, Maria, you hit the nail on the head yesterday. You said you thought we were probably treasure hunters and we were looking for a wrecker's camp. Well, Mary Trueblood's great-grandfather ran a wrecker's camp. He sacked treasure ships, so looking for the site of the camp is exactly what we're doing."

"I knew it." She slapped the table, rattling the four coffee cups. "Well, I wish you luck. I always thought it would be neat to find some gold coins down here. I've known several people who have. They didn't get rich, but—"

"We have an idea that his wrecker's camp was located at the vacant property behind the doctor's office. Where O'Neill and Malhotra do their business."

It's the best story we could come up with.

"Behind Malhotra and O'Neill's building? The fenced land where the Coral Belle stood?"

"Yes."

"But there was a hotel there. Not a wrecking camp."

Obviously there were holes in our story.

"Well, the information is a little sketchy, but maybe the camp was there before the hotel was built."

She nodded, thinking it through as a blue heron landed on the railing.

The pure-white egret looked up from his meal and squawked as the blue heron jumped down and paraded over to the plate of eggs. The egret flapped his wings and rose about six inches from the planked wooden floor as two seagulls swooped down, one landing on a chair, one on the floor. The egret and the heron both squawked, and I caught the dishtowel from the corner of my eye as it flew through the air, coming dangerously close to Em's head.

"Shoo, shoo!" The lady ran from behind the counter, picked up the towel, and rushed the blue heron, who wisely leaped to the railing and gracefully launched himself into the air.

The two seagulls frantically pecked at the egg on the floor, then took their leave, flying inches above us.

"Gotta love the peace and tranquility out here," Em said as she ducked.

And, to be honest, I did.

We'd finished our second cups of coffee. The birds had all flown away once the eggs were consumed. Green water lapped at the deck and a small sailboat almost brushed our railing as it headed out from the harbor.

"So, let me get this straight. You want me to drive down to the lot, walk down the south fence line, and see if there's any sign of your digging last night?"

"Yeah, sort of."

"But if the dogs ran you off—"

"Honest to God, Maria, you can't tell anyone about that." James's eyes were wide and he grabbed her hand across the table.

"Because you are afraid you'll get caught?"

"Because he's embarrassed that the dogs almost caught up with him." Em smiled. Always stirring the pot.

"Shut up, Em." He let go of Maria's hand and regrouped. "We left our shovels. But due to a boat arriving, we don't think they paid much attention to the—"

"A boat? At that hour of the morning? Maybe it was a fishing boat."

I leaned in. "We thought it was strange, too. Thirty-five people were on this boat. They all had suitcases with them."

Maria frowned, looking out at the water.

"Strange things happen down here. You just never know."

"Will you go look?"

She shrugged. "Why not? There are some nice cottages on that side of the property. I could just be scoping them out, you know, for possible sales."

Em had called this one right.

"Of course, I would like to be considered if you find gold coins."

"Yeah." James and I both shouted together. We weren't after gold coins. We were after pounds of gold bars. And this biker babe was going to give us a hand.

CHAPTER TWENTY-SIX

We stayed away, went nowhere near the scene of the crime. Maria met us at a Walgreens drugstore across from the post office.

"You're right. There are several small clearings where you can see into the property. Your shovels are there, just laying on the ground."

"And what about the ground?" James said.

"It appears to be dug up where the shovels are laying."

We sat in the parking lot, Maria on the soft leather seat of her Harley, the three of us on that cracked vinyl bench seat in the truck.

"If they'd sent those dogs in to run you off, they would have searched the area and confiscated those shovels," Em said. "As it is, they didn't even check the grounds. The entire emphasis last night was on that boat. Maybe the dogs were to protect whatever cargo they had. You said they all carried suitcases."

"Again, what time did that boat arrive?" I knew, but wanted to hear it again.

"Three thirty." Em pointed to her watch.

"So we dig at two thirty tomorrow morning. Just in case

there's another boat at the same time." I was determined to find what my shovel had hit this morning.

"I won't be there. That's past my bedtime, kids." Maria pointed to her watch. "Speaking of time, I've got a house to show. Remember, if you find gold coins—"

She twisted the handle, adjusted the Harley engine to a throaty roar, and pulled out onto Highway 1.

"Think she'll keep quiet?" I asked.

"I think she likes the idea of being a part of this little scheme."

"Gold coins and all."

"We'll dig tonight, pard, but," he turned to Em, "I hope we pay more attention to who shows up."

She bristled.

James drove back to Pelican Cove.

"This time, I'm gonna take a short break, partner. Not much to do till early this morning is there?"

I studied him as we pulled into the parking lot.

"She's married, James. You do know that."

"She's a big girl, Skip."

Em nudged me and I opened the door and stepped out.

"I'm a big boy," he said.

"Not necessarily a smart boy," Em responded as she walked away.

James watched her, then turned to me and shook his head.

"I think it was Will Rodgers who said it best, my friend."

"What was that, James?"

"He said, 'Never miss a good chance to shut up.'"

"I never knew the man."

"Yeah, well, he made sense."

James walked in the direction of Holiday Isle, and I assumed he'd be occupied for the next several hours.

CHAPTER TWENTY-SEVEN

I left Em at the poolside bar with the popular Bobbie as I headed out to the check-in, a small building at the front of the resort. Our resort.

The girl I'd talked to when we found the body was sitting there staring at her computer screen.

She looked up when I opened the door.

"Oh, wasn't that creepy?"

"It was."

Doing a mock shiver, she smiled at me. "I still get goose bumps to think that, you know—and you? You had to see it. Oh, my God. You had to look at the body. Was it gross?"

"It was."

She shuddered for real.

"I've got a question for you. Are you familiar with the water-front suites about a mile and a half down the road called Ocean Air Suites?"

"Sure. I've got a friend who cleans rooms there."

"Really? It's right next to that vacant lot, right?"

"Uh-huh. The strange lot that's fenced in."

"Who owns the suites?"

"You want to know who is her boss?"

"Yeah."

"Doctor James O'Neill."

"Really? The same guy who has the chiropractor business?" I don't know why that surprised me, but I wasn't expecting it.

She laughed. "He's an orthopedic surgeon. I think there's a difference."

"Something to do with bones."

She nodded.

"Do you know Doctor O'Neill?"

"Not really. He tends to keep to himself. Jan doesn't know him either. She says he doesn't show up very often. I think his practice keeps him busy."

"She's met him?"

"I think so. Maybe one time he showed up late in the morning with a group of tourists. Yeah. That was it. They were supposed to come in maybe two a.m. and the boat was delayed. She was cleaning rooms and he showed up with these people at nine in the morning."

"Okay."

"But the place is kind of weird. There are days when she'll get a call and they don't need her."

"Off season, when it's slow?"

"Not necessarily. It's like that whole group will check in really late, sleep all day, and check out the next night. Not till maybe eleven p.m. So they lay her off for two days and then she's got to clean every room the next day. Happens once or twice a month. She's looking at some other job opportunities because this one is shaky. But the economy being what it is—"

"People who check in late and check out late? Ah, tourists. Who can understand them?"

"I just know that we need them."

She smiled and looked back at her computer.

I joined Em at the bar, my beer already on the counter, light brown and bubbly, sparkling in the late afternoon sun.

Bobbie looked at me and frowned.

"My God, this girl, Amy," Em said, "with James, she's having an affair on top of an affair."

"She's on vacation, Emily. You can't have too much fun."

She smiled and sipped her beer, licking the foam off the top.

"Your good friend seems to have more fun than he should."

I agreed. But I didn't want Em telling me that. It was a guy thing. James was James. Em never seemed to get that.

"Hey, I found out something interesting. That motel, excuse me, those suites on the north side of the fence—"

"Yeah?"

"They belong to the orthopedic guy next to the Vein Care Center."

"So he's got an investment close to his office. So what?"

"Well, it's just funny. This Doctor Malhotra owns the boat dock property and Dr. O'Neill owns the suites. And early this morning we see the boat come in and people disappearing at the suites' side of the property."

"I think you're making too much of that."

"Maybe, but you factor in that there were attack dogs for security."

"I'm sure you'll figure it out."

"And the fact that Jan, who works there, says guests sometimes check in very late and check out late the next night. Don't most motels and hotels have checkout by noon?"

I very seldom stayed in a hotel. I could barely afford the rat hole we lived in outside of Miami.

"That's the group we saw. The early morning arrivals." Em looked me in the eyes. "By the way, you're getting pretty good at this detective business."

"How's that?"

"Look at all you've learned in the past twenty-four hours."

"I'm no closer to the gold."

"You've only been here a couple of days, boyfriend."

I liked it when she called me that.

Standing up, she motioned to me. We walked to the beach, and she took my hand. At that very second, life couldn't have been any better. Of course, that never lasts.

CHAPTER TWENTY-EIGHT

We had dinner at the Ocean View Inn and Pub. The place was on the gulf side of the Key and did not overlook the ocean. That didn't seem to matter. It was still the Ocean View Inn.

"Are you sure you want to eat here?" Em was watching ten guys across the bar, laughing loudly, cussing a blue streak, and slamming down their beers as fast as they could.

The bar/restaurant/inn was directly across the highway from Pelican Cove. It was close, walkable, and Bobbie volunteered that the bar food here was passable and it was cheap. She also said some pro football players owned the place and it was world famous. I sensed a theme in Islamorada.

The sign out front said: OLDEST ESTABLISHED LIQUOR LICENSE IN THE KEYS. Everything seemed to revolve around the Keys and alcohol.

Sitting down, I immediately saw there was something sunken into the dark wood bar. A small plaque was embedded there as well. "Spike from Henry Flagler's railroad," it read.

"Em, this is cool. It's a spike from Flagler's folly."

She gave me a suspicious look, then gazed up and down the bar. To her right was a guy who looked like an ex-football player. His curly hair hung in ringlets and his muscle had turned to flab.

Next to him were two older fishermen, the creases in their faces showing the effects of too many days in the sun. Judging by the empty bottles, they were well into their fifth round. Arguing about a football game or player, they went at each other.

"Sum bitch should have stayed a farmer. Never was NFL quality, Danny. Never was."

"Well I say he has two year, two years to prove his mettle. You just think you know it all and—"

"I'd lay a Benjamin down on that. He'll be gone in two."

I signaled the barmaid, a rough-looking woman with a weathered face and her hair pulled back in a knot. She wore a stained white tank top and sported an ugly red scar running down her right cheek.

"Two beers. Yuengling."

She stared at us sullenly and I thought immediately of Bobbie. Were all the bartenders in Islamorada surly?

We checked out the long bar and the far wall with pictures of fishermen, their catches hanging high, as we ate our fried ocean perch and french fries. Not the healthiest meal in the Keys, but the Ocean View was world famous. And that was something. World famous. It made us proud.

She set two more beers in front of us without asking, apparently signaling there was a two-drink minimum for the atmosphere.

Giving us a suspicious look, she said, "Where you from?"

"Miami," I replied.

In the din of laughter and conversation she shouted out, "Are you here for the tournament? You don't look like tournament types."

"I didn't even know there was a tournament."

She squinted her eyes, as if she didn't know whether to believe me or not.

"Swordfishing. They go out at night, three, four miles off-shore where the water's warm. They fish from seven till lines up."

"Lines up?" Em asked.

"Three a.m. They pull their lines. Second night the same thing. Whoever has the most weight, wins."

I wasn't much of a fisherman. "How much does a swordfish weigh?"

"Hundred, hundred ten. Wouldn't you say, Willie?" She motioned to an old leather-skinned man down the bar.

He grunted.

She put down our check, and I handed her the debit card. It's amazing how fast a thousand dollars can slip away. A nice resort, a few good meals, oil and gas for the truck.

"If you're not here for the tournament, what are you here for?"

"Just, you know, vacationing."

She stared at me for a moment. "Don't look much like vaca-tioners either."

Just then a cheer erupted on the other side of the bar, and a couple of men started singing off-key and loudly.

We walked out into the humid evening.

"Did you catch that, Skip?"

Walking across the deserted highway, she grabbed my arm.

"Big fish?"

"That's not what I was referring to."

"Then what?"

"She said lines up at three a.m., and we saw the boat at three thirty."

"You think?"

"Timing is suspect."

"Sure didn't look like a fishing boat. And I don't think you'd have thirty-five people out there. It just doesn't seem right."

"Seems funny they pull in their lines at about the same time you saw the boat."

My girlfriend is right more than she's wrong. I pondered the thought, and I was certain that was no fishing boat.

I heard the throbbing engine before I saw the headlight. A Harley-Davidson came roaring around the bend, and we both ran for the grass. I turned to look and couldn't make out much, except the driver was helmeted. Whoever it was, was riding like the wind. That bike blew by us and disappeared down the road.

"Could have been the gold fender," I gasped when we got to the other side.

"Could have been Maria Sanko." Em wasn't winded at all.

"Could have been our lives if we hadn't picked up our speed."

It was still early and Holiday Isle was cooking, the music and noise drifting across the water.

"Want to go?" Em was making the suggestion.

So we walked to Rumrunners and there were James and Amy, cuddling at the bar.

"Tell me, Skip, would you fool around with a married woman?" Em studied them for a moment.

"Doesn't every situation depend on the moment?"

She put her hands on my cheeks and stared into my eyes. "I don't know if I like that answer."

CHAPTER TWENTY-NINE

We met up in the parking lot at two fifteen. James and I both had smiles on our faces. I only guessed at *his* reason.

"What we have is a committed relationship, Skip," Em whispered. "Don't forget that word committed. Okay?"

I nodded. Em walked in and out of our relationship at her discretion. I felt I was lucky to have what was left.

"We can only hope that our shovels are still where we left them," James said as he pushed the pedal to the metal and hit fifty miles per hour.

We parked in a small lot a block and a half away, far enough from the vacant property, but close enough to make an immediate escape if things turned sour. And things already had a history of turning sour.

"Pray that Malhotra and O'Neill don't show up in a boat at this hour." Em closed her eyes as if in prayer.

Cupping my hands, I offered James the first chance to vault the fence. He cleared easily.

Em lifted me and I grabbed the top rail, awkwardly straddling, then jumping off the metal bar.

"You guys be really careful. Please."

The moon was muted behind a thin layer of clouds as we walked softly across the dew-dampened grass.

"Over there." James pointed to my shovel.

It was amazing that no one had checked up on our digging. They must have been used to having trespassers, those skinny dippers and the make-out artists. And apparently no one had ever done more than that—trespass. So no one was looking for trespassers who would dig the place up. It never occurred to them.

"You want to continue what you were doing yesterday morning?"

Picking up the shovel, I pushed it into the soft earth. There it was again. The sharp clink of metal on metal. It wasn't a stone. It didn't feel like concrete. I spaded out the sand, now digging deeper and out a little. I was about two feet into the soft sandy soil when I hit something else. This time it felt like a rock. Kneeling down, I buried my hand almost elbow deep.

"What do you have?"

"Concrete, James. It's flat and smooth."

"That's what you hit? Well, at least we've discovered the foundation."

"There's something else. Just give me a minute."

I thrust the blade into the ground and pried upward. Whatever the metal piece was, it gave just a little and I slipped the head of the shovel under an edge. Not enough to dislodge it, but it was a start.

"Got something?" He could sense it.

"Just hold tight."

Prying, I felt it give a little more, still covered with too much earth.

"No sign of any boats, pard. And we haven't heard a peep from our lookout. Keep digging."

Shifting my position, I started wedging the shovel around

119

the piece of metal. I could see it was small, maybe five by eight inches, and I pried again. It moved, and I was able to slip more of the shovel under the piece, carefully lifting it. Cradling it in the curved blade, I eased it out of the hole.

"A box. An old metal box." James removed it from its steel bed, brushing away at the dirt that covered the top.

I tugged hard on the top of the box, but it was either locked or corroded shut. Maybe both.

"Is this it? The information?" I studied the object.

"We could dig some more. Personally, I think we're damned lucky to have found anything, you know?"

I knew. It was a big area.

"Let's kick some of this sand back in the hole."

We smoothed over what we could in the dim light, then tossed the shovels up and over the fence on the south side. James started walking toward the fence that fronted the main street, on the west side.

"James," I shouted in a throaty whisper. "Over here."

Walking toward the Ocean Air Suites, I tried to visualize the exact path the boat passengers had taken.

"Trying to find the passage?"

"There's got to be a gate here. It's as simple as that."

We ran our hands across the metal framework, and James found it first.

"It's right here. No secret how they got out."

A heavy metal padlock hung from the outside latch.

"May as well go over here." He put the box under his arm as I boosted him and he jumped. Then I clawed my way up the fence, dropping onto the sandy beach below on the other side.

And there was James.

Between the guy with the diamond earring, and a third man dressed in a white shirt and gray slacks.

"I think I told you before that you were trespassing." I saw the gun hanging by his side.

I was speechless. We were caught red-handed. We'd been here less than three days and already James had been taken to the sheriff's office and it appeared that I would be next.

"I was—we were—looking for something that—" I had no story.

James stood there, his arms by his sides. No box.

Tell them the truth. It's the best I could do.

"We were looking for the foundation of the old Coral Belle Hotel. It was on this property and we—"

"I know where it was."

"Well, we were—"

The earring dude pushed his pistol into James's side and shoved him toward the first building.

"Are you calling the cops on us because we were walking on your sand? Really? That's it?"

As we moved, the guy in the white shirt and slacks finally spoke. "There aren't going to be any cops involved. We're taking care of this ourselves."

That's when we heard the motorcycle, the throbbing roar of a Harley engine, and saw the shadowy machine and its helmeted rider as they screeched into the parking lot of the Ocean Air Suites.

As the two men turned their heads in unison to see who had entered their space, I chopped at the gunman's wrist. I don't know why. I'm not a brave guy, but I sensed he wasn't focused and I hit him hard on the wrist, my hand throbbing for the rest of the night.

He jerked and the gun went flying as he spun around, looking at me in confusion. James turned to him, and with the palm of his hand caught the guy under his chin, snapping his head back. He fell hard on the shell parking lot as his partner reached for my neck.

Hearing someone running behind me, I assumed the worst. I swung wide and hit the man who was choking me right in the middle of his face. Even in the dim early-morning light I could see the blood from his nose as it spattered his white shirt.

The footsteps stopped and I heard a voice that I recognized. "Don't anybody move. I've got the gun."

CHAPTER THIRTY

Em stepped out of the shadows and leveled the gun at the gentleman in the now red-and-white shirt.

I let out a deep breath and backed away. She looked like she knew what she was doing, but you never knew.

"What the hell is going on?"

I turned and there was Maria.

"What are you doing here?"

Glancing at all of the players, she finally focused on me.

"Uh, you were checking on the old hotel, right? I couldn't sleep so—"

"You came down to check on us," I said.

"Yes. Yes, that's exactly why I'm here."

Em kept the gun trained on the guy with the bloody nose.

"Who are you?"

He scowled.

"No, I want an answer."

"I'm Doctor James O'Neill." A very frosty attitude. The guy wasn't happy with us, that much was clear. "I own this property, and, young lady, you and your friends here are in a lot of trouble. When we call the police—"

Feeling slightly braver, I stepped up to him.

"You were the guy who said 'no cops.' You were going to handle this yourself."

He wiped at his face, smearing the blood.

"So?"

"So it's obvious you don't want the cops involved. Maybe you're doing something here you'd rather not have them look into."

It was a shot in the dark, but he reacted by stepping back and raising one of his hands as if to say, "Stop."

"What do you think you know, son?"

"I don't know anything." I didn't want this guy coming after me ever again. "Look, Doctor O'Neill. All we did was walk on your property and you threatened us with a pistol. I think that any court of law would say that you were a little excessive with your proposed punishment. What were you thinking of doing? Shooting us? Pistol-whipping us?" I threw up my hands, emboldened by Em's power of the gun.

"Can I get up?"

The guy with the diamond stud.

"No." Her steely gaze never left O'Neill.

"So what are you going to do now?" The doctor returned her stare. "You see, this is what is known as a Mexican standoff. Neither of us wins. You walk away, we'll walk away. And if you stay away from this property, we'll forget your transgression. Is that an agreement?"

I looked at James, and he nodded. I looked at Em, and she held the pistol steady.

"Em?"

"Okay." She was pissed off at these guys.

Maria Sanko didn't say a word. I was sure that she was sorry she'd ever made the trip. Unless—

"It's an agreement." I nodded my head.

"Now, hand me the pistol." The doctor reached for the weapon.

"The agreement has been reached," Em said. "Nothing was said about returning your pistol."

The guy from the golf cart struggled to his feet.

"Give me the damned gun."

I was with Em. "No. You threatened us with this gun. We're leaving, but with the pistol. Right, Em?"

She nodded.

"I sincerely hope we don't meet again." The good doctor glared daggers at us. "I don't think it would be good for either of us."

"Doctor, we're never setting foot on your property again." I hoped we wouldn't have to.

I turned to find James, but he was already walking toward the street, moving very fast.

Em turned, lowering her weapon, and I followed her out of the parking lot. There's something sexy about a woman with a gun.

Maria walked to her bike and pushed the big machine behind us.

"Thank God you showed up." I stepped up beside Em.

"Damn, Skip. I couldn't be everywhere at once. I was on the far side and I heard the commotion. I got to you as fast as I could."

"Hey, you just said it. You couldn't cover three sides at once."

She squeezed my hand. "Skip, we've been through some things together, but tonight, realizing you guys could have been killed, I was really scared."

"Scared?" I couldn't believe it. "I never saw you so calm, so in control. And, Em, you made some impressive time getting over here once it turned into a free-for-all. You may have saved our lives."

"Skip, I saw the damage you two did. Very impressive. I never pictured you as a pugilist. I kind of like it."

It had surprised the heck out of me, too.

Maria caught up with us on the street.

"What the hell? That was scary."

I'd been thinking about it for the last two or three minutes. Turning to her, I asked, "Did you tell them we were digging tonight?"

"Them?"

"Dr. O'Neill and the other guy. Did you tell them about us?"

Her eyes got wide.

"Absolutely not." There was bitter acid dripping from her tongue. "What do you think I am?"

"Maria, I'm sorry," I said. "There were four of us who knew where we'd be tonight, and I can account for three of us."

"Oh, you son of a bitch." Her fists were clenched. "Just because they happened to be there you think that I called them and told them about you?"

The thought had definitely crossed my mind. It made sense. I may have been wrong. "Look, I'm sorry. I thought that—"

"You didn't think." She glowered at me. "I helped you do research, I offered my services to help you find this ghostly wrecker's camp and you accuse me of setting you up? You are a first-class son of a bitch, Skip Moore."

She straddled the seat of her Harley-Davidson, turned the key, and blew out onto the street.

Em and I watched her disappear.

"It seems we've upset several people tonight." Em let go of my hand.

"How else would they have been waiting for us at three in the morning? That's not the time of night two grown men walk the beach." I thought about that statement. "Unless—"

Em shook her head. "I don't think so."

"The good news is that we found a metal box."

"Really? The information you were looking for?"

"I think."

"Skip, that's fabulous."

"The bad news is that I don't think it made it over the fence. James didn't have it back there."

I had no idea where the metal box could be.

CHAPTER THIRTY-ONE

"Dude, she peeled out of here. What happened?"

"Skip simply asked her if she'd turned us in to Doctor O'Neill and company. A fair question."

He stepped back. "Never saw that coming."

"My God, James, she was the only other person to know what we were planning. I mean, I think they were going to kill us."

"Pretty serious accusation, amigo."

"And what did you think?"

He smiled. "Same thing. She knew about our plans. And, it was strange that she showed up at the exact time we were getting grilled by the doctor and his friend."

"We handled them though, didn't we?" I thought about how I'd hit O'Neill in the nose. One of the prouder moments of my life.

"Gave 'em the old one-two." James smiled.

"James, all of that hassle. And you never got the box, did you? Is it still on the vacant lot?"

He smiled. "As soon as I saw both guys were distracted, I

picked it up where I'd dropped it. Right by the fence." He reached into the truck and pulled out the old, dirty metal container.

I grinned. We were well on our way to finding the gold.

"I think I'll go to sleep and dream about piles of gold, gettin' bigger and bigger and bigger." James was smiling.

"*The Treasure of the Sierra Madre*," I said. No question. We'd both watched it one hundred times. Maybe more.

"Let's drive over and pick up the shovels," James said.

"Then I think we go back to the Cove and pry open the box."

"It's three thirty in the morning. Do we wake up Mrs. T.?"

"It depends," my best friend said, "on what's in the box."

We drove back, Em never saying a word, the gun in her lap. Ma Barker, Bonnie Parker, "Squeaky" Fromme–the woman who pointed a gun at President Ford. I had fantasies of Emily as a gunslinging moll.

In my room, we worked on the lid, prying with a metal nail file from Em's purse and a corkscrew that came with the room. James took the nail file and worked it up under one side. Then under the other. He slid it up between the box and lid on the front, and pulled back.

The file snapped, and half of the blade jammed between the lid and the box.

"Sucker is locked."

"Rusted shut," said Em.

"Both," I added. "If we had a blow torch—"

"A hacksaw," James suggested.

"A hammer." Em slammed her fist on the top of the box.

It popped open, the lid springing up and the rest of the nail file dropping to the floor.

"Whoa." James moved back.

"Oh, my God." I gazed into the container. A folded piece of paper lay in the open box, yellow and curled on the edges.

"Take it out," Em said.

"It hasn't seen the light of day for seventy-five years."

"If we want to know what's on it, we've got to take it out."

"Maybe we should wait." James wasn't sure we were making the right move.

I reached in and pulled it out with just the tips of my thumb and index finger. Careful not to do any damage.

It was crinkly and stiff like a cracker.

"Man, if we try to unfold this, it's going to break into pieces."

"We've got to see what's on that paper."

"James, we'll destroy it."

"Soak it in water."

"The ink could run."

"Skip, James. Do you remember where you were when I called you from Miami and told you about the letter I'd received?"

We answered together. "The library."

"What does that have to do with anything?" James gave her attitude.

"Libraries do more than check out books. You guys saw a lot of news clippings and magazine articles."

"Even some letters about the hurricane."

"Libraries fix old letters. Old newspapers. They must have a process."

"Oh." James nodded. "Once in awhile, you come up with a decent idea."

"I've bailed your ass out more times than I care to count, James. I've had a lot of good ideas."

He didn't say anything.

"I suggest we get some sleep and visit your friendly Islamorada Library first thing tomorrow morning."

We agreed and headed to our respective rooms.

It was probably five a.m. when I heard the doorknob turn.

The first thing I thought was that someone had made a mistake. They assumed it was the room next door.

Then I heard a clicking noise as if a key was being inserted. Pelican Cove still used keys, not the plastic slide cards that most places use.

"Who's there?" I sat straight up in bed.

Em shook her head, wiped the sleep from her eyes, and stared up at me.

"Skip, what's going on?"

"I don't know. Someone's trying to open the door."

My girlfriend reached for the nightstand drawer beside her bed and opened it.

Standing up, I slowly walked toward the door.

"Skip, step aside." There was urgency in her voice.

I took two steps back and heard the door handle turn again.

With a powerful thrust the door swung in, banging loudly against the wall. I saw a silhouette, both arms straight out in front.

"Get down, Skip."

I dropped.

The first explosion was deafening, and I could just make out the second one.

I looked up from my kneeling position, peering out the open door. There was no more silhouette.

"Are you all right?" She was shouting.

"What the hell happened."

She was standing by the bed in my T-shirt. Her blonde hair was disheveled and her face was ashen.

"Em?"

And then I saw the gun hanging from her right hand.

"He shot at us, Skip."

"And?"

"I shot him."

The outside lights shone bright through the door and I stepped out on the walkway. There was no one. Out in the parking lot the roar of a motorcycle split the night, then things got quiet again.

"There's no one here, Em."

She was suddenly by my side. Emily in my T-shirt, me in my boxers.

"Apparently, you didn't do any damage."

She knelt, running her fingers over the cement.

"Apparently, I did," she said.

She held up her fingers and they were stained with bright red blood. And there was a whole lot more of it on the concrete.

CHAPTER THIRTY-TWO

The couple from the neighboring unit stuck their heads out the door.

"Jesus Christ, if that was a bullet, it destroyed our TV and almost took us out," the guy said.

We heard commotion from down the hall and several other people stuck their heads out, trying to see if everything had returned to normal. I suppose it all depends on what you consider normal.

A guy with a dirty work shirt and thirty keys hanging from his belt came rushing into our room, walked to the headboard of the bed, and put his finger in the bullet hole.

"This where the bullet went through?"

I nodded.

"Damn. Gonna have to patch and paint." Apparently no sympathy for the intended victims.

He shook his head in disgust and walked back out.

"You could have been killed, Em."

"Back at you, Skip. We survived."

"You need to go back to Miami. This is definitely not a safe place."

"What? And leave you two guys on your own? Come on. The reason I came down was because I got the note saying someone wanted to kill you. You need me for protection."

She pointed her index finger at me, then poked it in my chest.

"Look, I may have screwed up on the surveillance thing, but give me credit, boyfriend, I've pulled my weight."

She had. No question.

James walked in behind Mrs. T.

"Boys, I think it's time we go home. Someone is serious about stopping this investigation." Mrs. T. appeared shaken.

As two sheriff's deputies paraded into the room, I pulled Mrs. T. aside.

"Mrs. Trueblood, I've got some really good news."

She looked skeptical. "I'd say we could use some right now."

"We found a metal box near the foundation of the Coral Belle. Inside is a piece of paper. It's old, it's brittle, and it's all folded up, so we're taking it to the library tomorrow to see how we can open it and make it readable."

Her mouth hung open as surprise flooded her face and all of a sudden I had the feeling that she never really expected us to find anything. And we'd pretty much expected that we would.

Ushering her out onto the walkway we walked around the bloodstains and I touched her shoulder.

"Did you hear me, ma'am?"

"Yes. Yes. You really found something? I mean, what else could it be? It's in the right spot, and you said it's old and—" She looked up into my eyes. "You still want to go through with this?"

"We are this much closer to finding the gold."

"You almost got killed tonight. I can't in good conscience ask you to stay on my account."

"What about the dead guy?"

She looked away from me and down at the pool.

"Obviously Mr. Weezle and Mr. Markim weren't in my employ at the time of Mr. Weezle's death." She still seemed rather cold about his death. "But you," she said, "you and your friend, someone tried to kill you."

"Twice."

"What?"

"It's a long story."

"James, I can't—"

"It's Skip."

"Skip, I will honor your offer."

"Really?" I was stunned.

"Really. You've put yourself on the line. If you find the gold, you get one million dollars."

There was the catch. Pretend she'd misunderstood. But hey, one million was still a heck of a lot better than the previous deal.

"With all respect, Mrs. Trueblood, it was two million dollars."

"Whatever."

From behind me I felt a hand on my arm. Turning, I saw Big D with a disgusted look on his face.

"You let people track through the blood here on this concrete?" Officer Danny Mayfair said with an accusing tone.

"I didn't exactly let anyone do anything. I don't remember being in charge of this crime scene."

"We need to talk."

And for the second time in two days I was interviewed by the Monroe County Sheriff's Department. This time it was more informal. I even knew the officer's nickname and how he got it.

CHAPTER THIRTY-THREE

"It's called deacidification." Kathy Ebert sat at her desk, piled high with papers and books, and the three of us were hanging on every word.

"And you do it here?"

"We do. On older books. Antiquarian collectors do it. There used to be a lot of acid in paper and, just like the piece you've got there, it turns yellow and crinkly over time. So the idea is to preserve the paper. We can stop the acid from doing any more damage with Bookkeeper Deacidification Spray."

"But we need to open it without destroying the—"

"Bookkeeper Solution is a nonaqueous, liquid phase process that uses magnesium oxide."

"A nonaqueous what?"

"Not important, Mr. Moore. Once we fix the letter, we'll use Bookkeeper. Right now we want to open your letter without, as you said, destroying it."

"And how do we do that?"

"We're going to treat it like a cigar. Put it in a humidor."

We watched as she pulled out a wet sponge, opened a box of Baggies, and put the sponge and our folded paper in one of the plastic bags.

"We expose the paper to as much humidity as possible. Then, tomorrow—"

"Tomorrow?" The three of us said it almost together. And we all three sounded disappointed. We had work to do and the letter was crucial to our investigation. We were hoping for today. She assured us she couldn't hurry the process.

"It's going to take about twenty-four hours. Minimum. Then, we'll try to unfold it. We'll apply some blotter paper to give it more moisture, loosen the fibers."

"And when you open it tomorrow?"

"Some of it will break. It's inevitable, considering the condition it's in. That's when we go to plan B."

"And that is?" Even Em was impatient.

"Japanese tissue."

"More moisture?"

"No," Kathy said. "This transparent tissue is lightly coated with an adhesive, like Elmer's Glue. It's actually a polyvinyl adhesive coating. We put the letter back together like a jigsaw puzzle. Then we place the strips of Japanese tissue over the broken areas, like tape. When we apply a warm iron, the strips literally melt into the paper and almost seamlessly hold the letter together."

James, Em, and I sat back in awe. Kathy beamed.

"We do it here from time to time."

"And we can read whatever is on the paper?"

"If all goes well, it should read as well as when it was written."

"This is great. So, you won't open it until we're here right?"

"It's safe. I'll wait until we're all assembled tomorrow."

I looked at James. If someone else read the information on

that paper before we did, they might just go find the precious yellow metal themselves. But I figured we could trust Kathy. We had to trust someone. And if you couldn't trust a librarian, who could you trust?

CHAPTER THIRTY-FOUR

The restaurant was old, made of wood and stucco and painted green. Bentley's Raw Bar was upstairs and it was all dark wood and small tables. The bar was well stocked, and as we walked by the cute barmaid smiled. At James.

"Debit card is going down fast." We pulled out chairs and sat down.

"Yeah, but Skip, since we found that letter, I think the lady is going to open up her pocketbook."

I'd held it in until I felt certain we'd have access to our letter. But I couldn't hold it in any longer.

"James, Em, this morning, after the shooting, Mrs. T. agreed that if we find the gold, we get two million dollars."

They were stunned.

"This is no joke?"

"No joke. I don't have it in writing, but verbally she agreed. Two million, my friend. Two million, Em."

James kept shaking his head. "Two million. Oh, my God. Two million."

The smile on his face went from ear to ear.

"We're still a long way from that precious metal, pard, but damn. If we just keep moving in the right direction."

We ordered appetizers that were surprisingly good. Gator tail, crabmeat balls, and escargot cappricio. Being the gourmet of the group, James was in his element. He still had dreams of being executive chef at some fancy restaurant. A million bucks could do a lot to advance his career.

"Buy our own place, Skip. Just like we talked about in college."

Em smiled. She tolerated us. Our fantasies.

"A million bucks doesn't go as far as it used to." Running her daddy's construction business, I figured she would know.

"Let me change the subject for a moment, guys. I've been thinking about these guys Malhotra and O'Neill."

"What about them?"

"Do they know that you've been digging on Dr. Malhotra's property?"

We'd been surprised they didn't know about it the first time.

"I don't think so."

"Do they know about the gold? Were they aware you knew where the map or whatever's in that box was? Is that why they were taking you away at gunpoint? Is that it?"

James washed down a gator bite with his draft. "I don't think they had a clue what we were up to."

"So why were O'Neill and the other guy so fired up to take you two away? They basically suggested they had some vigilante justice planned for you. That line about no cops being involved? I seriously think they were going to kill you. There had to be a reason."

And I thought she was right.

"So, even though it may not have anything to do with missing treasure, why do you think they wanted you out of the way?"

"Or maybe still do. Do you think that shooting this morning was set up by Malhotra and O'Neill?"

"Maybe, but you're missing the point."

We often missed the point. We specialized in missing the point.

"Why are they afraid of you?"

I shrugged my shoulders.

"Because you saw the boat come in. You were right there when it docked. The dogs ratted you out, and then later somebody recognized your truck."

"Because of the black stain."

"Right. So they were able to track it to you. What makes them so afraid of you? Why do you scare them?"

"Okay, Em, the boat." I sipped on my Yuengling. The restaurant was warm, with just some fans to cool it, but the beer was like ice and tasted perfect. "The boat is the key, right?"

"Probably, but why?"

James popped the last crabmeat ball into his mouth. Talking with his mouth full he said, "Something we saw."

"What did you see?"

"The boat." He was again missing the point.

"What else?"

"People getting off the boat."

"What else?"

"They were carrying suitcases."

Em nodded. "There's something else there. I'll be damned if I can see it, but it had to be right in front of your face."

"Em, if this has nothing to do with the gold, why should we be so worried about it? I mean, other than the fact that they were marching us away at gunpoint?"

Em rolled her eyes, as she often does when talking to James.

"Because somebody tried to shoot us today, James. And I'd

141

like to know why. Maybe saving our own lives is more important than finding the gold."

James swallowed the remains of his rich brown beer. Damn, it was nice to be on an expense account.

"We can save our lives by going home, boys and girls. Back to Miami, Em. Back to Coral City and our rat nest of an apartment, Skip."

The three of us looked at each other.

"And then again, maybe we can save our own lives and find this elusive gold," said Em.

"Yeah," I echoed her sentiments. "That would be nice."

We paid the check with Mrs. T.'s debit card and left a generous tip. We'd just hit the lady up for another thou. After all, we were worth a whole lot more than when we woke up this morning.

In the parking lot, James drained two more quarts of oil into our leaky old engine.

On our way back, he asked me about the computer.

"Glad you reminded me. Drive by the sheriff's office and I'll duck in and pick it up. Big D told me they were done with it."

"Big D?" Em asked. "He didn't seem to be a very big guy."

"Maria's ex. I asked her the same question."

"What did she tell you?"

"What do you think?"

Em dropped it.

"We might have another problem. They took Em's gun."

"Which isn't Em's gun," James stated.

"I'm not sure whose gun it is. It seemed to belong to the guy we met on the golf cart. The one with the diamond earring."

"We can always pray that it's not registered," Em said. "Because if it comes back that the pistol was stolen, I could be in some serious trouble. I'm pretty sure that the crime of stealing a weapon is a felony."

"Em, for God's sake, they were using the gun on us."

"Your word against theirs, James."

I could tell I was about to get a lecture.

"Think about it. Here's a guy who works part time at Cap'n Crab as a line cook who moonlights as a PI, and on the other side, there's a vascular surgeon with strong ties and strong business connections in his community."

She turned to me. "Here's a guy who dabbles as a private investigator and sells security systems to people who have nothing to secure, and over here there's an orthopedic surgeon, probably president of his Rotary Club and the fair-haired boy in Islamorada."

She waited, timing her delivery.

"Just who are they going to believe?"

She was right. I prayed that the gun wasn't registered to anyone. If it was, Emily could be doing time.

CHAPTER THIRTY-FIVE

"You go into the embassy, in character, during a party. Hide in plain sight."

I couldn't place it.

"Come on, man. Tom Cruise, nineteen ninety-five or six."

"*Mission Impossible.*"

"Yeah."

"And it has relevance because?"

"Something happened in plain sight and we're missing it, just like Em said."

James had actually agreed with Em. That was a surprise.

"A boat came in. People got off the boat."

Emily had gone to the room to freshen up. Guys don't freshen up. Splash some water on my face and I'm good to go. James and I sat in two beach chairs, staring out at the flat water and the clear blue sky.

"What did those people have?"

"Suitcases. All of them had suitcases," I said.

"Personal items or are they posing as tourists and actually smuggling something?"

"Whoa. That's a thought." I was impressed. James was really getting into this.

"What are they smuggling?"

"Okay, this is a stretch, amigo, but what if, what if this gold thing is out there. What if Weezle and Markim found the gold bars? Maybe in the ocean. Maybe they found a treasure map. What if these people are out there, diving and bringing back the gold bars in those suitcases?"

And just like that, I wasn't so impressed.

"James, that's really far-fetched."

"Yeah, maybe."

We sat there watching seagulls swirl around a small fishing boat that drifted offshore.

"Swordfish tournament going on this week."

He nodded his head. "This is the Keys, son. There are always fishing tournaments going on."

"This one runs from seven in the evening until three in the morning."

"And you think the boat coming in at that hour—"

"Em thinks."

"I think what?" She snuck up and put her hands on my shoulders. "I put the computer under the bed."

"And the gun?"

She smiled. "The thirty-eight? Where I can get it if I have to."

They'd released the pistol as well. With five shells left. There was a verbal warning to get it registered, so apparently no one had claimed ownership. And since there was no evidence that she'd shot anyone, they gave it back to her. I decided she was the perfect person to be the keeper of the pistol—KOTP.

"I was just telling James that you thought the timing of the fishing tournament and the boat coming to dock at three thirty might be tied together."

"Just a thought," she said. "And, by the way, I'm going to the drugstore. Got to get a new nail file after my last one went to the good of the cause. Want to come?"

What I really wanted to do was drive. Her Carrera was hot and I'd never been behind the wheel of a Porsche. The black beauty had three hundred forty-five horsepower. The powerful V-6 was meant for speed, but during our short trip to the store she kept it at forty-five. No, she did not let me drive.

"It's brand-new, Skip. You know how I am with my cars."

I did. She rode them hard, kept them for a year or two until she was tired of them, then got rid of them. And when she would go on hiatus during our relationship, I was always afraid that was what she was doing to me.

She pulled into the parking lot and I grabbed her arm.

"Check it out."

Parked on the right side of the store was a black Harley with a gold fender.

"There's got to be more than one, Skip."

"Park in the other row so we can see who gets on it."

"What if this person works here? We could be waiting a long time."

She pulled in and we waited. Ten minutes went by and we looked at each other.

"Private investigators do stakeouts that last hours. Days."

She was right. The two of us were impatient after ten minutes.

"Give it another ten."

"I guess my nails can wait that long."

Ten minutes to the second he walked out the door. Slight build, in a short-sleeved shirt and jeans. I studied him as well as I could, trying to see if he resembled Todd Markim, Weezle's partner. He had a similar look, but I'd only seen the Internet

Yellow Pages ad, and at this distance I wasn't quite sure. What we both noticed was his right arm.

From his wrist to his elbow it was wrapped in gauze and bandages.

"Could've had an accident and scraped it pretty bad," I said.

"Could have scalded it. Maybe he was cooking and accidentally spilled boiling water on it."

"Maybe he was working on the bike and—"

"Let's say it, Skip. Could be a flesh wound from a bullet."

The man pulled on his helmet, gingerly, and headed out into traffic.

"Okay, okay, the nail file can wait." Em gunned the engine and we were in pursuit.

CHAPTER THIRTY-SIX

We left Islamorada, heading south. Em put two or three cars between us and the biker, but considering there is only one road and just two lanes almost all the way to Key West, hiding from anyone was going to be tough. At least the rider didn't know the Carrera. We didn't think he did.

"This could be a wild-goose chase." She kept her eyes on the road, looking very sexy behind the wheel of her new sports car.

"Could be. But we're kind of at a standstill until we read that piece of paper tomorrow."

"If this guy is Todd Markim, have you thought about what you're going to do? I mean, you have nothing on him except that he's a private investigator who's gone missing. He didn't steal anything from Mrs. Trueblood, did he? I mean, he's allowed to walk off the job, right?"

"Yeah."

"You have no evidence that he murdered the guy in your room?"

"No."

"We're really not sure he was the one trying to get into our room this morning." She hesitated. "The one I think I shot."

"No."

"Just wondered what you were planning." She never looked at me, just kept her eyes on the traffic up ahead.

But of course, this was a jab to let me know that I never plan. Whatever happens, happens. I don't know if it's my philosophy of life, or if I just don't bother. Either way, it's probably not a good strategy for a PI.

"Maybe I'll talk to him. Ask him if he or his partner were the ones who threw paint at the truck and took a shot at us in our room. I'll ask him if he's the one who bashed in his partner's head."

She smirked.

The speed was about sixty and with no lanes for passing, everyone evened out. Our myopic view was caused by mangrove trees growing high in the water on both sides of the road, so we just stared ahead. At more road. Crossing a bridge, I finally got a view of the open water, a brief look at where the blue sky met the blue of the gulf on the horizon. Florida was full of visual delights.

From a side road a box truck pulled out, blocking our view of the cars and the bike up ahead. A crudely painted sign was scrawled on the side.

HAULERS

"Damn."

"Skip, it's not like he's got the option to lose us. I mean, we'll see him if he gets off the road."

And we did. But too late.

We passed a sign that said: LOWER MATACOMBE STATE PARK AND CAMPGROUNDS. A moment later, we drove by the paved road that exited right, into that very park, and we saw the motorcycle as it rounded a curve on that road and was lost in the trees. He'd gotten away.

"Damn." This time it was Em. "I'll find an exit and turn around."

Thirty seconds later she braked and pulled the Porsche off onto a bare patch of earth. Spinning around, she pulled up to the highway and waited another two minutes while a stream of vehicles paraded by. Finally, we crossed the road and reversed direction. This time she made the exit, slowed down, and drove back into the trees that had swallowed the biker and his ride.

She stopped the car and while the engine idled, we took stock of the park. In front of us was a scattering of tents and booths—signs of an art festival or craft show. The closest paintings were hanging from the sides of a tent and they appeared to be crude oils of African masks.

To our right was a small concrete block restaurant with a sign that said: HOMEY KEYS COOKING. There was a scattering of pastel yellow, blue, and pink tables down by the water. A family of four sat at a blue table, eating sandwiches and watching pelicans scoop fish from the water into their deep bills.

"So, where did he go?" My eyes swept the location.

To our left was a gravel parking area where maybe twenty cars and trucks rested, two of them with trailers and boats rigged for fishing. There was no sign of the black bike. A young man with a long-billed cap and a deep tan stepped out of a pickup at the end of the row and walked toward us. As he passed I shouted out the window.

"There's a campground here?"

"There is."

"Where?"

He pointed to a narrow road back between some more trees. I nodded and Em eased the car in that direction.

"Your Porsche is going to stick out like a sore thumb."

She raised her eyebrows and turned to me. "Please, don't refer to my automobile as a sore thumb. Got it?"

"Yeah, but you know I'm right."

"Then I'll park it and we can walk."

And that's what we did.

The campground was maybe half a mile back from the main park area, and on our short nature excursion we got to see more trees. A lot of trees.

Finally, we came to a clearing and there were rows and rows of campers and tents. The campers were the expensive ones that you can pull out the sides to make more room, and the Air Stream shiny aluminum trailers.

Fancy names like North Ridge, Holiday Rambler, and Coachman were printed on the sides of some. There were also campers that looked to be on their last leg, campers with dents and cracks, and tents that were stretched taut over poles. There were several lots with what looked like blow-up rooms and in the distance, I saw outhouses.

We walked together, eyeing the paths that ran between the temporary homes. A little girl with pigtails came racing out between two campers on a Big Wheel and almost took my left foot off, and not ten seconds later a dirty-brown mongrel mutt leaped at us, baring his yellow teeth. I jumped back, almost falling on top of Em, but the dog was restrained by a chain attached to a post driven into the ground.

"Do you anticipate any more attacks?" Em asked.

"I didn't anticipate the last two."

We kept walking, staring down each path, hoping to see some sign of the bike or the biker, but there was no sign of the black Harley with the gold fender.

"He may have grabbed a sandwich back at the restaurant and taken it with him on the road. There's no proof that he's here."

She might have been right, but I took her hand and tugged her along. I hadn't given up hope. But as we ended the walk, coming up on the last row of campers, I had to agree. We'd lost whoever it was we were following.

"Well, damn it. It wasn't supposed to happen like this."

She squeezed my hand.

We reversed our course and headed back the other way, still pausing to see down the rows where cars and trucks parked on small crushed-seashell lots. I felt it in my bones, this guy was back here.

"Don't see it, Skip."

"Could be pulled up beside a trailer or tent. We'd have to walk every path."

"We can do it, but I think someone might get a little suspicious of this couple that's scoping out the campground."

"Good point."

We walked back through the trees and headed for the Porsche.

I looked down and kicked at a beer bottle that lay on the ground. Watching it land in a clump of brown grass, I raised my eyes to see a man walking toward us. In his hand was a helmet, and he was swinging it back and forth.

Turning my head, I nudged Em. She turned as well and we stepped to the side of the narrow road to give him wide berth.

"Is that him?" She said it in a coarse whisper.

"I don't think so."

I risked a glance as the man walked past us. His eyes were focused ahead and he paid no attention to us.

I felt my heart literally jump in my chest and my stomach took a dip, as if I was on a roller coaster.

"Skip, for God's sake, what's wrong?"

I couldn't talk. Couldn't utter a single word. I froze in place, trying to catch my breath. Sweat broke out on my forehead and for a second I closed my eyes, trying to gather my thoughts.

"Tell me." She grabbed my arm, shaking me, but it did no good.

"You look like you've seen a ghost."

I just kept nodding my head up and down.

I had seen a ghost. The person walking down that road was the dead guy. I would have sworn on it. The same guy that I saw in our room at the Cove, the blood from his head seeping into the carpet.

CHAPTER THIRTY-SEVEN

"Peter Stiffle was the name of the dead guy."

"James finds that amusing," I said.

"The name?"

"Yeah. Not the death."

"James would."

"Could have been his twin, Em. This guy today looked just like him. Minus the cracked cranium." I shuddered, thinking about that gruesome scene.

"Let's walk through the case."

She was driving back, the road almost empty and she had opened it up to eighty. My car, James's truck—they had no idea what eighty was. Forty, fifty, that was a stretch for them, but eighty?

She goosed it up to ninety for a short stretch, but brought it back after a couple of seconds.

"Mary Trueblood hires Markim and Weezle. They agree to help find the gold." Em was reciting from the story I'd told her.

"Right. And she waits for six months to hear from them.

When she checks in, they've disappeared. Their phone is disconnected, their website is gone, and a personal check turns up nothing."

"And she waits six months?" She had the speedometer up to ninety again. "Six months before hiring you?"

"That's what she said."

"Okay, maybe." She stared out the windshield, seeing the same trees and pavement that I saw. A monotonous blur of green and gray.

"But she must have given them some clues. They didn't just drive down here and await further instructions. I mean, she told you guys about the Coral Belle and you found," she paused, slowing down as we approached traffic ahead, "well, we're not sure what you found."

"There's always that." I was worried about what we'd found. "But, we'll find out tomorrow. I can't believe it's not good news."

"So these two investigators disappear and you and your partner look them up on the Internet. If memory serves, you went to the Yellow Pages online and found their firm. Right?"

"We did. Right there, as a matter of fact." I pointed out the window at The Green Turtle as we cruised by.

"You've got an idea of what they look like."

"We do. We saw their pictures on the web."

"And when James discovers the body in your room, he's convinced it's one of the investigators."

"I was convinced, too. It wasn't just James."

"Okay, so you're both positive that the victim bleeding all over your carpet was Weezle."

"Yes."

"And today, not more than thirty minutes ago, you are certain you saw the same man who was killed in your room at the Cove."

I nodded. "I'm glad you timelined it, Em, but the fact remains, I saw a ghost or someone who looks exactly like the dead guy, Peter Stiffle."

Em took her eyes off the road for a second, looking at me. "We call the sheriff's office."

"The less of those guys, the better."

"No, no. Not to tell them that there's a ghost. What we need is verification. Of the dead man's identity."

I thought about that for a minute.

As Em pulled into the parking lot at Pelican Cove I said, "He could have called himself Weezle or Markim. In reality I suppose he could be Peter Stiffle."

The corners of her mouth turned up. She seemed to be somewhat amused herself.

"Yeah, there have got to be a lot of guys out there who are dying to change their names to Stiff from Weezle or Markim."

"Stiffle."

"Whatever. Skip, we need to know, once they've taken the fingerprints or whatever else they do for identity check, who the dead guy was. Then, we'll figure out who the live guy is."

"The ghost guy."

"He's not a ghost." She opened her door and stepped out.

"No?"

"Guaranteed."

"Great. I was beginning to wonder."

"Trust me on this one." We walked to the stairs. The elevator took too long.

"You're sure it wasn't a ghost?" Playing with her.

"Positive."

"And just how can you be positive? That's a pretty bold statement." I paused, then remembered one of my favorite movies.

"You're talking ghosts here, for God's sake."

"Skip, I know we're talking—" She took a deep breath. "Your humor isn't exactly on target today. We're talking about dead people, and for some reason this ghost thing is not funny."

She drew a deep breath, rolling her eyes at me. "But the line you just handed to me is a quote from the Patrick Swayze and Demi Moore movie, *Ghost*. Right? I got that, didn't I?"

She'd nailed me.

"Well, there's got to be an explanation other than your ghost theory. I'm wondering if you weren't wrong about the dead guy's identity."

"I'm starting to doubt it too. Different name, and then I see who I think is the real Weezle at a state park."

Em went up to our room. James wasn't in his, so I walked over to Holiday Isle, hoping I'd run into my partner. I was pretty certain he'd be entertaining the married Amy since she was leaving for her other life tomorrow. Back to the husband and kid.

I wondered how it was to want the things that you can't have. And then it hit me that maybe Amy was able to pull that off. She wanted a fling when she wanted it. A serious relationship when that suited her.

And maybe that wasn't so bad. Maybe it kept things in balance.

And, I couldn't wait to tell James the ghost story. He'd have some take on it. I'd also remembered a quote that I wanted to run by him. It was from the first *Ghostbusters* movie. I was sure he'd remember it. It was only eight words long, but it described what I hoped was going to happen with this entire case.

We came, we saw, we kicked its ass.

CHAPTER THIRTY-EIGHT

The lovebirds were at the bar, the bad guitar and singer drowning out any chance that James would hear me yell his name. The second-floor, open-air bar was fairly crowded with a bunch of middle-aged people down from Miami for some race. They sported race hats and T-shirts with race car numbers on them, and names that I didn't know. Bottles of Budweiser lined the bar top and brightly colored race banners and checkered flags hung from the rafters.

Walking to the back of the bar, I put my hands on James's shoulders.

"James, we need to talk."

"We can talk here."

"No." I motioned to the stairs that led to the mini-tiki huts one flight up.

He leaned into Amy, saying something in her ear. She shrugged her bare shoulders, and we walked up the steps.

I told him about the body double, and he gave me a skeptical look.

"Skip, I'm about as positive as I can be that the dead guy in our room was Jim Weezle."

"And I saw him today. I swear I saw Weezle."

"Impossible. He was dead. That wasn't some sleight of hand trick. Some magic. I mean, I got hauled down to that jail because they thought I had something to do with it and—"

"I know. I know. But James, somehow there are two different people. One dead, one alive."

"I don't know what to say."

"Em's calling the sheriff's office right now. We're going to confirm the dead guy's real name."

James didn't even smile this time. He sipped his Bud and stared out at the water over the railing.

"Got a thought, amigo."

"About the ghost?"

"No. About the boat." He turned and looked at me. "We got nothin' till tomorrow morning when we hopefully get to read that letter."

"Agreed."

"Well, I say we make another trip to the vacant property this morning. Three thirty in the a.m."

"Are you crazy?"

"We position ourselves on that residential side and watch through the openings in the trees. I want to see if another boat comes in."

"James—"

"We don't have anything else to do, Skip."

"Sleep might be a good thing."

"You can sleep anytime."

"And what's it going to prove? If we see the boat?"

"Then we'll know it's a regular occurrence. We'll find out if it's the fishermen who are in that tournament. We'll pay more attention. And, before all the stores close, why don't you go to that camera store up by O'Neill's and Malhotra's office and get a couple pairs of binoculars?"

Running up and down the highway, we'd seen the store three or four times.

"James, those cost some serious money."

"Dude, we need the equipment. It's for the job. If the lady is willing to up our pay to two mill, she'll spring for the glasses."

"And why aren't you going to get the binoculars?"

"Skip, this is Amy's last night in town. We want to make the most of it."

There are times when I want to punch him right in the face, but he wouldn't understand.

We drove to the camera store, then to the drugstore for the nail file.

"The guy who was killed came up as Peter Stiffle."

I kept both hands on the wheel. I didn't want to piss Emily off by driving with one hand, and besides, the car felt more alive when I was totally engaged in the driving process. I know, it was about a two-mile round-trip drive, but hey, it was a Porsche Ca-rerra. And this time I was in control.

"Damn. So it must be Weezle that we saw." She stared out the windshield.

"Who is Stiffle?" I asked more rhetorically.

"No idea."

"By the way, Mrs. T. went online and put five hundred more dollars on the debit card. She thinks we're onto something. That's how we got the binoculars."

"Skip, I hope we are on to something, but you do realize that investing fifteen hundred dollars in a venture that is expected to gross forty-four million isn't exactly a commitment of faith." She watched me, either to gauge my reaction to her comment or to make sure that I was treating her precious auto with the proper care.

"I get that. But she hasn't said no to anything so far."

"When daddy has a multimillion-dollar project, when anyone in our business has even a million-dollar project, there's a lot of up front money. The lady should be happy to come up with whatever you want. The return on investment is going to be huge. Unbelievable."

Return on investment. I remembered enough of my college business courses to know she was right. One hundred percent right.

And I remembered the story of Mel Fisher, who searched the bottom of the Florida waters for sunken treasure. His oldest son and his daughter-in-law were both killed in a dive while looking for gold. Now Mel was someone who seriously had an investment in his project.

She picked out a six-dollar file when cheap emery boards would have done the trick, but I guess she can afford it, even without the debit card from Mrs. T.

"So we're going tonight?"

"James thinks we need to get to the bottom of the boat thing. Find out why O'Neill threatened us."

Em took a deep breath as I pulled into the Cove. "I think he's right."

"Really?"

"I do."

James was agreeing with Em. Em was agreeing with James. That almost never happened. I looked up above to see if the stars were aligned, but it was still daylight. I made a mental note to check on that later in the evening.

CHAPTER THIRTY-NINE

We walked almost half a mile, the humidity so thick you could cut it with a knife. I'd worked up quite a sweat when we finally arrived.

"They could still identify the truck," James said. "I think it's best that we parked way back there."

So far no one had noticed the plate. I mean, how often do you check your license plate? The guy we took it from had a white truck, we had a white truck. He had a Florida plate, we had a Florida plate. Unless we got stopped by the sheriff for some violation, we were good. And the other guy, whoever he was, would never be the wiser. Until he went to register for a new plate.

"Em, are you sure you want to be a part of this?"

"I've told you before, Skip, you need someone to bail you out if you get in trouble. I've kind of grown used to the job."

In the dim light, I saw James frown. At least he didn't agree with everything she said.

"It's just three o'clock. Three o'clock, it's lines up." Em walked down the tree-lined street looking for clearances we could see through. "The boat should be here soon."

"This isn't private property, correct?" James was right in checking.

"Shouldn't be. It's a public street that runs right down to the water. And this is the public sidewalk that runs along this short section of the street." I was pretty sure about this.

"So no doctor or guy on a golf cart can run us off?"

"I suppose they could, but we can stand our ground."

"You guys have binoculars," Em said. "I've got this." Reaching into her purse, she pulled out the Colt .38 snub-nosed revolver.

"Preparation gets the job done."

"And we've got the tools."

We knelt across from a cement block house, a dim porch light eking out a meager halo. The rest of the street was dark and the moon was barely evident in the cloudy sky. Perfect for our hiding.

Talking in hushed voices, we swatted at mosquitoes and made plans if someone saw us.

"The dogs, what if they recognize the smell? What then?" James was thinking of those bare fangs.

"They didn't bother any of the passengers. I think they only attack when they're told to." Em had already figured it out.

The night was deathly silent, only an occasional vehicle humming along back on the highway. I thought about the sound of a steam locomotive and the long blast of the engine's horn as it traveled down to Key West. Chugging along, some of the cars would have carried the common folk, Skip and James. Crowded together with screaming children and their parents.

Then there would have been cars for the wealthier set, like Em and her dad. And finally there would have been cars for the railroad execs and the superrich. Must have been quite a time.

We heard the truck, the muffler maybe a little loose. The beams swung from the main road and even though we couldn't see it, we knew someone was pulling into the motel. Or the suites.

Or whatever they were. And I could hear high-pitched whines, like someone almost crying.

"What?" I whispered.

"Doesn't sound human," James remained kneeling, staring through the break in the hedge and trees.

Again I could hear it. Like a little baby just starting to cry.

There was a rattling of metal and I put the glasses to my eyes, scanning what I could see of the vacant lot.

"Over there." James was pointing to the northeast corner of the fencing. The same place we'd climbed over yesterday and landed almost in the lap of Dr. James O'Neill and his sidekick.

I looked and saw the gate opening. It could have used a little WD-40 as it squeaked and groaned, the hinges rubbing metal on metal.

"There are the whiners."

Sure enough, two dark dogs—I would have guessed Dobermans—came parading through the entrance. Short ears and a stub for a tail, they whined, straining at the leashes that one man held in his hand. I was pretty sure it was the guy that James laid out when he hit him with the palm of his hand.

"What if they—"

"They won't, Skip. Anyone could walk this street or sidewalk. They can't just attack everyone."

I just prayed that those two dogs didn't have a good memory of our smell from two nights before.

As I reflected on that spirited evening, I saw the pinpoint of light maybe half a mile out on the water. It got bigger by the second, and I was sure it was the boat.

Em strained to see it without the glasses. She kneeled down beside me and tapped me on the shoulder. "Want to share?"

What the heck, she'd let me drive the Porsche.

"It's a big boat, maybe bigger than the other night," I said.

The boat slowed, and I could hear the twin props kicking in

164

to slow the vessel. The captain had probably thrown her into reverse. The vessel was now almost coasting to the dock. The man with the dogs tied the leashes to a post, then threw a rope to someone aboard.

And the cast of characters got larger as Em handed me the glasses. I observed another person walking in from the Ocean Air gate. Magnified and in the light of the boat, I could make out his stiff appearance, and what appeared to be salt-and-pepper hair, a beard, and mustache.

"Can't prove it, but I think it's Dr. Malhotra."

"Guy who shares the building with O'Neill?" James peered into the darkness.

"The same."

"The plot thickens, grasshopper."

I just nodded, not understanding any of it.

"So those two guys are partners in whatever venture this is." James spoke softly, still watching through his new binoculars.

"It would seem."

The boat's light went out, plunging the property into darkness. Now a flashlight played on the deck as passengers disembarked. As before, they had suitcases and this time I noticed there seemed to be a mix of women, men, and even some children. All of them carried luggage.

"This is not a fishing boat. You don't take kids on a boat for tournament fishing." I was sure of it.

Em tapped me on the shoulder again. Whispering, she said, "But, you could use the timing of the tournament boats coming back to blend in." She paused for a moment. "Lots of boats all coming to shore at three thirty. What a perfect cover, Skip, don't you think?"

"So no one would be suspicious of a boat landing at this hour of the morning?" It made sense.

She nodded.

But why would they want to keep it a secret? Smugglers? Something in the suitcases. Gold?

"Drugs." James said it with conviction. "They're bringing illegal drugs in. Perfect. Two doctors are importing illegal narcotics."

"Doesn't sound right, James."

"I'd bet on it, Skip."

And then we heard someone yell, and it echoed off the water.

"Mas rapido."

And then another voice. *"El barco está saliendo."*

There was a semi loud "Hush. *Silencio.*"

Then, all you could hear were feet on the deck, on the dock, and we watched as the passengers disappeared into the trees.

James stood up as the engines reversed and the boat backed out to sea.

"I would bet you that someone rakes the sand over there."

"And I would bet that the cleaning service will have tomorrow off. Then they'll have to come in the next day and clean all of those rooms from these late check-ins." I remembered the conversation with our desk clerk at the Cove.

"Damn. There's something there we weren't supposed to see. And maybe somebody tried to shoot us today because we did see it." James stretched and we started walking the half mile back to the van.

"Something in those suitcases."

We walked back in silence, each of us rerunning the scene we'd witnessed. Something worth holding us and threatening us with a gun.

A night bird's shrill call startled us.

"What were they saying back there?" James got into the truck and Em and I climbed into the passenger side.

"Obviously it was Spanish."

"I hate to say it, Skip, but I think James may be right. They could be smuggling drugs. Using kids, men, women—"

"Anybody remember high school Spanish?" I asked as James turned the key.

And turned the key. And turned the key.

"Guys, I think our battery just died."

CHAPTER FORTY

It turned out that Em had AAA coverage. They'd come, tow the truck, and drive us back to the Cove. So she called them on her iPhone. It also turned out that we had to wait two hours, so we walked. That only took about an hour and fifteen minutes.

We crashed for three hours and then the phone rang. I was groggy, tired, and sore and not in the mood to talk to James or whoever was making a conscious effort to bother me.

"'Lo."

"Skip, it's Maria Sanko."

I couldn't think of anything to say.

"I want to apologize for the way I acted the other night. The other morning. You probably had a right to accuse me of—"

"Hey, I'm sorry. I actually appreciate the fact that you came out to see how we were doing. Looking out for us."

"I was out there because if you found gold, I wanted some."

I wanted to believe she actually cared about us, but then I remembered that we'd lied to her the entire time we'd known her.

"So, what do you want now?"

"First of all, did you find anything?"

I was quiet for a moment. Lying to Maria was becoming a habit. I hated to do it, but—

"No. We were chased by dogs the first night and the second time we went, well, you were there. You saw what happened."

"Yeah. What was that all about? I didn't tell anyone you were going to be there. I hope you'll believe me."

"Do you know those guys? O'Neill and the motel manager?"

"I know who they are. And I've pitched Dr. O'Neill some property recently. There's an old motel down where Zane Grey's fishing camp used to be, south of here. It's in foreclosure, and I was trying to interest him in buying it. Maybe fix it up, give it the Zane Grey western theme and, you know."

I didn't. Zane Grey had been a western novelist, and I knew he'd frequented the Keys, but that was about it.

"So, Maria, you know him, this O'Neill?"

"He called me yesterday."

"Wants to buy your motel?"

"No. That's still for sale."

"What did he want?"

"He knew I was the one on the Harley. He wanted me to give you a message. He said he wants you to stay off his property, stay away from the medical building, don't go near the vacant lot, and, oh, he wants his gun back."

"Well, you delivered the message. Now, I've got to get back to sleep. It was a late night." Lots of messages being delivered.

"He was pissed, Skip. And he's usually a very nice man."

He certainly hadn't shown that trait to me.

"I'll take it under advisement. Thanks, Maria."

"Skip. If there's anything else I can do—"

I hung up. There wasn't. At least not then.

Em drove to the library, the three of us squeezed into her two-seat sports car. James cursed the entire two-mile trip.

"Are you going to be able to squeeze a battery for your truck out of your employer, James?" Em asked. The spymobile still sat half a mile from the infamous vacant lot that we'd pillaged.

"I certainly hope so, because I swear we're not going back with Skip and me in each other's damned laps."

She just smiled as she pulled into the library parking lot.

"Guys, I have some good news for you."

Kathy motioned us into her office, the makeshift lab.

"The paper has moistened considerably. I think we can make this thing work with a minimum of effort."

She had already removed the folded letter from the jerry-rigged humidor, and thankfully hadn't opened it yet.

"I've got the strips. We can paste this thing together and I will be happy to share it with whomever you want. But," she hesitated, "I would like the permission to print the contents in our newsletter."

I shivered. The contents could be worth millions of dollars. Millions.

"I'm afraid that we can't promise that, Kathy." I didn't want any stipulations on what we had to do.

She glanced at the damp piece of evidence. The piece of paper that could dictate our future livelihood.

"It's historic." As if that gave her the right.

"And, it's private. It actually belongs to our employer's great-grandfather and I'm afraid we can't authorize that the contents can be made public."

She frowned. Librarians probably think that everything that is readable should be made public.

"You'll ask her?"

"We will," I said. But the answer was a given.

She started unfolding the ancient piece, very slowly unwrapping it. With a damp sponge she moistened the creases, and sure enough, the paper responded. The first fold-over flattened out without any damage to the piece.

The second fold was more troublesome and even with extra moisture it cracked.

"You'll have that," she said, working with her hands like a surgeon.

There were more cracks and it was obvious that some of the paper would need adhesive.

Our archivist worked for forty minutes, slowly unwrapping the old message. When she was done, we had six pieces of paper. I'd tried to read some of it, but the way the letter unfolded, the writing was mostly on the underside of the paper.

When she finally turned one of the six pieces over and we studied the words, I saw James with a big grin on his face.

L dp vdih.

With the first group of letters I knew *we* were safe. It was all written in code.

CHAPTER FORTY-ONE

She'd sprung for the new battery, and James was happy.

Mrs. T. had the template and she worked on it at the desk as the three of us sipped mai tais on her balcony. Yes, we were guests at a resort. But there were certain levels of resort living and this lady was right at the top. The room was better, the view was better, the drinks, hand delivered from the bar, were better.

"Kathy was disappointed." James was leaning out over the railing, watching two girls in bikinis sunning themselves poolside.

"First of all because she couldn't read it and secondly because we wouldn't let her make a copy of it." She'd asked again if the contents could be kept at the library. I politely declined. The lady was nice and had seriously helped our cause, but—

"It was truly impressive how she melted the Japanese tissue into the paper." Em had been fascinated with the process. There was almost no sign of the breaks in the original manuscript.

"Kids," she called from inside.

When we stuck our heads in the door, she motioned for us to come in.

"Sit down."

"Good news?"

"I don't know."

She stood up and handed Em a piece of the resort's stationery with the translation of the coded document.

"This is from my great-grandfather, Matthew Kriegel. He was on the island when the hurricane hit. Please, read it."

Em nodded and read out loud from the translated version.

I am safe. For the moment. As you know, I was entrusted with over 2,000 pounds of gold to be used in the purchase and upkeep of properties for the railroad. The future of the railroad at this point would appear to be in grave jeopardy. The rails themselves are twisted and uprooted everywhere you look.

At this very moment there are crews arriving by boat to search the island for bodies, of which there are many, lying on the ground, hanging in the trees, their decay causing foul odors that spread for miles. There are hordes of men coming in and looting what remains there may be of people's homes and businesses, (although little remains at all) and there is utter chaos among the people who survived.

Medical care is slow in coming and I myself am in need of someone to help mend a broken arm.

That being said, I am still responsible for the gold that I brought with me. I trust no one, but must trust someone. Even if I were in excellent physical condition, I could not move the heavy crates. There is no one to take the gold back to the mainland so I am exploring several options.

Em looked up. "I can't imagine how bad things were. And to be reading a firsthand account—"

James tapped his foot. "The gold, Em. He's about to tell us what happened to the gold."

She glowered at him and continued.

Miracle that it is, the cases are unharmed. Ten heavy wooden containers with the gold still inside, these wooden crates of riches are as sturdy as an oak. So, their being yet untouched, I can have them moved several places. Hiring a few good men, I can put them on small boats and drop them off at sea. I cannot get a boat back to Miami at this time. A good place would seem to be the rocks that are directly off the resort (which no longer stands) called The Millionaire's Club. Corporate giants had built a spur off of our railroad to park their private railcars when they visited this fine establishment.

I shook my head. "There were the regular railroad passengers, then there were these guys who had their own railcars. I can't imagine what that would have been like."

Em continued reading.

The other choice I have come up with is to bury them on land, although the chance of digging very deep is fraught with danger because we are only inches above the water table.

I intend to explore both options. If I bury the gold, it will be on the property of The Millionaire's Club. I will estimate the longitude and latitude of that location. The crates are 14½ by 9½ and 6 inches deep. They weigh approximately two hundred pounds each.

I pass this information to you, my darling wife, and hope we are connected in the not too distant future. However, things are in upheaval and every minute brings a new disaster or gruesome discovery.

My arm aches, and I am feverish. I fear that the rotting corpses will spread disease. There is already some talk of burning them in a mass funeral pyre. I pray that I will not succumb to an early death and be one of those whose ashes are cast to the wind.

I am burying this letter in a metal box and you alone have the location of that box. Please, pray for me, but if I do not return you will have the yellow treasure to do with what you will.

Longitude: 80° 37′ 40″ W Latitude: 24° 55′ 30.72″ E

"And that's it."

No one spoke for at least a minute. We were busy absorbing what we'd heard. Finally Mrs. T. broke the silence.

"Matthew Kriegel was protecting the company assets. I was a little worried that I was going to find out he'd basically stolen the gold."

"Kind of like we're going to do?" James had to smart off.

"We've gone over this before, Mr. Lessor. There is no railroad company. In fact, there really wasn't one after the hurricane. It went belly up."

I didn't mention that the gold would have helped their financial situation.

"He didn't trust anyone." Em stood up and walked over to the balcony door, breathing deeply. "Can you picture that? The stench of dead bodies everywhere, this poor guy with his arm broken, feverish. Who knows what was going through his mind? None of these people had ever witnessed this kind of devastation before."

"What's important is that we've got two places where he may have hidden the gold. We've got a serious treasure hunt." James had a grin plastered on his face.

I surveyed the assembled party and we all had a smile. Except Em. After reading about the death and destruction, we'd found the pot of gold at the end of the rainbow. Now all we had to do was dig it up.

Who was it that said, "Nothing is as easy as it seems?"

CHAPTER FORTY-TWO

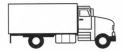

"I think he had it shipped out to the rocks." James was speculating.

We sipped more mai tais at the poolside bar and stared out at the water. Up until now, the idea of actually finding forty-four million dollars' worth of gold was somewhat of a pipe dream. I thought it was possible, but I had no idea how it would feel.

Now, I could taste it. Feel it. Dream it in 3D. I was convinced that Kriegel had made this fortune accessible. And that meant that James and I and Em would be rich.

I'd checked it out at the dive shop. It was very doable. "I can dive it."

"Skip, this is risky." Em seemed concerned.

"Cheeca Rocks, Em. They have a supervised dive site out there. I can veer off and check out the territory."

I'd taken a course at Samuel and Davidson University (Sam and Dave U) and learned the basics of diving. I mean I was certified, but with limited experience. But how tough could this be? Cheeca Rocks was a regular site, and was only fifteen to twenty feet deep at its deepest point. No big deal. In fact, for an experienced diver it would be almost claustrophobic. I was far from an experienced diver.

"Pard, your diving experience, this is awesome."

James had majored in parties and sex. I was close behind, but in this case I'd taken a class that actually made a difference. Should have called it Treasure Hunting 101.

"It does make more sense to check the dive site first. We can't just start digging at Cheeca Lodge. I mean, they may call the sheriff." It was obvious James wanted no more run-ins with the law.

I unfolded a map I'd picked up at Holiday Isle's dive shop.

"It's here." I pointed to the spot off the shore.

24° 54′ 245″ N and 080° 36′ 885″ W.

"But if it's a popular spot, wouldn't someone have found the cases by now?" Em always saw the other side.

The same thought had run through my head. Thousands of tourists had visited the spot, snorkeling, scuba diving, and if the crates had been left out there, someone would have found them years ago.

"What kind of camouflage would they have?" James asked.

"Coral."

"That's it?"

"That's a lot of camouflage. I would guess you could accumulate several feet of coral in seventy-five years."

"Accumulate? So it would grow over the cases?"

I'd read about some of Mel Fisher's treasures that had been encrusted with coral. It was hard to make out the items at all. Only because he knew the location of the ships that he investigated did he find a lot of the valuable pieces.

"If Kriegel swore the guys who hid the gold to silence, there would be no reason for anyone to suspect that a treasure was just offshore."

"So there would be no way of detecting any gold?"

I shrugged my shoulders. "I don't know much about metal detectors, but I would guess there are some devices that can find gold. Especially if there's that much down there. Ten crates should set a detector off, I would think."

I was still skeptical. Ten crates of gold? Boated out to the rocks? It was a little too much to hope for.

Mrs. T. came down the steps.

"I cannot impress enough on you that we need to be very quiet about this. Even when you're talking among yourselves. If there's a chance that our property still exists, I don't want anyone getting wind of our expedition."

"We aren't going to say anything to—"

"Mr. Lessor. You admitted to telling your employer where you were going."

He quieted down.

"Mr. Moore, you not only told your lady friend where you were, but you invited her to join us."

She was right. Neither of us kept a secret very well.

"If we are to keep this project to ourselves, then you will have to measure every word you speak."

"What's the project?" Bobbie walked over, eyeing our empty drinks.

James looked at Mrs. T. and rolled his eyes.

"Just a little history thing we're working on," Em said.

Bobbie pointed at the empty drink glasses, then motioned toward the male bartender, busily mixing a drink on the other side.

"Did Scotty get you?"

Without missing a beat James looked her in the eyes and said, "Nobody gets us Bobbie. That's the problem."

She looked puzzled as she walked away to wait on a heavyset older couple. Probably in their late thirties.

178

CHAPTER FORTY-THREE

"So you're lookin' for coins?"

The wizened old man looked like he was straight out of central casting. He had fine white hair tied back in a ponytail, and his brown leathery skin threatening to crack at the creases. A short shoot of hair stuck out from his chin; a beard that had never really taken off.

"Yeah. Coins." James nodded.

"Lots of people find coins. I swear there's still millions of dollars to be had, right offen these shores."

"You think?"

I frowned at James. Don't be a smart-ass. The idea was not to draw any attention to our mission.

"Yes, sir." His voice was high pitched, and I decided he reminded me of old Ben Gunn from *Treasure Island*. Gunn was the pirate they left behind on the island to guard the treasure. A crazy old loon.

"From Gasparilla to Bowlegs, them pirates were a burying bunch of thugs. And if it weren't the pirates, then it were them wreckers who'd scavenge all sorts of riches off them distressed ships that ran up on the rocks." His eyes were wide open and his animated speech told me that he had a passion for the stories. "And they buried their treasures. 'Twas the only way to keep 'em safe."

"We think there are coins off the coast, maybe a quarter of a mile. So, we wanted to know if you've got a metal detector that works under water."

He stroked his stubby beard, and stared at the two of us. "We'll get to that in a minute."

Em and Mrs. T. were back at the resort. Four of us descending on a small one-man shop like this seemed a little much to take.

"Now you'll be needin' a small boat."

He stepped around the worn plank-wood counter and motioned for us to follow. We went through the main room with an air compressor and tanks to a dark backroom that smelled of grease, gasoline, and oil. He pulled on a rope, and a garage door opened onto some old gray wooden docks and the bright blue Florida sky.

What had once been white paint peeled from the old boards and several of the docks leaned as if pushed by a giant wave or wind. I was reminded what waves and wind can do in the Keys.

Five small boats floated in the water as we walked out onto the rotting wood. A seagull lazily lifted off a post and landed on a dock forty feet away. The old man stepped up to a bobbing dinghy, big enough for four people and a couple of extra tanks and that was about it.

"Said you just needed maybe a quarter of a mile, right?"

"Yeah."

"This would do the trick."

James gave it a suspect glance. "It doesn't leak, does it?"

"Leak?" He almost shrieked the word. "Good Lord, son, I personally check each boat when it comes in."

James bit his tongue and kept quiet.

Sun beat down on the bleached wood and I inhaled the odor of rotting seaweed and washed up marine life. I hadn't been diving since college, and most of the training took place in a safe pool. This was going to be an experience.

"Now, you boys can obviously go somewhere else, but you're gonna pay a lot more. I'll make ya a really good offer. We'll do this boat—nothin' fancy you understand—then we'll rent you the mask, the tank, and all the divin' gear and then you want a metal detector, am I right?"

"And you rent those too?"

"Well, I have one here. I'll let you rent it, although I can't speak to its ability."

"Never tried it?" I asked.

"No. You see, I found it. Sort of."

"Found it?"

"Came back in one of my boats. Must have belonged to this guy who rented the boat. I had to hire a kid to take me to the boat, 'cause the diver left it about a mile out."

"I don't understand. Somebody rented a boat from you, then just left the boat and the metal detector a mile offshore?"

"Didn't exactly just leave it. This guy ran out of oxygen and died out there."

"Oh, shit." I turned to James. "Do not say anything about that to Em. Or anybody. You got that? She'll freak."

"Trust me, pard, I got it."

"So, you got yourself a boat, diving gear, and the dead guy's metal detector."

"How much?"

"How long?"

"Half a day." I figured we weren't going to dig it up and bring it home the first trip out. We just needed to see if there were crates of gold. Then we could make our plans on how to haul it out. One thing at a time.

"Three hundred fifty dollars. Payable in advance on account of—"

"Yeah," James said, "you pretty much told us. On account of —"

We'd decided on the next morning. Go out at seven thirty before the scheduled dives and plan on coming in between ten thirty and one in the afternoon.

"James, you're driving the boat, right?"

"I am."

"Em, you're kind of the lookout. If things get strange, if someone shows up who looks like there might be trouble, you're going to figure out how to get rid of them."

"And if I can't?"

"I don't have the answer, but for God's sake don't leave me down there by myself."

We sat in Mrs. T.'s room, sharing a pepperoni and mushroom pizza from Boardwalk Pizza. When James heard that Boardwalk Pizza was right in front of the sheriff's office, he almost refused to eat it. But the pizza was pretty good, and again, the lady was paying.

"My question is this." Mrs. T. sipped from a can of caffeine-free diet Pepsi. "How are you going to know if there's gold down there? We've already discussed the fact that it may be overgrown with coral. Lots of coral and seaweed. So even if you're lucky enough to actually find the spot, how will you be able to tell through the coral and everything else?"

I had the answer.

"Skeeter has a JW Fishers Pulse eight K metal detector."

"Skeeter?"

"Skeeter," said James.

"And just what exactly is a Fisher Pulse thing?" She threw her hands up, obviously confused. I understood.

James grabbed at the last piece of pepperoni and mushroom. "We looked it up on the Internet."

"And?"

"And, it's a gold detector equipped for use underwater as well as on land. It can find gold and silver six feet from where it detects the metal. So if there were six feet of coral or silt or whatever, this baby should find it. It's got an underwater earphone that I can listen to and it's weighted so it will stay in one spot and not drift around in the water. I think we lucked out on this one."

She appeared to be significantly impressed. "So this expedition is an additional three hundred fifty dollars, right?"

"Gotta spend it to make it." James smiled.

"I want to say that you boys, and you too, Emily, you have shown me a great deal of ingenuity. I was skeptical at first, but you've found the letter, you made arrangements to have it put back together, and now you're set for the dive tomorrow." She smiled, a smug look on her face. "Emily, despite my initial concern, I think you were an excellent addition to the team."

James glared at Mrs. T.

I would have felt a whole lot better if the event had been set with a more high-profile dive shop, but the consensus was that using this little hole-in-the-wall guy, it would remain more secret. The fewer people who knew about it, the better.

"So it's all set. Tomorrow morning you'll make the dive and we'll see what we can find." Mrs. T. stood up and basically herded us out the door.

The three of us walked down the stairs to the beach, hearing the loud laughs and music coming from Holiday Isle and Rumrunners.

"You're supposed to dive with someone else." Em eased into a lounge chair, looking across the water at the world famous tiki hut bar. "I've read enough to know that it's stupid to dive alone."

"Buddy diving would be the safest thing to do," I had to

agree, "but hey, no one here dives, Em. Besides, it's two feet to twenty feet. Hardly a depth that I should have a problem with." Considering I hadn't dived in three years, any depth could cause a problem. But my macho instinct had kicked in.

My instructor used to dive solo. However, I will always remember her instructions. "Wait until you've had at least a hundred dives before you try it. And even then, remember that when you're solo, no one has your back. No one."

"Pard, I know this may be a stretch, but we've already told Skeeter that you're going down to look for coins. No big deal about that, right?"

"It's our cover, James. That's what we decided."

"Right. So what if we tell that cover story to someone else?"

Em gave him a disapproving glance. "Who else do you want to tell? We could take out an ad in the local paper—"

"Just a thought, folks. I know a diver who can be suited up and ready first thing in the morning. And as long as we don't tell this diver the real reason we're going down—"

"James, this isn't a good idea."

He nodded. "Oh, and it's a good idea to send you down there by yourself. Especially after the story Skeeter told us about —" he stopped, a chagrined look on his face. "I'm sorry, Skip."

"What story? What did this Skeeter tell you?"

"It's nothing."

"Tell me." Em's signature stone-cold instruction.

With that tone of voice, I had to. Damn James. Can't keep his mouth shut.

"Some guy died on Skeeter's watch because he ran out of oxygen."

She stood up and grabbed my hand. "You shouldn't be out there by yourself. A million things could happen. You need backup. I hate to admit it, but James is right, Skip."

I hate to admit that James was right? This was not a good sign.

Wait until you've had a hundred dives before you try solo. A hundred? Hell, I'd had about ten open-water dives. Ninety to go.

"So who's this backup?" I couldn't wait for James to tell me.

"Amy. She decided to hang out with me for a couple more days."

"Oh, come on, your married girlfriend?"

"That's the one, Skip. And she's way more experienced than you are."

CHAPTER FORTY-FOUR

Clear your regulator. Clear your partially flooded mask. Breathe without your mask. Swap the air supply from your partner. All the rules that went through my head. What had I signed on for?

Why would anyone in their right mind want to escape the earth's plentiful supply of oxygen and dive deep beneath the ocean for a brief glimpse of what lies below? Knowing that their breathing supply was sorely limited. Knowing that with a couple of short, quick breaths, they could die.

I pulled on my bathing suit and watched Em out of the corner of my eye.

"What are you doing?"

"Getting ready," she said.

"Em, that's a thong, for God's sake."

Her tan thighs, butt, abs and everything else were well defined and the brief suit showed it all off.

"Skip, stop it. It's not a thong."

"No. You look—you look fabulous." I remembered how she looked last night *without* any of this brief cover-up, but that was a private moment. This was on display for James and anyone else who cared to look.

"Thank you."

"It's just that James and—"

"Oh, for crying out loud. This is what I brought, and this is what I'm wearing."

"For that reason only?"

She turned and shot an angry glance over her shoulder as she adjusted her breasts in the thin material of her bikini.

"And just what does that mean?"

"We have a visitor. I've seen her in *her* bikini. Is this by any chance a one-upsmanship?"

"Would you rather I wear a sweat suit?" She turned to me, displaying a very scantily clad perfect torso. "Or do you want a frumpy one-piece that looks like something your mother would have worn?"

I studied her.

"Do you?"

The answer was no. No. No. No. However . . .

I loved to check out her body. And the fact that there might be a jealousy contest between the two ladies actually excited me. But I had to admit I didn't like the idea of James seeing all that I was intimate with.

"So, the way Amy looks has nothing to do with—"

She punched me on the arm. Not a light punch by any means. She could have done damage to a pro boxer.

Em wore a cover-up and carried a beach bag as we stepped into the truck. Amy, James, Em, and I. Amy had a cover-up as well. I was anxious to see her outfit revealed.

"Amy, do you have your own mask?" I was renting mine.

"I do," she said. "I haven't had that many dives, but enough that I know I don't want someone else's mask and mouthpiece."

I nodded. That would be a preferable situation. My own mask and mouthpiece. Perfect. However, I never thought this hobby would be more than a college credit course.

James turned the key and the engine roared. A new battery had solved the problem. We pulled out of the parking lot and drove south to Skeeter's Dive Shop.

"So, Amy—" Em started the conversation with nothing to say. Do you mention the husband? The kid? The guy she came down with? Or the affair with James? It didn't seem to matter, she was a part of the team. This Amy—no one seemed to know her last name—was my backup. I'd been told that a backup was sometimes useless unless they were good friends. A backup had their own agenda and often was off on that task, rather than watching your back.

As we pulled into the parking lot of Skeeter's Dive Shop, I thought about that. Maybe I should have just done a solo dive.

I wished to God that I had decided to do that. Then Amy took off the filmy cover-up.

This twenty-three-year-old girl had the figure of a goddess. I must have been staring at her perfect narrow waist and hips and legs to die for.

"Settle down, big boy," Em whispered in my ear as she shed her cover-up.

I turned and was once again in awe. My girlfriend had a fabulous body. I saw James, his eyes wide open and a leer on his face.

Skeeter had the boat ready and all the diving gear was neatly stowed.

"Here's your detector. I put in some fresh batteries, and I even tested it. Seems to be working just fine."

Amy and Em cast a wary glance at our boat, but James and I stepped in, the little ship rocking back and forth. If we hit any waves, I had a feeling this thing could go over in a heartbeat.

"You know where you're headed?"

I nodded. I didn't think we needed a GPS for this trip. It was just off the Cheeca Lodge dock.

"Okay, you have that boat back by one p.m. or there'll be a full-day charge, you understand?"

"Got it."

We helped the girls in, and they put on life preservers.

Untying the two ropes, Skeeter tossed them to us as James started the motor. Fifteen seconds later, we were headed out to sea.

"Everything okay back there, little buddy?" Leave it to James to start with the Gilligan references.

The engine was loud, and combined with the wind, it was hard to hear, so we spent the next ten minutes in silence, watching for the long pier.

James had the throttle pushed all the way, but the boat crawled. If we had planned on going any distance at all, it would have taken all day to get there.

Finally, the pier came into view and James veered out, approximately a quarter of a mile off the end.

"Nobody out here."

He slowed down, from what must have been ten miles an hour, to an even slower cruise. Looking back to the shore I could make out the Cheeca Lodge, the location of the Millionaire's Club back in the thirties.

"How deep is it supposed to be, Skip?" Amy leaned over the edge and looked into the murky water. The boat rocked slightly and we all sat still until the swell subsided.

"Skeeter says anywhere from two to twenty feet. I think the gold—the coins—are probably in the deepest part."

She nodded. "And how big an area are you going to explore?"

I had no idea. "We'll play it by ear. Or until the air supply runs out."

Em grabbed my jaw and squeezed. "Please, don't say that."

We sat there for a minute, the boat gently drifting, water lapping at its battered fiberglass body. The sun was still low in the morning sky and the blue-green water reflected orange rays that bounced along the surface of the ocean. James tossed in the anchor and the rope went down quite a ways.

"What do you estimate?"

"Fifteen, twenty feet."

"A real treasure hunt." Amy seemed ready for the adventure. I wasn't so sure that I was.

"Pard," James pointed at me, hoisting a plastic bag he'd carried on board. "I brought binoculars."

"I don't think those amount to much underwater."

"I'm using them up here. Keep surveillance on top of the water. You keep an eye on what's going on down below."

"I was just curious why you're diving here?" Amy was going to analyze the situation. That couldn't do us any good. "I mean, Islamorada has all those Spanish ships that went down in the seventeen hundreds. I hear that a lot of divers find coins on those expeditions."

"Yeah, well we have information that says this is a good spot." I was hoping to shut down this line of questioning.

She nodded. "What's the next step?"

"We dive."

"Tanks have been checked?"

I nodded my head. "Yeah."

The old man seemed like he knew what he was doing. Still, some diver who'd used Skeeter's services had run out of air and we were using the dead man's metal detector. I was a little nervous.

"Hey, Skip," Amy was strapping on her tank. "Have you ever dived naked?"

Em looked at her, James looked at her, and I stopped midprocess for a second. The image of this lady diving with nothing—

"Have you?" I asked her.

"I have. It's a kick."

"Let's not try it today while you two are underwater, okay?" Em didn't sound too happy.

I pulled on my flippers and, sitting on the side of the boat, we adjusted our mouthpieces and masks. I thought about what I was doing. The detector in hand, I realized I had no business being here. But then, what was new? Every time I get into a project with James Lessor, I end up in over my head.

Amy flipped over, entering the water, and I followed her, leaving James and Em by themselves for who knew how long. That was going to be crazy time.

CHAPTER FORTY-FIVE

I'd forgotten how peaceful it could be. We were no more than fifteen feet down, and the maximum was going to be twenty, but serenity settled in quickly. I could hear the bubbles as I released my air, filtered by the steady hum in my earphone. *Don't forget how to breathe.* Amy was up ahead, her cute butt bobbing as she kicked her flippers. Already I questionied her as my partner.

Working the wand of the detector, I ran it over the ocean floor. Slowly, with the earphone attached to my right ear, I heard the low pitch of a hum. The pitch would rise when I found any metal of consequence.

I'd looked it up on the web, and apparently minerals in the water weren't enough to set it off. I kicked, and moved another ten or fifteen feet, trying to keep the anchor as my focal point.

Out of the corner of my eye I saw Amy, gazing at the coral and the school of black-and-white sheepshead that went swimming by.

I kept moving, running the wand along the bottom. At the most I had sixty minutes on this tank. There was a spare in the boat, but if I did my job I might not need it.

And I was breathing too fast. *Settle down. Relax.* I remembered the instructor telling us, "Breathe slow and not too deep." You could use a sixty-minute tank up in twenty minutes if you weren't careful.

I saw a bigger fish in the distance, murky until it came closer. A long gray nurse shark about nine feet long. I shuddered. They were usually harmless, and typically hunted at night, but I'm not a fan of sharks, period. I stopped moving and after observing me for several seconds, the shark swam away, his body twisting in the water. *Let the air out. Slowly. Conserve your air supply.*

Amy was oblivious to the shark, darting here and there and not checking on me at all. It was okay. I didn't want her to be too observant.

The crates would be a little over fourteen inches long, so if I found something, the signal should go for over a foot. I was out from the anchor maybe one hundred feet, so I started to retrace my path, only this time sweeping the wand across the path I'd made. Back and forth, twenty or thirty feet either way.

Nothing. After about ten minutes I decided to have James move the boat. Signaling Amy, we swam back to the anchor.

I pulled myself up after her, feeling pretty good about how I'd performed. I'd figured it out, and remembered most of the important points. Hey, I was still alive.

Ten minutes later we'd anchored the boat in a new position and were getting ready to go back down.

"Did she take off her clothes down there?" Em asked.

I didn't respond.

When Amy and I dropped off the boat, I found the water a little deeper. Coral grew everywhere. Brain coral, star coral, fire coral and I played the wand right beside it. I didn't want to injure any of the stuff, but at the same time I wasn't going to let a small amount of coral get in the way of forty-four million dollars. There had to be a way.

Back and forth as Amy would spot a school of parrotfish, angelfish, or a formation of coral, and go after it. Nothing, nothing, and nothing.

And then I heard it. The low gentle hum of the detector was stronger in my ear, then very strong, like a siren. I swear it sounded like a fire engine. Then quieter, then back to the steady frequency. What the heck? I ran it back and there it was again.

Stopping directly over the loud noise, I swam down, pulling up the metal detector and staring at the loamy soil beneath it. There it was. An irregular circle, corroded metal, sitting on the ocean floor. I picked it up, studied it for a few seconds then dropped it in the pocket of my swim trunks. Maybe it was a coin. Maybe it was a piece of cheap metal.

Moving back and forth over the loamy bottom I listened intently. Just that constant hummmmm sound. Then there was another rise in volume, the sirens at full volume, and I stopped. Same scenario.

A semiround piece of metal, covered with corrosion. I pocketed the piece.

Back and forth, back and forth. Nothing. After twenty minutes I found Amy admiring the coral and totally oblivious as to what I had been doing.

I pointed up and she nodded. We found the anchor and rope and rose to the surface, kicking with our fins.

"So what do you think, amigo?"

"I got nothing, James. It's a big, big ocean."

"Yeah, but if that gold . . ." he hesitated, "if that collection of gold coins is there, it would be well worth it."

I nodded. "I want to check those coordinates again, James."

"Then I hope we're wrong."

I gave him a puzzled look. "Wrong about what?"

"The location."

"We don't know if we're right or wrong."

James cast a quick glance at Amy who was in conversation with Em.

"Skip, take the glasses," he handed me the binoculars, "and look off the starboard bow."

"Starboard?" the boat shifted, turning with the slight breeze.

"Behind us, damn it. About the end of the pier. Coming this way."

I trained the glasses in that direction and saw a small boat.

"Wow. These things really have some power."

"Look closer, amigo. Much closer."

Staring through the glass, I adjusted the center wheel to bring everything into focus. It took several seconds.

"I've got it homed in. Now, what am I looking for?" I'd trained the lenses onto the approaching boat.

"You can see the occupants?"

"Yeah."

"And you can make out their faces?"

"I guess. What am I supposed to be looking for here, James?" I was looking and trying to shed my tank at the same time.

"Damn it, Skip. Look."

"James, I've got my eyes on the—" I stopped. I stopped taking off the tank, stopped talking, and just kept the glasses aimed directly at the boat.

"I thought you'd get it."

Todd Markim and Jim Weezle were headed directly for our boat, and we had no backup plan.

CHAPTER FORTY-SIX

Their craft didn't seem to be much bigger than ours and it did not appear that they were moving very fast. Probably a cheap rental from a place like Skeeter's.

As I pulled in the anchor, James started the boat.

"What's wrong, boys?" Em saw the look of determination on my face.

"We've got friends." I pointed toward the shore.

"Let me guess. Markim and Weezle?"

"Yes, except that Weezle is dead."

"Obviously not." She rolled her eyes. "Or are we on that ghost thing again?"

"What is going on?" Amy stared at us, obviously a bit confused.

"Two guys who want the same thing we want."

"The gold coins?"

"The gold." I looked back and saw they were gaining ground, or in this case, gaining water. "The gold coins."

"Are they dangerous?"

The engine chugged and our boat slapped at the water.

James shouted above the noise of the engine, the water, and the wind. "We don't know, but we're not going to stick around and find out."

"I've got something just in case," Em yelled out.

"What?" We all three harmonized.

She reached into her beach bag and pulled out the .38 revolver.

"You carry a gun?" Amy's eyes were wide open.

"Just a little precaution."

Watching her drop it back in the bag, I said, "Just a little protection."

"That too."

We ran parallel to the shore, waiting to see if they followed us.

The breeze picked up as James angled back toward land, the little craft buffeted by the stronger wind.

"You okay?" I asked.

"We're making headway." He looked over his shoulder, his hair blowing in the wind. "Are they coming?"

I looked back with the glasses as we bounced across the waves. I could smell the salt in the air.

"It appears they are right about where we were."

"Dude, do you think they've got the same information that we have?"

"Don't know," I shouted. "So far, ours hasn't panned out too well."

I felt the Velcro pocket of my swim suit.

"Hey, James, I may have found some coins."

He spun around. "No shit?"

"No shit. I'll show 'em to you when we get back."

It took us almost forty-five minutes, but we finally docked at Skeeter's. The wizened man came sauntering out, eyeing the boat for possible damage. There wasn't a spot on the boat that wasn't damaged. Dinged up, banged, bruised, and battered, the body still held together. All of the damage had been done long ago.

"Them fellas find you?"

"Oh, no, don't tell me," I couldn't believe it yet I could. "Them fellows?"

I knew right away who it was.

"Let me guess." I stood there in front of him and told him exactly what had happened. I knew it before James or Em did.

"Two guys asked about us, where we were going, said they were supposed to meet up with us and you told them exactly where we were going and that we'd rented the metal detector, right?" I'd bet two million dollars on it.

"Yeah." Skeeter had a wide grin on his face, so proud of himself that he'd turned us in.

"So they found you." The grin exposed two missing teeth in the front.

"Oh, yeah." James nodded his head, his arm around the lovely Amy's waist. "They found us."

"Well, I'm gonna guess that you are done with the equipment?"

"We are," James said.

"Skeeter, I'd like to rent this detector for the next several days."

James spun around and stared at me.

"Full-day rental?"

"Yeah."

"Well, I guess I can do that. Prepaid with a credit card or cash?"

James hauled out the overheated plastic and handed it to Skeeter.

"You boys should have just brought one with you, like your friends."

"The two guys? They had their own?"

"Did," he said as he swiped the card. "I'm surprised they didn't show it to you. Same make and model."

The Harley was in the parking lot, a dusty black one with a gold fender. There was no question who was out at Cheeca Rocks looking for gold.

"Show us the coins, amigo."

In the truck I pulled the two pieces from my pocket, and handed them to James.

"So much crud on them, it's hard to tell."

"Coral encrustation."

"Don't get technical on me, bro." He turned the key.

I knew right away that I'd been dissed. James didn't believe there was any value.

And again he turned the key, and turned the key.

"Open the hood." I climbed out of the truck.

"You don't know the first thing about an engine." James's face was getting red. He was not a happy camper.

"Open it."

He pulled the lever from inside. "Didn't we just put a new battery in this damned truck?"

"We did. That's why I want you to pop the hood, James."

I lifted the white metal and stared at the oil-soaked engine and the new battery. Somehow the red cable had come off of the brand new battery. I slipped it back on, twisting it to make sure there was contact.

Climbing back in, I said, "Turn the key."

After two tries, the engine fired.

"Okay, what did you do?"

"Somehow the cable came off the battery."

He nodded. "I think the guy at the garage knew what he was

doing when he replaced the battery. So there must be another explanation."

"I think we know the other explanation." I motioned to the motorcycle, down the row from us.

Em pushed me toward the door. "Let me out for just a moment."

"Sure. What's up?"

She pulled the new metal nail file from her bag. Of course the modern, well-equipped woman carries not only a .38 caliber revolver with her, but also a heavy-duty steel nail file.

Sliding out, she moved past me, and as she brushed up against my thigh I could smell the suntan lotion she'd applied, mixed with a slight odor of sweat. I was in love.

Walking to the black cycle she took the file and shoved it into the rear tire. Harder and harder, twisting.

"Em. What the hell?"

Now she had two hands on the file, forcing, twisting, pushing.

"Girl," Amy shouted out from the backseat, "what are you doing?" There were notes of fear and anger in her voice. "That's someone's property for God's sake. You can't just—"

Em turned and shot her a cold glance. "I could ask you the same question. What the hell do you think you're doing?" She took a deep breath. "With other people's property?"

Amy drew back, recoiling with a little fear.

"But I'm lady enough not to interfere with your multiple boyfriends and your marriage and maternal status." She turned her head sharply, looking back at her work so far.

A second later she looked back at Amy with a burning, smoldering look. "Please, kindly shut up and let me finish." She drove that blade, peeling off rubber, striking, digging.

Amy didn't say another word. And I could see in his eyes that James was torn. Em had ripped his new, married girlfriend, the girl, who was my sidekick in the brief dive expedition. But she, Em, was standing up for me, for James, and for the truck. There was a lot to be said for that.

Em twisted that sharp piece of metal, turned it over and over again, and finally the file snapped in her hand. She turned to me with a defiant look, then a smile spread across her face.

"I got through."

"Yeah?" I walked over and bent down. Half of her brand-new file was embedded in the rubber tire.

Very faintly I could hear the thin hiss as air escaped the tire.

"But now you've got to buy another file."

"Uh-huh. But this time I'm charging it to Mrs. T. She's the reason we're here, right?"

CHAPTER FORTY-SEVEN

Driving north, there was dead silence from Amy.

I pointed to the jewelry store on the left side of the highway. It was a white building with blue trim and a blue neon bird above the door.

"James, The Blue Heron Jewelry Shop."

"What?"

"Pull in. Let's have somebody look at these coins."

He had a smirk on his face. "Pard, I seriously doubt if those ugly things are worth much. If anything."

"Humor me, my friend."

Cutting across traffic, he drove into the parking lot.

"Do you know, Skip Moore, that in the years that we've dated you have never invited me into a jewelry shop?" Em sounded a little peeved. "You've never even suggested that we look at anything."

"Well, I—"

I wasn't sure what the insinuation was. I didn't have the kind of money to be able to afford jewelry. I mean, with Em it was pretty much pizza, a movie, and a sweater or a CD for her birthday or Christmas. Maybe a good book, but forty or fifty bucks was about my limit.

Amy kept silent. Since the dustup with Em she hadn't said anything. I glanced at her, but she kept her focus straight ahead.

The four of us stepped out of the truck.

Walking into the little shop, I was immediately taken with the emerald fish, gold birds, and silver sand dollars that adorned the shelves. Rings, pendants, and bracelets sporting jewel-encrusted crabs, conch shells, and pelicans were laid out on soft velvet inside glass display cases. Maybe this is what Em had been hoping for. Everything was sparkling and elegant.

"Cheesy," she said.

It was a good thing I hadn't bought her jewelry. She wouldn't have liked anything I would have picked out.

"Can I help you?" A soft lilting voice broke the silence.

The guy was dressed in a tux shirt with an honest-to-God hand-tied bow tie.

"Do you appraise old gold coins?"

He smiled.

"Of course." His voice almost condescending.

"Well, we found what appear to be coins while we were diving and wondered if they had any value."

"Oh, how exciting. We just love old gold coins."

"We're not sure they're gold, but—" I had my reservations about this guy. "So you've had some experience with—"

"Sir," he held his hand up, "we are in the diving capital of America. Of course we've had some experience."

I handed him the two coins.

Studying them for a moment, he nodded. "Let me take them in the back room for a moment. I'm going to apply some soap and water. If that doesn't give me what I need, then we'll try some ammonia."

"That's all safe?"

"Of course." He sounded offended. I didn't mean to question his expertise, but it was just that if they had any value at all—

"I take a soft toothbrush, and—" he paused, looking at James. "I should introduce myself. I'm Louis. Would the four of you like to come into my back room? I promise," smiling at James, "all I'll do is try to clean the coins."

My partner shuddered.

The two coins soaked in detergent.

"Every couple of weeks someone comes in with coins, just like these. There are millions of dollars in gold and silver out there."

As if we didn't know.

"It's just so exciting when someone actually finds something of real value. Real pieces of history."

He carefully removed them from the solution and took a toothbrush to the pieces, gently working it back and forth.

"If it's gold, the metal will be soft and we have to be gentle. Don't want to scratch the surface. If it's silver, it will be soft too, but there are some harsher chemicals we could use."

Finally, he put the two pieces in ammonia. "Don't worry, boys, it's safe." He never acknowledged the ladies.

Ten minutes later, he was working the toothbrush over the coins. Soft strokes, running over the surface.

"Oh, I just love this," he said. "Look."

Wiping a paper towel over one of the coins he smiled and, even though some of the corrosion remained, I could see part of the yellow surface.

He beamed at James. "They are gold coins. Probably from one of the Spanish wrecks that sank in the seventeen hundreds. Of course all that would have to be documented, but—"

"How much are they worth?" James wanted to get to the heart of the matter. Never one to smell the roses.

The bow tie guy stroked the coin lovingly.

"Oh, retail value would probably be at about fifteen hundred."

There was a hush in the room. Em glanced at me with a surprised look on her face. James's mouth was frozen open. Amy stood back, not quite sure what to make of all this. She had assumed the coins were the reason we were here.

Finally, I asked for clarification. "The two of them might be worth as much as fifteen hundred dollars?"

"No." He folded his arms over his chest. "That's not what I said, that's not what I meant."

I knew I hadn't heard that correctly.

"What I said was each coin is probably worth in the neighborhood of fifteen hundred dollars."

"Whoa." James was asking for a time-out.

"We might get as much as three thousand dollars for those?" He pointed to the two pieces now lying on paper towels.

"Very likely."

James looked at me, licking his lips.

"Dude, we weren't hired to find gold coins."

Amy said, "I thought that's what you were looking for."

Behind her back, he rolled his eyes.

"What's your point?"

"His point is," Em stepped up, lifting the coin and admiring the yellow portion that was visible. She admired the exquisite engraving on the actual surface you could see, "Mrs. T. wants the 'other' gold."

Looking at Amy, she nodded her head. "You know, the other coins."

"Okay." Amy was confused, as she should have been. "But I'm not sure I understand this."

"We know the coins we are looking for. These are not those coins."

"So these coins are ours." James put his arm over her bare

shoulders. "You see, Amy, these are not the ones she hired us to find. Skip found gold coins that are legally ours. Isn't that great?"

"Morally, ethically—" Em gave me a thumbs-up.

We'd actually made some money on this expedition. And that didn't happen very often with our ventures.

CHAPTER FORTY-EIGHT

We were silent on the drive back to Pelican Cove. There was shock over the value of the coins, and an uncomfortable aura over the parking lot blowup between Em and the lovely Amy.

"Well," I tried to start the conversation that needed to happen. "That was a real shock. I mean, that's a lot of money."

No one offered any response. I figured Amy and James were both pissed off. At Em and at me. It was an awkward moment. James focused on the road and no one else offered any comment.

We pulled into the resort parking lot, James parking right below my unit. His room was just down the way.

We all sat there for a moment. Finally James reached into his T-shirt pocket and pulled something out.

"Pitch his card, Skip." He handed me the flowery business card the jewelry clerk had offered him. On the back was the guy's cell phone number.

"You sure, James?" I shouldn't have goaded him, but it was second nature. "He seemed awfully interested."

James gave me a grave glance and again he shuddered and stared out of the windshield, looking at the pool.

Closing his eyes as we all sat there, he let out a long sigh. It had been a long morning. A long afternoon.

Turning to Em before he got out of the truck, James put a hand on her shoulder.

"Look," his hand tightened, "I realize that Amy doesn't have all the facts about what just happened." He glanced over his shoulder at Amy, the bathing suit beauty. "So, I'm going to explain everything to her in a minute."

She gave him a wry smile.

"James," I said.

"No, no." He held his hand up, stopping me from getting involved. "I'll do what is right. Don't worry, pard."

Hesitating, he looked at my girlfriend, "I'm just saying, Em, I appreciate what you did back there. The tire and everything. Standing up for us. It was time somebody let those guys know that they can't keep messing with us."

Em nodded.

"I just wondered what you would have done if the nail file hadn't worked."

She smiled. "I would have taken out the revolver and put a bullet in their engine block. Think they would have gotten the message then?"

My girl had turned into this gun moll that even I didn't recognize.

CHAPTER FORTY-NINE

I had never experienced a morning so full of events. Diving with Amy, finding the gold coins, discovering that our two nemeses, one of whom we thought was dead, had followed every step we took and were now trying to find the gold, watching my girlfriend destroy the front tire on their Harley-Davidson, and having James and Em actually on the same page.

Three thousand dollars. In the history of our independent business adventures James and I had never made that much money free and clear. Mrs. T. was picking up the tab for finding her relative's stake in this hunt, the gold bars that were worth forty-four million dollars. This money, the value of the coins, would be clear profit.

And I wondered if Weezle and his friend had found more coins. Maybe they would give up their search for the gold bars. I doubted that. My real fear was that they would find the sought-after gold bars and that I had missed them.

Em went to the room and I wandered out to the beach, watching a lone guy on a bright yellow sailboard as he maneuvered it over the water, catching the breeze wherever he could. It was a big ocean. Trying to find ten crates of gold in that massive body of water was practically impossible.

But then again, I'd found three thousand dollars' worth of gold coins in about ten minutes and that was by accident.

Walking by one of the docked boats, I nodded to the older man sitting in a deck chair, thumbing through a magazine.

He glanced up as I walked by. "Interested in fishing?"

"No, not really."

"I know this island like the back of my hand. And the waters. You can ask anybody. I find the fish when no one else can." He tilted his long-billed cap up on his head, his weathered face smiling.

"I'm sure you're good."

"Good? I'm the best." He stroked his chin. "You got any friends who are looking for a charter—half day, all day, you send 'em to me."

"You know the area pretty well, right?"

"I do." He slowly stood up, thrusting his hands into his khaki cargo shorts and twisting his neck as if it were stiff.

"What do you know about Cheeca Lodge?"

"Fishing?"

"I was thinking more about the property."

"What about it? You know they rebuilt some if it a couple of years ago. Place had a big fire and they had to close up. Some guy tossed a cigarette on the thatched hut bar on New Year's Eve. Nasty situation. But it's a fine resort. Fanciest one in this area. Very modern, upscale—"

"Quite a bit of property?"

"Oh, I'd say. Got a golf course, big pool, and lodge. Plus all them bungalows. But it's a bit pricey."

"Quite a history." If the gold wasn't buried in the ocean, Kriegel said it would be buried somewhere on that property. Where

Cheeca Lodge now stood. Hey, it wasn't the size of the ocean, but still a sizable area to cover.

"Started out the settlers built a two-room schoolhouse and a Methodist Cemetery."

"So now there's this fabulous resort—"

"And an old cemetery."

"The cemetery is still there?" We'd heard that, but I still had a hard time believing it. You don't have an old cemetery on a resort property.

"Yep, right on the beach beside the swimming pool."

I wondered if they sold that photo on a postcard. "Swimming next to dead people. Wish you were here."

"Pinder Cemetery. Used to be called that. Named after Etta Pinder. Died sometime around nineteen fourteen. Now they call it Pioneer Cemetery, but it's still there. The statue kind of guards it."

"Statue?"

"The broken-winged angel. I think she was there before the hurricane back in thirty-five. She's still there, in the middle of that plot of ground."

I was trying to picture this ancient, deteriorating cemetery and this high-class resort coexisting.

"The resort is—"

"Built up around it."

"So you're swimming, fishing, laying out in the sun and there's this old cemetery right beside you?"

"That's exactly the way it is."

"And the bodies are above ground?"

"No. Buried under the ground."

Again I remembered the letter we'd found. Kriegel was concerned that if you dug straight down, you'd hit water before you could bury anything. His assumption was that the land was almost at sea level.

"Why are you so interested in Cheeca?"

"I want to visit."

"It's a private resort. They got a gate with a guard. You're a guest or a vendor or you don't get in."

We'd hurdled bigger obstacles than Cheeca Lodge.

"So, unless I pony up for the room rate, I can't visit?" I asked the old captain, even though I wasn't sure he had the answer.

"Well," he stretched his arms and took a deep breath, "I told you I know this island like the back of this hand—" the gentleman passed his hand in front of my face. "If you pull up to that gate and say you want to visit the Methodist cemetery, they cannot deny you a visit. It's an official historic site."

"Really?"

"They don't want everyone to know that, but the Methodist church still owns the cemetery and anyone, even you, can show up and be admitted. I mean, they do have this very pricey resort and all."

"What's your name?"

"Here's my card."

I looked down to read it.

Al Amero. Fishing expert and boat captain.

"Mr. Amero, I'm Skip Moore and I will tell anyone who wants to know that you are the finest fishing guide anyone could want."

He gave me a broad smile and shook my hand.

"I do the best I can, young man."

"You've been a big help."

"Things are a little slow right now. You might want to get out there and start spreading the news, know what I mean?"

CHAPTER FIFTY

I found him at the pool bar, no surprise.

"Where's Amy?"

He rolled his eyes. "I stopped by the bar next door and she's in deep conversation with another guy. Some salesman named Trump from Illinois." He took a swallow of his draft.

"Yeah?"

"I suggested we split for some private time, but she's telling me that she's not done yet and she's kind of into this guy."

"She said that?"

"Implied it."

"Imagine that."

"Imagine what?"

"She's married, having an affair, decides to have an affair with you, then finds someone else attractive. I mean, what are the odds?"

"I thought you'd have a little more compassion, amigo."

"I don't."

"I got that."

He was silent for a moment. I could hear the gears working in his head. Finally, he looked at me.

"Well, it's obvious that Em isn't on board with this either. Maybe I should stay away from women who are in a relationship."

"Or multiple relationships?"

He nodded.

"James, I want to take the metal detector to Cheeca Lodge. Tonight. After dark. There's some exploring that needs to be done."

"We can do that."

"We've got to tell them that we are there to see the cemetery."

"Dude, I'm really not into cemeteries."

"Dude, you suggested that we get involved in this project. If you don't want to deal with it, we can kiss our two million commission goodbye."

He hesitated, then said, "Why a cemetery?"

"You remember, Cheeca Lodge has a Methodist cemetery? All we've got to do is mention that we're there to see the cemetery and it's a guarantee to get onto the property through the private gate."

"But it's still private property, Skip. We go tooling in with the truck and they're going to send us packing."

"They've got to let us in. It's a deal they made with the Methodist church."

"So you're going to take the detector to Cheeca Lodge?"

"I am. We'll go in late afternoon. Then when it gets a little dark—"

"Amigo, where do we start looking?"

"Well," I'd thought it through and was pretty pleased with my plan. "There's a golf course, a beach, of course all the buildings—"

"Man, if that stuff is buried under the buildings I don't see how we could ever get it up."

"There's a big pool—"

"When they dug the pool, somebody would have found it if that's where it rested."

"There's only one thing left, James. And it was there in nineteen thirty-five."

"Whoa." He gave me a big smile, his eyes opening wider. Motioning to Bobbie, he said, "I'm buying this guy a beer. He's a genius."

She nodded. "What kind?" She still didn't remember.

"Whatever he's having," I said.

"Oh," she brightened up. "Yuengling."

James looked out at the water, focusing on something inside his head, the vision I'd painted.

"Pure genius. This guy Kriegel is walking around, maybe he even gets a ride down to this Millionaire's Row where the fancy house had been, and he's thinking about where to bury his gold."

I nodded. "I'm thinking that the gold was still on the train. The railroad cars were scattered everywhere, but maybe this freight car was still closed. And these crates had to be solid. Put together really well. So Kriegel has a little time before the looters get here and he's checking things out."

"He gets this far and finds out there's a cemetery. And it's still there."

"That's where I'm headed."

"Bodies buried?"

"Under the sand. The only damage to the entire place was the angel statue. There are bodies from the late eighteen hundreds. Just headstones above ground."

"Nobody is going to dig up bodies."

"No decent people. Zombies, maybe."

He frowned.

"So, if someone did stumble on one of these buried crates,

accidentally," he rubbed his chin, "they'd think it had something to do with dead people. A wooden box in a cemetery? Maybe a pet coffin?"

"Doesn't this make perfect sense?"

"Skip, it does. It would be like hiding something in plain sight. Anyone who found it wouldn't understand its significance."

"You'd think it would be a pretty safe bet."

"We're on for tonight, pard."

"A little exploring." Hiding in plain sight.

Kind of like the boat people down at the vacant property. I'd bet money they were smuggling something in plain sight. I wouldn't bet our two million dollars, but I'd bet money.

"Hey, Skip," James scrunched his shoulders, ran his fingers through his hair, and shook his head. In his best Rodney Danger-field imitation, he said, "Country clubs and cemeteries are the biggest wasters of prime real estate."

That one was a freebie. I think we'd both memorized every line in *Caddyshack*.

CHAPTER FIFTY-ONE

I carried the shovels, just in case we decided to dig tonight, and Em had the metal detector.

"Suppose we can stop in for dinner?"

"We'll give it a try," James said. "Once they let us in, they may as well take our money."

We went through the gate with no trouble.

The guard said, "Oh, you're here to see the cemetery, our historic site?"

"Yeah. History," James said.

He handed us a pass and motioned us through.

When we arrived at the circular drive, the guy at the lodge walked out with a question mark look on his face.

Studying the truck he said, "Are you a vendor?"

Was it so hard to believe we were guests? Dressed in T-shirts, shorts, and flip-flops, I thought we fit right in.

"We're here to have dinner and see the cemetery." Em smiled at him and that seemed to get the job done.

"Very few people come here to see the cemetery."

"We have family buried there and—" James trailed off.

"Well, certainly, sir." He stood there in his crisp white shirt, white cargo shorts, white socks, and tennis shoes, holding his hand out.

"I'm sorry," staring at the nametag on the attendant James said, "Jack, where do I park?"

"Sir, I'll park the—" he surveyed the truck, "the vehicle."

"No problem, I can—"

"Sir, I will valet the vehicle."

"Let him park it, James." It was obvious that Em had valet parked before. James and I, never.

Reluctantly, James handed the man the keys, and we got out of the truck.

"New experiences, Skip. That's what I'm all about."

I just shook my head.

We had a nice dinner. Better than we ever ate. I had shrimp and scallops. Em had an Asian dish I'd never heard of, and James had lobster. My best friend and girlfriend got along like brother and sister. They fought the whole time, but kept it down so we didn't get thrown out.

Sitting out on the patio, a candle burning softly at our table, we smelled the ocean air, listened to a classical guitar, and had a glass of wine. It was what civilized people seemed to do. No Yuengling beers tonight.

Afterward we walked out to the cemetery plot. It was about the size of a postage stamp. Small, crowded, covered with sand, and a very strange addition to the beach. The statue of the angel was there, complete with a broken arm and wing done in the '35 hurricane.

A wooden fence surrounded the burial ground but we were able to walk inside and survey the stones. Mounted on a post was a metal plaque that declared the cemetery was deeded to Richard Pinder in 1883 by President Chester Arthur. At least President

Arthur did something with his short career. I knew nothing else about his presidency.

"So, what do you think, pard?"

Dusk had settled, and while several couples strolled the beach, most of the diners and outdoor folks had headed for their rooms or whatever nightlife they could find.

"Think the truck is unlocked?"

"Hard to say. I've never had a valet park my truck before. Em, do they, these valets, do they lock your vehicle?" He spoke with an affected British accent, mocking the valet and probably Em.

"Em?" I looked at her with what I hoped was a pleading expression.

"I know, you want me to go ask the attendant. You think because I'm a girl they won't ask what's going on."

"Because you're a very attractive girl," I said.

"And I sometimes get tired of playing that role. Skip, James, they may ask us to leave. We've probably overstayed our welcome. I mean—"

"Give it a try?"

She threw her hands up. "Okay."

She was back in three minutes with the detector.

"Truck was unlocked, and parked on the circle in front."

"Probably because they thought we'd be short timers. They assumed we'd leave soon after arrival so they parked us close by." That made sense to me.

"I think it's because the truck gives them some prestige. They parked it in front to show off." James hadn't lost his bad phony British accent.

"That's it." I glanced around the property and there was no one. Rooms on higher floors looked down on the plot, but their curtains were drawn.

"I'm just going to sweep the perimeter." The idea that had seemed so dead on, that had sounded so plausible, now seemed like a dumb idea. There were dead people under this ground, not buried treasure. And what happened if there was metal in a casket—for whatever reason—and we dug that up?

"James, I hadn't thought about it, but what if there's a metal casket? I don't want to dig up dead people. Isn't that against the law?"

"Son, if we haven't broken some laws already—"

"Yeah, but I'm not comfortable with making a mistake like that. Let the dead rest in peace and all that."

"Some article I saw at the library, Skip. It said that the caskets buried in Pinder Cemetery were wooden."

"Why?"

"This story pointed out that first of all there weren't many metal caskets made. Maybe for the superrich. And, the landowners didn't want the metal corroding and leaching into the beach."

"Talk about early environmentalists." Truly amazing. Some of these caskets were from the 1800s and people were already going green.

Still, I was having second thoughts. I'm not the most religious guy, but upsetting the spirit of a dead person didn't seem to be the kind of thing I wanted to be doing. But here we were. And I had the detector in hand.

"We'll observe." James stepped back.

Plugging in the earpiece, I slowly swept the detector back and forth as I walked on the outside of the cemetery. Occasionally there would be a minor increase in the hum of the machine and I could see the needle move a little on the meter, but there was nothing that got my attention. Of course, I knew absolutely nothing about the subtleties of the JW Fishers Pulse 8K metal detector. Maybe I was passing over silver earrings or gold necklaces. You couldn't dig every time an increase in the volume occurred.

"Nothing too surprising here."

"Sweep the cemetery, Skip." Em was standing with James, the two of them watching my face for a reaction. Well, they couldn't hear the fire engine siren, so they had to rely on my face.

Slowly, sweeping inside the picket fence now, over caskets and bodies that lay rotting under this gray-white sand. And there was the rise in volume, where the siren sound got louder then dropped back to normal. Not having a clue about corpses, I assumed that a rusty old belt buckle or a pair of wire-frame glasses was giving off a signal. Maybe some brass buttons on a gentlemen's coat.

"Metal handles on some of those coffins?" I heard Em as she watched my face.

As it got darker, I worked toward the center, sweeping as my compatriots stood on the sideline.

Side to side, front to back I swept the wand. The ebb and the flow in my earpiece kept me focused and several times I thought there might be something. But there had to be a long siren in my ear. The length of a crate of gold. A small coffin of yellow metal. I swept over and over, and the darker it got the more intense I was. I wanted this more than anything. Find one coffin of gold. That's all I asked for. One sign. Something that told me I was on the right track.

Finding a wooden box in a field of coffins. Hiding in the open.

I was in a zone. Sweep this way, then that. Over a grave and then over empty space. Were there spirits who would speak to me? Maybe spirits were the reason there was a volume increase. The sirens that I heard could certainly be the sound of spirits. Tortured souls who died in a devastating wind storm. Ghosts who were haunted with the pain and the devastation of the hurricane of '35.

Sweep, sweep and I was on the darker side of the plot when I heard the voice.

221

"Okay, folks, time to go home."

I lifted my eyes from the ground and watched Em and James being led away. The security officer stood behind them, prodding them to the lodge. In the dark he hadn't seen me. I'd totally been ignored.

I stared at them until they disappeared into the night. I didn't have my cell phone and wondered how I would contact them. Putting that out of my head, I concentrated on the sweeps.

Over and over, back and forth, and only small responses. I stepped out of the fenced-in area. If someone had buried wooden caskets of gold, why would they take a chance that they would accidentally stumble on a real casket with a body inside? Better to bury them on the perimeter.

I swept five feet out around the fenced-in property. Ten feet out. Then fifteen.

I heard the fire engines. My heart started racing as the sirens got louder and louder, louder and louder. Over a foot of high-volume sirens. This was exactly what I was looking for. Then it tapered off.

My hands were shaking. Could be something else. But the size, the intensity of the signal—

I wanted to dig. Right now, but the shovels were in the box truck. I was elated, flushed with success, and scared to death that I'd be found. I was certain I could be arrested for what I was doing, but the idea of finding any part of forty-four million dollars was overwhelming.

What was under the sand?

Studying the ground I'd covered, I noticed there was no headstone. It was definitely outside the fenced section of sand. That didn't necessarily mean that a body wasn't buried there. Old tombstones had a way of wearing down, falling down or being stolen. But still, it was one more sign that this could be a crate of gold.

I ran the detector five feet away, then ten. There was nothing. One crate of gold? It was hard to imagine that they'd only buried one. Maybe one on top of the other.

Out of the corner of my eye I saw someone approaching. Maybe that same guard. I switched off the detector and walked quickly to the building directly in front of the cemetery. Sliding around the corner, I kept walking. No one followed me.

With deliberate strides I reached the gate, hoping I hadn't been completely deserted. If they wanted a share of the treasure, James and Em had better be waiting for me when I got outside.

CHAPTER FIFTY-TWO

The truck was across the street, parked under a scrawny palm tree. I could see them in the soft glow of a streetlight, a worried look on Em's face.

Walking up to her window, I tapped lightly on the door and she jumped.

"Skip. For God's sake, you could have given me a heart attack, I mean you should at least—"

"I found something."

Through the open window, James whispered, "No shit?"

"Whatever it was, it was the perfect length, a little over a foot long and the signal it gave off was really strong."

"Still," Em being the voice of reason, "it still could be just a piece of metal."

"Listen," I handed them the detector through the open window, "the signal was about fifteen feet outside the cemetery."

"So hopefully it's not buried with the bodies."

"We don't know. But I feel a little safer." I was semiconfident that there would be no interference with dead bodies.

"Dude, what do we do now?"

"We had maybe twenty minutes that they left us alone back there. Then you two were unceremoniously escorted off the property, right?"

"About twenty minutes."

"So from the time we started sweeping the property until you met the guard, twenty minutes passed."

They both agreed.

"Well, I spent another twenty minutes covering the ground before I saw a guard coming in my direction."

"So, if these guards have a routine, we should be able to figure out their schedule," James said.

"Exactly. I'm guessing they cover that area every twenty minutes."

"So we know how much time we have to work with," Em jumped in.

"And," I concluded, "we found out on the vacant property that it isn't that difficult to dig. It's sand. I mean, we should be able to determine what is buried there in twenty minutes. Two shovels, two diggers."

James and Em were quiet. We could hear a night bird somewhere in the distance and the drone of some tree insects. Occasionally there was a car or truck up on the main highway.

"We're talking about digging in an old cemetery, right?"

I'd been leaning into the open window, so I opened the door and climbed in beside Em.

"Technically outside a cemetery."

"What if, and I'm just saying, what if we put our shovels through the top of a real rotted wooden casket? And we go right through to a skeleton?"

James, who always talked a good game, was having second thoughts.

"I don't know. I don't know how I'd feel, James."

"And if we don't, if we don't do this, then we'll never know if it's the gold or not, right?"

"We'll never know." I agreed.

"And it's our job to find out." James was searching for courage. "We were hired to find this stuff."

"We were. But part of our job isn't to break the law."

Another silence.

Finally Em spoke. "You guys know that I usually try to pull you back. I don't want either of you getting in over your heads, but you usually manage to do that anyway, right?"

We both nodded.

"But in this case, if you're careful, I think you've got to go for it."

"Seriously?" I couldn't believe she was 100 percent on board with this.

"Seriously."

"We could get in a lot of trouble."

"Could."

"Serious trouble."

"You're digging in the beach, right?"

"Duh." James frowned.

"That's what people do. They dig in the sand. Kids do it. Adults do it. If you're at a beach, it's natural to dig in the sand."

One of the few memories I had of good times with my mother and sister was going to Miami Beach and burying my ten-year-old sister up to her head. She was fine with it and Mom and I dug the hole with our hands. Marie lay in the sand cavern and we covered her up to her neck. Then I drew a butterfly around her head. There must have been ten people who came up and took pictures, and my sister was the hit of the beach. For about ten minutes.

"It's just a strip of sand. As long as you're not digging in the graveyard, it's just the beach. I think we're okay. Seriously."

Em was buying in. I was amazed.

"Let's go back to the Cove. Tomorrow night I think we've got some serious digging to do."

"You know what happened the last time we dug, amigo?"

I did. We'd found a treasure map.

"Our luck is on course," James said.

"In this case," Em was smiling, her hand on my knee, "I don't think it was luck. I think you guys have done some really good investigative work. You're putting the puzzle together."

"Yeah." James had a smug, satisfied look on his face.

"Swing by the vacant property," I said.

He turned off the highway and went back a block to the fenced-off boat dock.

"What are we looking for?"

I glanced at my watch. Eleven fifteen. Something that the girl at the front desk had said. That guests checked in at the Ocean Air in the very early morning and checked out very late at night.

"I don't know, just cruise by."

James slowed down to a crawl and we passed the camouflaged property, then the Ocean Air Suites.

"Whoa. Hold it."

James braked.

We gazed back into the parking lot, sizing up the big tour bus parked in front. Its parking lights were on and with our windows down we could hear the hum of the big diesel engine.

"They're just dropping off a late tour group. No big deal." James shrugged his shoulders.

"Maybe." Something was nagging at me. Tour buses don't usually drop people off around midnight.

"Guys, I don't think we want to sit here and debate what the bus is doing here. We've already been in trouble for hanging around this property."

James pulled out and drove back to the highway.

"Park it over there, James." I pointed to a deserted gas station. It was dark and there was no one around.

"Skip—" Em was not happy.

"Five minutes. Just watch the road over there, where traffic comes out from the Ocean Air."

"Another one of your stakeouts?"

"Five minutes, Em. And the last stakeout turned up someone who looked a lot like Jim Weezle. We did have some success, am I right?"

She had nothing to say.

We waited, our engine running.

"Maybe it's a good time to give the old girl a drink."

James turned off the truck, went to the back, and came back empty handed. "No more oil, Skip. Not a good thing."

"How long can we make it?"

"Won't be many more miles she'll be bone dry. It'll freeze up the engine and we'll grind to a stop. Not a good thing at all."

"It'll be nice when we get a new truck."

With two million dollars, James could buy as many trucks as he wanted.

"What are we waiting for, Skip?"

And that's when the big fancy tour bus pulled out, moving onto the highway headed north.

"We were waiting for that," I said. "James, can you follow the bus?"

He started the truck and drove up behind the bus staying with it for a couple of minutes.

"Still don't know what the purpose of this trip is." He kept his eyes on the vehicle in front of us.

"Can you pass him?"

"At this speed, yeah."

I felt the truck pick up speed. Maybe two or three miles an hour.

"If that bus was going fifteen miles an hour faster, probably not."

It would be a good thing when James got a new truck.

Flooring the gas pedal, we eased around the lumbering bus.

"Look up at the windows."

Em and James glanced up at the row of windows.

"What do you see?"

"People. In every seat." Em nodded.

"So they weren't checking in." James was confused.

"No, they were checking out. At eleven thirty p.m. The whole group." I was confused.

"Something very strange about that operation."

"They're smuggling stuff," James said. "Drugs. Drugs or gold."

CHAPTER FIFTY-THREE

At seven o'clock in the morning the room phone rang. Em never budged, so I reached across her and grabbed the receiver.

"Hello."

"Skip?"

"What?"

"This is Maria Sanko."

"Maria, Maria, if we find those coins, I promise you that—"

"Skip, I have a friend who would like to talk with you."

I was still working the cobwebs out of my head. We'd come back to Pelican Cove and probably drank a little too much red wine and beer. We were pumped up with the prospect of actually having found something. Then we tracked down Mrs. T. who was at Rumrunner's bar, and when we got her on board with the gold fever, we drank some more. I think she bought the entire bar a round. James's ex, Amy, was nowhere to be found.

I was a little fuzzy.

"Do you hear me?"

"Why does someone want to talk to me?"

"This gentleman is Bernard Blattner, a gentleman who is almost one hundred years old. He has some information he'd like to share with you."

I was slowly waking up. I stretched the phone cord as it tightened over Em's throat. She jerked up, awake and short of breath. Pulling the cord from her neck, she ducked under it and headed for the bathroom.

"Maria, I don't understand."

There was a long silence on the other end.

Finally, "Look, you and your partner have used me several times in the last couple of days."

It was my turn to be silent.

"You've played plumbers, historians, and treasure hunters. And I've gone along with you, largely because I was sucked in on several of your ruses, but also because I find you both charming con men. I tend to have a soft spot for guys like you."

I wondered if her husband, who lost the motorcycle in the divorce settlement, was one of those charming con men. She'd apparently outconned him. She now owned the Harley-Davidson.

"And what does he want to talk to us about?"

"Listen, I feel we had an unfortunate moment, and I'd like to help you guys out. Over the years I've sold a lot of property to Bernie. The gentleman has a lot of knowledge about Islamorada. He's lived here all his life, and he may be able to help you find your hidden treasure."

I hesitated and my heart jumped. "Our what?" How the hell did she know about the treasure?

"You know, your wrecker's camp. The gold coins or whatever it is you're looking for."

"Maria," I was thinking this through, "if this old guy has information why hasn't he dug up the treasure himself?"

"No, no. He can give you some history about the wreckers,

some idea of how it all worked. I thought it might be beneficial. That's all. Unless, you've found what you're looking for?"

"No. We haven't."

"I'm not trying to interfere, but if you guys want a little history, from someone who's seen it all, then this might be your chance."

I was suddenly wide awake. Someone who had actually survived the storm. One of the handful of people who'd been alive and stayed alive during the massive hurricane that blew away Flagler's Folly. This is what we'd been waiting for. He may or may not have information, but this was a true survivor.

"Yeah. Sure. Of course. We'd love to talk to Mr. Blattner."

"Okay then. I can have him visit you guys or you can—"

"This would be great. I owe you an apology. It's just that— could he meet us here this morning sometime? If he's not busy maybe."

"Skip?"

"Yeah?"

"He's ninety-nine years old. How busy do you think you'll be at ninety-nine?"

"How about around ten?"

"Make it eleven. I don't think his pacemaker starts till then."

I smiled. We were going to talk to someone who had actually been there when that train blew off the track. When a twenty-foot tidal wave rose out of the ocean and tore the tracks from their foundations. When almost every building in the town was ripped from the ground and destroyed and when five hundred people were killed by an act of God. We were going to talk to someone who'd lived through it. I was excited and terrified at the same time.

We were sitting at a white, glass-topped table by the pool when I heard the roar. Looking out into the parking lot, I saw the

Harley, a blur of shell dust rolling over the ground as Maria screeched to a halt.

Behind her, a slim, frail man with wispy-white hair pulled off his helmet and struggled to step off the bike.

Like a true lady, she walked around and helped him, waiting until he was steady and on his feet.

Shuffling his feet, the old man moved forward, seeing us as we stood around our table.

"Well, hello children." His voice was dry and breathy and his old face pulled tight on his skull. It was the eyes that were still young. My grandmother used to call them smiling eyes. I'd always asked her how eyes could smile, and she'd just give me that look—the smiling eyes look.

James, Em, and I nodded politely.

I was surprised that Maria had come. And yet I don't think I expected a ninety-nine-year-old man to drive himself. Still, riding with Maria Sanko? At my age I'd be petrified. The old guy must have had nerves of steel.

He reached out, shaking our hands as we introduced ourselves.

"Glad to meet all of you. As you may know, I almost didn't make it here this morning."

"Oh, my God." Em reached out and took his withered hand. "What in the world happened?"

"Ms. Sanko was driving."

His eyes sparkled and he barely kept his mouth from smiling.

"Mr. Blattner, we have some questions." I didn't want to discuss this in front of Maria, but it was our one chance to get all the information we could.

"Shoot."

"You were here when the hurricane of thirty-five hit?"

"I was. Damndest storm I've ever seen."

"You were—" James was fishing.

"I was twenty-four years old. I worked on the pineapple docks."

"The boats came in from Cuba, right?" I was seeing it all in my mind.

"They did. Loaded with pineapples and limes. Most of the time they'd come in on freight cars, already loaded. It was my job to get those cars onto our spur tracks up to the main track and head 'em up to Miami."

"So they were already packed in freight cars? All you had to do was get them on the tracks?"

"Well, it wasn't as easy as that. Took four of us to get the car off the boat, down the dock, and to the spur."

"Lots of physical work."

"You bet."

He smiled at Em. Almost like he was flirting.

"And we'd sort and load some of the local farmer's products on those docks too."

"So there were pineapple growers down here?"

He nodded, his white hair falling over his face.

"There were. They ended up hating us, the railroad people."

"Why? Weren't you shipping their fruit to Miami as well?"

"At first we did. We shipped pineapples grown right here. But they wanted a lot more money than the Cubans. We wanted to help out the local farmers, so for a while anyway, we used to take old scrap iron from the railroad and add more weight to the local producers' crates of fruit. That way, they'd make more money. We'd hide small pieces of iron in the shipment, but somebody up in Miami found out that we were adding iron to increase the weight and they stopped buying shipments of pineapples grown in the Keys. We had come up with the idea, so the farmers blamed us for the loss of business."

It sounded like a James Lessor scam. Add some iron to the package so you could bill extra. As long as no one figured it out. He pushed his hair back. "Same thing that happens today, young man. Foreign countries are willing to work cheaper. Folks in Cuba could and would do it for a whole lot less. So, with our services and the cheap fruit from Cuba, we eventually shut out the local grower. Those growers threatened to shut us down, but it never happened. Took a two-hundred-mile-an-hour wind and a tidal wave to do that. And the wind and water did that very effectively."

James had both hands folded on the tabletop. He glanced at me, then looked at Bernie, ready to ask the serious questions.

"Mr. Blattner—"

"Bernie."

"Mr. Blattner"—he couldn't do Bernie—"where were you when the train blew off the tracks?"

He smiled. "We had an old shack where we could take a break from the hot sun. We could go into the back room of the shack to, excuse me, ma'am"—he looked at Em—"relieve ourselves."

"That's where you were?"

"I was. But when the tidal wave broke, I believe I was running like the wind. That's what I remember. I don't know where I thought I was going, but I was running."

We all took a breath. The horrific storm scared me in the present. I couldn't fathom how it must have been back in Bernie's present.

"Can we talk about what happened after the storm?" Em asked.

"We can talk about anything you want to talk about, beautiful lady." He gave her a wide smile, his crooked yellow teeth showing.

"Did you get a look at the train?"

"Oh, yes. Cars all over the place. Some of them were five hundred feet away from the track. Funny thing was, the engine never fell over. Heavy metal engine it was, and it never went down. Almost everything in the town, in the entire area, went down. But not old four forty-seven. Nope. Stood as a tribute to the strength of the railroad and I took that as a sign that we'd be back again."

"Didn't happen, did it?"

"No."

"Mr. Blattner," I started.

"Bernie."

A ninety-nine-year-old guy was not Bernie. I had some respect for my elders.

"There was a man from Miami on that train. He was in the finance department for the railroad." I did not want to go there because up until now we seemed to be the only ones who knew about the gold. Well, not counting Stiffle, Markim, and Weezle.

"Was he killed? Most of 'em were."

"He was the great-grandfather of the lady who hired us. Look, I know it's a long shot, but it seems there were very few of you left. You might have run into this guy. He had ten small wooden crates and he was looking for a place and for someone to help him bury them."

He nodded. "Jackie Logan worked with me on the pineapple docks. Strappin' young boy. We both worked with our hands, arms, backs, and legs. Couldn't be in much better shape than we were back then." He smiled and sat back, his mind drifting into nineteen thirty-five.

"So this guy, Matthew Kriegel, he was looking for someone like you. A survivor who could do some heavy lifting and someone who might know the island."

Nodding and smiling, the old man folded his hands on the table.

"We didn't hurt for work for the next week. We collected

bodies, with masks on our faces so we wouldn't get sick. Boy Scouts from Miami come down, I believe, and helped."

James cleared his throat. "Do you remember anyone asking you to help bury some wooden boxes?"

"This all has to do with the wrecking camp?" Maria looked confused, but that was to be expected. We'd made a game out of confusing her.

"Then there was the cleanup of the train itself. And pickin' up debris all over the island. We'd set up tents, unpack medical supplies when they got there, but it was a slow process, yes it was."

"But no wooden boxes? None that you can remember?"

A white seagull with a black face hovered overhead, checking our table for a sign of food.

"There was a guy."

"What guy?" I didn't want to seem too anxious, but I was.

"Offered to pay me and Jackie five dollars if we'd help him load some crates on a horse-drawn wagon. That I do remember. Those were good wages."

"Oh, my God." James's eyes were wide open. "So you do remember this guy. And you worked for him?"

"Jackie and some of the Negroes took the job. Those crates were heavy, Jackie told me. And me, I was still employed by the railroad and I was cleaning out the cars, thinking we could salvage some of them."

"This guy, the one who employed Jackie—" I had to ask the question.

"It was a long time ago, young man. I don't remember everything because I think we were all in a state of shock. God all mighty, no one had ever seen that many dead people. Friends, a girl I had dated, my boss."

"Do you know where they took the crates?"

"I remember he had a broken arm. Just hung loose by his

side. And he wasn't well. I believe he may have died of fever if it's the same man. Some did."

Em finally spoke. "Bernie"—no respect for the old man—"you have a fantastic memory."

"It was a horrifying time, young lady. Something you can't put out of your head, hard as you try."

"Bernie, did Jackie ever tell you where they buried the crates?"

"I believe he did."

"Where?"

"It comes back to me. All that death and destruction. Limbless bodies, animals dashed on the rocks, and corpses hanging high in the trees where the tidal wave washed 'em. And that odor. The stench of rotting flesh."

"Bernie?"

"I never knew what was in those boxes, but he told me they buried the crates, the ones from the train that we never saw the insides of. They buried them in the old Pinder Methodist cemetery. Kind of fitting, don't you think?"

"And Jackie?"

"Never saw him again after that. I did hear that he moved to South America and bought some plantation down there, but I never knew for sure."

CHAPTER FIFTY-FOUR

"Skip, we're going to be rich." James had dollar signs in his eyes. "Rich, I'm telling you."

"Don't call me Rich."

He smiled. We sat in our room, waiting for Mary Trueblood to come in. I'd called and told her we had some big news.

"James, we're dealing with a cemetery plot. A place where they bury people. Souls are interred there. You realize this is not something we can just explore with no consequences?"

"We're dealing with the property around the cemetery, amigo. Around the cemetery. Not in it. Em made a good point. There's a big difference. This is on the beach, amigo. Ten crates of gold. Oh, my God, Skip. Over forty million dollars' worth of precious metal. Not only will we get two million, but our company will be mentioned everywhere. Think about it. The publicity will be overwhelming."

He was practically foaming at the mouth.

"Skip, I think there's a very good chance you've found it." Em was smiling a very wide smile.

"Have you guys lost all your senses? There's no guarantee that—"

"Amigo. Did you not hear the old man?"

I had.

"Let me ask you two something." I was now the voice of reason. "Have you ever thought about how we're going to dig it up and remove it from a five-star resort? Have you?" I heard myself getting louder. "Under the scrutiny of guards every twenty minutes, not to mention people watching from their windows? People in the pool, on the beach. You guys are acting a little crazy, you know? What do you want to do, just pull a bulldozer up and start tearing up the beach?"

Like that would ever happen.

"Whatever it takes, buddy." James was lit up like a Christmas tree.

"Skip," Em was not far behind him. She had always been the voice of reason. Not any more. So it seemed a little strange to me that I was asking for some sanity. "Maybe we go to the authorities. We get Mrs. T. to admit to them we've found buried treasure. We get our money, the state of Florida gets theirs, and Mrs. T. still comes out a multimillionaire."

That was a concept I hadn't considered.

"But what if the Methodist church says it's theirs?" My thought.

"Point well taken," James said.

"What if Cheeca Lodge says it is theirs?" My thought.

"Another point to Skip," Em said.

"And what if the town of Islamorada says it's theirs?"

There was a knock at the door. Mrs. T. had finally arrived.

"We've got some pretty exciting news about the lost treasure," I said as I opened the door.

Maria Sanko stood at the entrance, her face in a knot of anger.

From the back of the room, James said, "Oh, shit."

"Suppose you tell me what was in those crates. You've been yanking my chain since we met, boys, and you," she pointed to Em who was sitting on the bed, "the three of you must think I'm pretty stupid."

"Look, Maria," I started the explanation, "we're working for someone. We have an employer. If it was just us, we'd work with you, but we have to explain everything to—"

"To whom?" Mrs. T. walked up behind Maria.

"You two may as well come in." They entered and stood in front of us, both of them with arms folded across their chests.

"Have a seat." There was one place on the bed, and Maria sat down on the floor.

I told Mrs. T. about Mr. Blattner and what he'd said. Then I told her that Maria suspected we were being less than truthful in our explanation.

"Do you want to tell her what we're doing?"

Mrs. T. suddenly looked very tired. She'd been carrying the weight of this story for over six months and right now, when we could smell victory, she was facing all kinds of problems.

"Oh, hell. She might as well know the whole story. But if she wants a cut for bringing in the old man—"

"We really should give her something," Em said, "latecomer that she is."

Mrs. T. gave her a death stare. "One hundred thousand. If, if we find all ten crates. And if we don't, we give her—" she paused, looking exasperated, "we give her our undying gratitude. Okay?"

Maria nodded. It was probably better than she expected. Yet here was a lady who got her husband's motorcycle in a divorce settlement. She could probably get a lot more out of Mrs. T. if she wanted to.

"Done."

"Maria, make yourself worth one hundred thousand dollars.

Tell us how to get ten crates of gold out of that resort with no one interfering." I was anxious to get a different take on the situation.

Maria smiled. "Ah, a challenge."

"Yeah." I smiled back at her. "And keep in mind that there are two other treasure hunters who are looking for the same gold. Dangerous dudes, I might add."

Without a pause she said, "You know what I'd do?"

James rolled his eyes back in his head. "No."

And she proceeded to tell us.

CHAPTER FIFTY-FIVE

"You know, eventually we all have to get back to our day jobs. Especially if this doesn't work out."

We grabbed some burgers across the street at the Ocean View. Sitting out back on picnic tables we looked over the bay.

"If we're due a break, and I believe we are," James drummed his fingers on the rough tabletop, "Maria had a brilliant idea."

"Don't hide what you're doing." Em took a bite from her sandwich and sat back, obviously impressed with Maria's savvy.

"Exactly," he said. "Do everything in plain sight. If you're blatant about it, people accept it. It's when you sneak around like we've been doing, that's when you get caught."

"Do you think she can pull it off within twenty-four hours?" I asked. I had serious reservations.

"That cash incentive that Mrs. T. offered should motivate her."

"I can't believe that people are that gullible." Em shook her pretty head, her golden hair swishing across her face. Maybe I just had gold on the brain.

"She hasn't pulled it off yet." Maria seemed a little too cocky. A little too sure of herself.

"No, she hasn't pulled it off yet, but I'm betting on her, Skip."

"What surprised me was that Mrs. T. agreed to fund the project."

"Again," Em pointed her index finger at me, "it's not a lot of money considering the payout. Skip, for a profit of even ten million dollars you would spend at least ten percent. Forty million means she could commit up to four million dollars. I'll bet she hasn't committed five thousand dollars. I'll guarantee this lady hasn't even come close to that amount."

She'd poured about two thousand dollars into our account and maybe she'd fronted Weezle and Markim. Not a lot considering what the reward might be.

"If she gets her money, she stole it for a song. As for Maria Sanko, the girl has a lot of moxie." Em smiled.

"Moxie?"

"You know what it means."

"I've never heard you use that word."

"Well," Em looked at James, "moxie is my middle name."

"Wait," he said. "I know this one." He studied the water for a moment as a sailboat drifted across our horizon. "Parker Posey in *Party Girl*. I'm right, aren't I? Ninety-five, ninety-six?"

"I loved that movie. Always remembered the quote."

I should have been proud of her, but somehow she was invading our turf. Movie quotes were for me and James.

We drove back to Cheeca Lodge, telling the uniformed gate attendant we wanted to see the cemetery.

"We're getting a lot of action on the old place."

"Oh, really?"

"You're the third people today. I'll go a month and not have anyone ask to see the old graveyard."

"Three people?"

"Yeah. Some single guy, then two people actually asked if there was a room that overlooked the place. I checked it out. Nobody has ever, ever asked for a room with a view of the cemetery. At least as far as we can tell."

"Really?"

"They asked for a view of the plot. Seems they have family that traces back to this piece of property."

"No kidding?" James said.

Handing us a pass, the gate attendant pointed us in the direction of the Methodist property.

It was mid-afternoon and the temperature was up in the mid-eighties as the valet drove off in James's truck.

Standing outside the fence, I gazed at the angel who had watched over the little graveyard during the worst storm in history. There she stood, surrounded by the beauty and the opulence of one of the finest resorts in the Florida Keys. The pool, ocean, suites, bar, and restaurants were just a stone's throw away.

"This is the spot." I walked it off. "There could be another nine boxes that surround the cemetery. They wouldn't have interfered with the bodies, being fifteen feet away from the picket fence, but chances are no one would mess with them."

"This evening we'll know for sure."

Maria had phoned Em. Everything was a go and the plan would go into action in the next three hours. In less than two hours, Maria Sanko had received the blessing of the hotel to dig up a portion of their precious beach and explore its suitability for sand sculptures. And they had no knowledge of what the real purpose was. The woman was a miracle worker.

Pacing the circumference of the cemetery, I happened to look up at the main resort building, directly to the west. Drapes in one of the bottom floor windows were open and there were two faces staring out at us.

245

I froze, realizing someone was watching. Someone was aware that we had an interest beyond the history of the dead bodies.

I froze, recognizing those faces. Markim and Weezle.

CHAPTER FIFTY-SIX

"Dude, you've got to be wrong."

"It was them, James. No question."

"I checked at the desk. No such persons."

"Look, they were there."

"She looked it up. The desk clerk said absolutely no one has checked into that room yet."

Closing my eyes, I pictured those two faces, staring intently at the three of us. As soon as I looked up, they disappeared. Either they ducked out of sight or vacated the room.

"James, it's never that hard to get into a vacant room. The maid is in there and you walk in and ask if she can come back later, or you catch a door when someone walks out and you grab the handle before it closes all the way."

"It's that dark side of you, partner. That's what intrigues me. That you think about things like that."

I glanced at my cell phone and saw it was almost time for Maria to arrive. Glancing up, I saw her coming out of the lodge with a guy about our age.

"Skip, James, Emily, this is Diego. He's in charge of special events here at the hotel."

He shook our hands. "I am delighted that you two want to do a practice session here. I understand your benefactress will pay us one thousand dollars for this evening."

We both just nodded our heads.

"You must be very good sculptors."

"Up and comers," Maria said. "They've won some contests in Europe, right boys?"

We nodded again.

She laid a hand on his arm. Surveying the beach, she looked up and down, then back at the cemetery.

"Diego, do you know anything about sand?"

"No."

I saw a look of relief on her face. "Good. I mean, let me tell you a little bit about what we're looking for and why the boys decided to use your beach to work on their project."

She bent down and picked up a small pinch of sand.

"We're looking for very small grain size. Maybe point one to point three millimeter grain size. And, we're looking for sand with sediment still intact. You see, clay particles and other sediment help the sand pack hard. That's what we're looking for."

"Is that what we have?"

She shook her head. "Hard to tell. We're going to be bringing a dump truck load of similar sand and a small backhoe loader. We may mix our sand with your sand. It should give us a stronger bond, better packing."

"A truck and backhoe? On our beach? You didn't say anything about a truck and a backhoe."

Maria smiled and shook her head. "Diego, please. Understand that that's why we're coming in later, so we can do this in relative privacy. No one will be on the beach at that hour and—"

"A dump truck? And a backhoe?"

"Diego,"—like a nurturing mother—like someone who was looking out for his best interest, like someone who wanted a one-hundred-thousand-dollar commission, "you get to keep the sand. And I know how it's important to renourish your beach. It's really a win-win proposition. It's going to work out very well for you."

The man frowned. "It is a worthwhile project, but—"

"We've brought yellow tape to cordon off this area. We'll run it from the building to a post out by the water. For safety reasons, you understand. We can't have people anywhere near us."

"And you're going to do this when?"

"Around eight or nine o'clock this evening. While we can still see, but most of your guests will not be outside."

He was biting his lip. "A backhoe and a dump truck. It seems like an awfully big undertaking for a practice session."

"Think about this, Diego. If the sand works, you're going to have what may be an award-winning sculpture on your beach tomorrow. You'll have it as long as you can preserve it. And, as the boys compete in national and international competitions, you'll be able to say that Cheeca Lodge had the first. The original sculpture. A giant sand sculpture of a futuristic seahorse."

"Okay, okay. We want to do this. We'll make sure that we keep people away from your operation. Just put the rest of my beach back the way you found it." He let out a deep breath. "Please?"

She smiled and touched his arm. "You're not going to regret this, Diego. It could be a huge project."

He was worried about the temporary truck and backhoe loader on his pristine beach, but dead people were right beneath the surface. I was just hoping that we didn't unearth any of them.

We hung out by the pool, Em in her white shorts and blue halter top, James and I in cutoffs and sandals.

"I still don't see how we're going to load ten crates."

"If those crates are really there," I added.

"Dude, you found one."

"Maybe."

"Ten crates, about two hundred pounds each," Em said.

James just smiled, taking a swallow of his beer. "Hey, this Sanko chick has got us this far. Ingenious, I say. Really."

"High-end sand sculpting. I saw some of those down on South Beach one year." Em sipped a rum and Coke. "Angels, naked women, Neptune, sea serpents, castles. The ideas were fabulous."

I'd made several sandcastles as a kid. Small ones, using milk cartons as molds, but the role we were playing took things to an entirely different level.

"I want to know what happens tomorrow when Diego comes out here and there's no sculpture. I mean, what happens when he calls Maria and says, 'Hey, where's my one-of-a-kind world-famous sculpture?'"

I didn't want to be here to find out.

"Maybe the sand wouldn't bond, or one of you got sick. You had a fight and broke up, you decided not to share your idea with the world at this time. Come on Skip, James. You're both born storytellers," Em said. "Surely you can think of a dozen reasons for why there's no sculpture tomorrow morning."

James was silent for a moment. He had picked up a cheap cigar from a shop up the street and lit it, puffing until the smoke streamed from his mouth. He quenched his thirst with the last swallow of beer and looked at me.

"Wonder if there's serious money in sculpting sand, Skip."

"James, we don't know the first thing about sand sculpting."

"Think about it, amigo. No bosses. You get to play in the sand and water all day," he glanced at Em, "work on a beach surrounded by bikini-clad girls who are oohing and ahhing about your work."

"You're crazy."

"Maybe not. I say we at least look into it." He lay back and closed his eyes. "I Googled it, Skip. Fifteen to thirty thousand in prize money in these contests. And you're kind of like the rock stars of the beach, huh?"

"James, we're about to embark on a project that could gross us two million dollars. And you want to play around on the sand for fifteen thousand dollars?"

I know, it sounds absolutely crazy, but James is always half serious about his business ideas. Myself, I didn't want to travel the world with a butter knife, cutting and smoothing lifeless sand into art forms.

It was eight o'clock when James and I ran the yellow tape from a pole by the building to a pole by the ocean, effectively cordoning off our section of the beach and the little cemetery.

At nine, the dump truck pulled up followed by a flatbed truck with a backhoe loader on the back. I have to admit I got a chill. Funded by Mrs. Trueblood, Maria Sanko had gotten us everything we needed.

Em, Maria, and James watched the perimeter. I supervised the dumping of a load of sand. After we'd created a mountain of the silicate and dirt, I helped the two drivers roll the tractor off the flatbed.

As advertised, the machine had a backhoe on the rear, and a bucket loader on the front. You could dig up the wooden crates with the hoe, then lift them into the truck with the front-end loader. Pretty cool.

The driver of that vehicle reached over to the passenger seat and pulled out my metal detector. The JW Fishers metal detector.

I was convinced we'd be stopped. There was no way that anyone was going to allow us to dig up ten wooden crates and then load them on a truck. We were crazy to think that Maria

Sanko had a good plan. It was a terrible plan. And on top of terrible, there was a great chance that the crates would be rotted, so we'd be faced with everyone seeing that there were crates of gold bars surrounding the old cemetery.

If there was any gold. Hell, I'd probably found a metal casket that had been buried in the last seventy-five years. This was a bad idea, a very bad idea and I—

"Hey, kid, where do you want me to start digging?"

I didn't want him to start digging at all. I was ready to call the whole thing off. Of all the hare-brained schemes—

"Here."

I walked off the spot where the metal detector had gone off.

"Man, be careful."

"We're going to scrape away one layer at a time. Inches. I understand the sensitivity of what you're doing. You've got some ancient wooden cases and you don't want to destroy them."

A very cool operator.

While he scraped, I swept the detector ahead. Nothing. Farther. Nothing. So possibly Mrs. T. had spent a lot of money on a project that was not going to produce anything. I swept farther ahead and there it was. The sound came out of nowhere and scared the crap out of me. I actually jumped. The siren was loud in my ear and very fast. Woooo, woooo, wooo, wooo. I felt a chill up my spine.

Clenching my teeth to keep from grinning, I fanned it lengthways and it stayed loud for over a foot, then tapered off.

Two possible miniature coffins. I glanced up at the windows facing the cemetery plot. They were dark. Behind the black glass could have been the eyes of two private detectives, watching our every move, but I could see nothing.

"Kid." The driver was motioning to me.

"Yeah?" I was anxious to find the next one.

"There's a wooden crate. Just like you said. Do you want me to work around it and put it in the truck? Time to decide."

There was no question.

"Yeah. Dig it up."

"Tell you what, just a point I should make."

"What's that?"

"If this is bodies we're diggin' up, there's a pretty stiff penalty for that."

"These crates aren't that big."

"I probably shouldn't admit to this," he paused, "but I actually done that before. Dug up a body. Just don't ask why."

He pushed the backhoe into the earth, pried up the wooden box, then turned around and lifted it with the front loader. It looked right. Pretty much the dimensions that were outlined in Matthew Kriegel's letter. And hopefully there was two hundred pounds of gold inside. We'd know soon enough.

CHAPTER FIFTY-SEVEN

They came up one after another. Box after box and I was ready to scream. James and Em left their posts periodically to run over and see the wooden crates.

"Team, we've got to make sure no one gets close to this site." Maria would motion for them to go back and guard the borders.

"Don't know what's in these that you want, but the boxes are well preserved." The dump truck driver stood there, puffing on a cigarette.

I was in awe as I ran the detector over another box buried about five feet below the surface. The boxes were in great shape.

"Silicate." Maria Sanko had walked up and heard his comment.

I pulled out my earplug. "What's that?"

"Sand is made of silicate. It's the prime ingredient of beach sand."

"And?"

"Under the right circumstances it gets into wood and literally petrifies it. Silicate is probably what has preserved the wood."

The lady was a fount of knowledge.

After five boxes we huddled together, high-fiving and slapping each other on the back. The two drivers must have thought we were crazy.

"Guys, here's my new idea."

Her original idea had been a winner, so we were eager to hear the latest.

"Let's have Hank fill in the holes with fresh sand. I'm simply going to tell Diego that we had to push the sculpture back one night. Something came up and we need another evening."

I pointed to the truck, loaded now with five identical wood containers, metal banding strapping the lids on tight. "But we've already got five of them in the truck. Why not go for—"

Softly, she said. "We're not sure what's in those boxes. And we can't be sure until we get to a more private location. We're taking them to this warehouse that I rent and we'll see if we're on the right track."

The evening air had cooled, and Em shivered. I put my arm around her, and looked at James.

"Sure. Maybe we've pushed our luck enough for one night."

No one had bothered us. No one had come to watch the two sculptors at their task. Thank God.

"Then it's agreed? We've gotten this far, let's not tempt fate."

Everyone nodded their heads as our two drivers stood off to the side.

"If we have success,"—even in the dark I could see the gleam in Maria's eye—"we will ask to come back tomorrow night. I don't think your banker will argue about spending the money for one more evening of digging."

"Damn," James whispered. "This is so much worse than waiting for Christmas."

James, Em, and I headed for our box truck. Maria got into the dump truck to give the driver directions and to make sure that he followed them. Right now we couldn't trust anyone.

Our guy with the backhoe smoothed the old and new sand from our pile into the craters we'd created.

"They were heavy." James kept his eyes on the road, following Maria and the wooden crates. "I tried just lifting a corner of one. I'd bet on two hundred pounds. Ladies and gentlemen, I think we've struck gold."

Em grabbed my thigh and squeezed. "I think there's one heck of a chance. I mean, it was just too perfect."

"We should have loaded them all." I wished we'd taken that risk.

"Skip," she nudged me, "if there's something else in those crates, the remains of someone's pet, or god forbid a small child, we'd have had to bring all ten caskets back and rebury them."

"Yeah. Well—"

"Dude, we're gonna be rich. I can feel it this time."

I felt it too. There was electricity in the air. Everything pointed to our really having found the mother lode.

"We're buying a new truck, partner."

"Agreed."

"And quitting those horseshit jobs we've got."

"Amen."

"And you're going to buy me some expensive jewelry, and not those crappy sea-creature jewels. Got it?" Em punched my shoulder.

I got it.

"We'll buy a fleet of trucks, Skip. Start that rent-a-truck business we talked about."

"How about your restaurant on South Beach?"

"That, too. It's going to be a party place."

"Em, James, there might not be any gold in those boxes."

We all three laughed.

CHAPTER FIFTY-EIGHT

We'd driven about four miles south when the dump truck's turn signal flashed right. James slowed down and turned off onto a crushed-shell road. The half moon was brilliant in the black sky as we followed the narrow path for two hundred feet, then saw a row of metal huts. A dim spotlight hung from the main building of the complex. The truck in front stopped, so we braked and stepped out of the vehicle.

I can truthfully say this was the most exciting, exhilarating time in my young life. I had never felt such a mixture of anticipation, fear, and confusion. Even Em, who was used to money, used to developing big projects, was shaking. We were about to discover what our treasure was.

"How are we going to unload?"

I shrugged my shoulders as Maria Sanko came around the side of the main building, riding a bright yellow forklift.

"Question answered, son." James grinned. We'd made a wise choice in finally confiding in her.

We worked getting the boxes off the truck, then sent the dump truck driver on his way. I did have thoughts that he might come back. If he suspected there was a big score, what was to stop him? But he waved and left the little storage facility, pulling back onto the highway.

In the yellow light, the four of us stared at the five crates lying an equal distance from each other on the ground. I'd never seen a prettier sight. There was a moment of silence, then my cell phone rang.

"Damn."

"Who is it?"

I didn't recognize the number.

"Well, answer it." Em was staring at me.

"Hello."

"Skip Moore?"

"Yes."

"This is Mary Trueblood."

I let out a long sigh of relief.

"What have you found out?" Lots of tension in her voice.

"We're just getting ready to open the first five crates."

"Five? Not ten?"

"I'll fill you in later."

Maria produced a pair of tin snips and started working on the first crate. Four corroded metal bands wrapped around the boxes and she cut each one. They were thin from the years of exposure and separated easily.

"Mrs. T., we're getting ready to open the first crate."

She was silent, probably praying. Forty-four million dollars in precious metal. I couldn't fathom that kind of wealth.

James and Em walked over and pulled on the lid. It wouldn't budge.

"Here, look." Maria pointed to the edge of the lid. "It's nailed shut."

"Whoever packed this wasn't taking any chances." I shrugged my shoulders. "Now what do we do?"

"Take this wrecking bar," she picked up a crowbar from the ground, "and pry it open."

"What else do you have in your bag of tricks?" James asked.

"Hey, I'm here to help you guys."

"And you're here for one hundred thousand dollars."

"That, too."

"It'll be just a minute, Mrs. Trueblood. We're working on getting the top off. Do you want me to call you back?"

"No. I'm staying on the line."

I slipped the phone back into my pocket, still connected, and went over to help. James took the first shift and he wedged the bar into a thin crease between the top and the side boards.

"This wood is solid."

"Almost like petrified?" asked Maria.

"Yeah."

"Silicate," she said.

He pried and worked that bar. We heard a creak and knew that the wood was separating. Slowly.

Occasionally we heard traffic from the road a couple hundred feet away. A rumbling truck, a car with a bad muffler, a motorcycle, a diesel engine bus. We were aware of them, but concentrating on the task at hand.

"I wish I had more of those pry bars," Maria said.

I was working it, Mary Trueblood still connected in my pocket. I'd pry and hear the creak, and the top would be just a little looser.

Half of the top was now almost free. Em took the bar and started working on the end of the box. For a slight girl, she's strong. She put her weight to good advantage and worked her way around to the far side.

"There's got to be an easier way," I said.

"More wrecking bars," said Maria, "but the Ace Hardware is closed."

"Let me take it again." James took the metal bar from Em and started prying, going faster now that the wooden top was almost free.

"Keep on prying, folks."

The sinister voice stopped us in our tracks.

"And when you're done, step back from the wooden box."

We all spun around, for the first time seeing the two scruffy guys in the dim light. The dark-haired one with the three-day growth on his face held a pistol, aimed right at Emily.

"Markim and Weezle?" James had a frozen look on his face.

"Keep prying that lid."

"Or is it Markim and Stiffle?" I asked.

The other guy, a little chubby and with lighter hair stared at me. "Stiffle is Weezle's brother. Was Weezle's brother."

"Twins?" I knew it was no coincidence.

"Keep prying."

James set the bar, and I watched him, his hands now shaking.

"Adopted?" Em studied the duo.

"Yeah. Different families. Different last names." Weezle sneered at her, the gun never wavering. "My brother was an idiot. We sent him to find the translation for that letter the Trueblood lady gave us."

"Whoa. She gave you the letter."

"We couldn't figure it out. Didn't have the code. When you two showed up with her, we figured that she'd translated it."

"And that we had the translation?"

"Keep prying." Markim stepped a little closer, his gun pointing at James's head.

The wood creaked and James moved down a couple of inches.

"And why did you kill him?" Em kept pressing.

"We didn't know you had the translation. But my dumbass brother went to your room instead of the lady's room. By mistake. Your reservation was in her name. Then the idiot calls me on his cell and is going on about how this lady's room has guy's clothes and everything. I figured that he's in the wrong room, and Mark-im and I were tired of covering his sorry ass."

"So you killed him? Pretty serious action for someone who gets the wrong room."

"I went up to straighten him out, and we got into a fight. He hit his head on the little dresser and," he paused, "you got a brother?"

I didn't. James didn't. We were like brothers, and there were times when I'd like to kill James. Still—

"No."

"I don't either. Not any more." He smiled, a cold, calculated grin.

"We kept bailing his ass out, over and over again," said Mark-im.

I did understand that.

"Keep prying."

James worked the bar again. He glanced up at me, cocked his eyebrow and I knew what he was saying. Two of them and a gun. Four of us. If we get the gun, we win. What do you think, pard?

Wiping sweat from his forehead, James looked once more at me and I nodded. These guys had taken a shot at Em and me, so I was certain they'd think nothing of shooting us now.

"It's almost off. You guys want to step up here and see what we've got?"

Weezle took two more steps and took his eyes off James, staring at the box with its raised lid.

James threw the crowbar as hard as he could, hitting Weezle across the face. Markim stopped, stunned, and I turned and hit him on the jaw. Dèjá vu. And all of us heard the explosion as a gun roared.

CHAPTER FIFTY-NINE

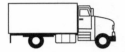

I stood there dazed, hearing the muffled voice.

"Are you there? Are you alive? Are you there? Answer me."

It took several seconds to realize it was coming from my pocket. Pulling the phone out, I shouted into it. "I'm alive."

Taking a quick survey, I saw James standing by the box, Maria cowering behind the forklift, Weezle unconscious on the ground, and Markim kneeling, holding his shoulder where blood was seeping onto his shirt. And then there was Em, standing behind the wooden coffin, her right arm hanging by her side with the pistol in her hand.

"Yeah. We're all alive."

"What was that dreadful noise?"

I took a deep breath. "Em shot Markim, and James took out Weezle with a crowbar."

"Oh, my God. What have you gotten yourselves into?"

I swallowed hard. "We're about to find out, Mrs. T. I really think I need to call you back later." With that, I clicked off the phone.

Maria had duct tape. Rolls and rolls of gray duct tape.

A forklift, a pry bar, duct tape? "What do you do with all this stuff you've got in your rental unit?" She seemed to have every tool imaginable.

"I rent properties, Skip. You need a variety of things to manage properties. I probably should take a course in plumbing, so I would have all those tools and wouldn't have to rely on phonies like you to fix my leaks."

She tossed a roll to me and one to James and we proceeded to wrap up the two PIs. We taped their arms to their sides, their legs together, then we repeated the process, over and over.

"Maybe Markim will bleed to death?"

"Nah. You shot him once before, Em. He's a tough one."

Weezle's face looked like he'd been in a heavyweight title bout. The crowbar had crunched his nose and split his lip, and there were purple bruises forming under both eyes.

"Finish opening the crate." Em turned her attention to the box. With all the excitement and the rush of adrenaline, we were at an emotional high. We had to get back to business.

I took the crowbar, wiped it on the damp grass to remove any blood, and continued to pry, leveraging my weight, my strength, to pull up the last couple of nails. I then worked around the wooden lid, prying it free. We all gathered 'round as James lifted off the cover.

"You know, we had that letter before you did," Weezle said. We'd propped him up against the forklift and a little blood was still running from his lip. "That's when we decided to find this treasure ourselves. Just the two of us. Without anyone interfering." He sniffed. "Problem was, we never figured out the damned code. So we followed you guys. We figured if the lady was with you, she'd know where the treasure map was located."

And James and I had decided to follow them, just in case

they knew more than we did. That didn't seem to be the case.

Weezle spoke like his nose was stuffed up. Actually, it was broken and the blood probably had filled his nasal passages.

"If there's any gold in those boxes, some of it should be ours."

The low-hanging light cast shadows, but we could see inside. There was a top layer of rocks, pieces of coquina and limestone that covered the surface.

I reached in and tossed them to the ground, anxious to get to the bottom of things.

Lying on the bottom of the box were small chunks of rusted iron.

"This is not possible." James stood back, a stoic look on his face.

"What's the purpose?" Em stared into the box, shaking her head.

"It's only one crate." Maria looked at the four unopened crates on the ground. "There are nine more crates. Let's not give up so fast."

Our two trussed captives looked up from their position on the ground.

"No gold?" Weezle croaked.

I bit my bottom lip.

"No. No gold. Congratulations," James said. "It appears that you guys gave up your business to find some stones and old pieces of iron."

There was a long sigh from Markim. He hadn't bled to death. Yet.

We picked the fourth crate, just to make it a random search. Twenty minutes later we popped the top. Rocks. More rocks and iron.

"Why would someone bury rocks and iron?" Maria looked like she could cry.

I sat on the ground, closing my eyes, and remembering the conversation with Bernie Blattner. It came back to me and for a moment I was almost nauseous.

"Jackie Logan."

"Who?" James was propped up against a tree.

The quiet of the early morning was cloying, and it was almost by necessity that we made noise.

"Come on, man." I was shouting. "Jackie Logan. Bernie Blattner's coworker."

"What about him?"

"Remember the story? The local pineapple growers needed to make more money, so what did Bernie and Jackie do?"

"Oh, my God. Oh, my God." Em had finally gotten the message. "They'd add scrap iron from the railroad to the shipments of fruit to up the price. It translated into more pounds of fruit. Until they got caught."

"So?" James looked back and forth at the two of us. "So?"

I turned to him, raising my arms, my palms up.

"Oh, my God, Skip." He shouted the name just as I had. "Jackie Logan. That bastard Jackie Logan."

"Son of a bitch figured it out."

"The rich son of a bitch. Damn. And this poor Matthew Kriegel, looking out for the Eastern Railway Company, is dying of fever—"

"Probably did die of fever, James. No one ever found him or the boxes. But Jackie Logan, he figures that with the right weight and the metal straps, the nails in the lid, it would take someone a while to figure out that these boxes didn't contain the original gold."

"Jackie Logan. He figures out those boxes are worth more than five dollars to haul them to a graveyard." Em sat on the corner of the box, her chin in her hands.

"He and the guys who helped bury the crates, dig them up,

open them, lift the gold, fill 'em back up and somehow take off with all of that treasure." I knew in my gut that's what had happened.

"And anyone from the railroad who dug them up would assume they still had the gold." It was all making sense. "It gave Jackie more time to get away."

"Only," James said, "no one ever came back for the gold. Until now."

"Who's going to call Mrs. T.?" Em was always the pragmatic one.

"She'll be devastated." Maria had only met her once, but knew the lady would not be happy.

"Jackie Logan. What did he end up doing?" James was pissed.

"Split the loot with the black guys who helped him, buried boxes of rocks and iron to approximate the weight of gold, and went to some other South American country. Bernie said he bought a plantation down there."

"I don't believe it. I don't believe it. I do not believe that we've been screwed like this."

"Worst part of this, James. What do you think is the worst part of this entire experience?"

He thought for a moment. "That we don't get the money?"

"No. That we can't go after the damned guy. Jackie Logan is long since dead. I'm sure of it."

"Point well taken, amigo." He breathed deeply. "And the money is long since spent, Skip."

"There's probably one more person who should feel worse than we do."

"Who's that?"

"Bernie Blattner. Bernard."

"Oh, yeah," Em said. "He turned down the moving job so he could help the railroad. And how did that work out for him?"

TOO MUCH STUFF

I felt like I'd been kicked in the stomach. Somebody had kneed me in the groin, or taken away my oxygen. There was no gold. There was no treasure. No dreams, no more surprises.

Well, that wasn't entirely true. We had a couple of surprises left.

CHAPTER SIXTY

Maria borrowed the private investigator's Harley with the gold fender that had been parked about halfway down the shell road and took off for home. We'd called the sheriff's office and left a message for Big D. We also told him who had killed Stiffle at Pelican Cove. We told him that Weezle was the same guy who took a shot at us at the Cove and whose blood had stained the walkway outside our room.

Then we called 911 and told the concerned lady who answered that there were two badly injured men at a storage lot off of the highway just south of Islamorada.

It was Em's idea to visit Mrs. T. in person. I figured she'd still be awake, and we would break the news to her gently.

"Skip, it's not the end of the world." Em was already sitting pretty good. A new Porsche, a rich daddy. James and I didn't even have a running start.

"I know. But this was going to be huge."

"Think about Mrs. Trueblood. I mean, she expected forty million dollars. Forty million, Skip."

"She did. All we expected was—"

"Two million, compadre." James shook his head, driving north on the highway. "Two million dollars. I think we'd already spent it."

We drove past the strip club, empty now at three in the morning, and down to the post office. I was the first one to see the flashing blue-and-red light.

"James. Cops."

"Damn. If we had a new truck we could outrun 'em."

"So they got the message about Weezle and Markim?" Em didn't seem too concerned.

James pulled over, gritting his teeth as the uniformed officer approached.

"Mr. Royster, I need to see your driver's license."

The young man stood ramrod straight, his hand out for the piece of plastic.

"I'm not Mr. Royster."

"Are you borrowing his truck?"

"I don't know who the hell you're looking for but I'm not—"

I reached across Em and hit him on the shoulder.

"What the—"

"James. Tell the officer."

"Tell him what?"

"We were going to report the license plate tomorrow. You know, we'd talked about driving down to the station and—"

I saw a glimmer of light in his eyes as he realized what was going on. We were driving on a stolen plate. Some guy named Royster was the owner of this license plate.

"Is this your truck?"

"It is."

"Is that your plate?"

James looked at me.

"No, sir," I said. "We believe somebody switched plates with us for some reason We have no idea why, but we just noticed it today. Well, tonight. So we thought that we'd report it first thing this morning."

And, as I said it, I thought about cameras being everywhere. Maybe they had a security camera outside the strip club where they had digital images of James taking the plate from Royster's truck and putting it on ours.

I saw the second set of lights, then the third. Three patrol cars were now parked by the side of the road.

"Are you employed by Doctor Praveen Malhotra?"

James looked at me, fear in his eyes. We'd gone from being almost killed to discovering that our fortune had vanished. Now the reviled law enforcement agents were ready to arrest us on identity theft.

"No. I think there's been some misunderstanding."

Two more officers walked up and the three of them had a short conference.

"James," I whispered quickly, "this Royster, he could have switched the plate with us, right?"

"Why? Why would he switch plates with us? I mean, I know why we switched plates with him. So we wouldn't be identified, but—"

He was back at the window. "If you refuse to surrender your driver's license, you'll have to come with us. This truck has been identified as one of several vehicles transporting illegal aliens to Miami."

"What?"

And there it was. Transporting illegal aliens. That was why Royster could just as easily have switched the plates with our truck. And it was just our luck. The one truck that we picked, the one plate in all of the Florida Keys that we stole, was owned by someone who may be a federal felon. What's the line? If it weren't for bad luck, I'd have no luck at all.

He'd drawn his weapon.

"Exit the vehicle and open the back of your truck. Now."

James bristled, I scooted out and helped Em. She clutched her bag by her side.

"Open it, sir."

My best friend's hand was shaking as he released the lever. The door creaked and rattled as it slid up and I remembered thinking we should use some of that WD-40 on our truck.

Four officers surveyed the empty interior with flashlights, causing a lightshow that bounced off every strut, panel and floor screw. I think they were genuinely disappointed that we didn't have people stowed in the back.

One of the men finally picked up the magnetic sign, studying it for a moment.

"You gentlemen are plumbers?"

I shot James a dirty look.

"No. Came with the truck."

"I'll need to see all three of your licenses."

We pulled them out and handed them to him. After carefully inspecting each one, he handed them to another officer who walked to his car. They were going to check the computer and see if we had any priors. I'd seen enough TV and movies to know how this worked.

They escorted us back into the truck and we sat there and waited. And waited. And waited.

Finally the original officer walked back to the truck.

"Sir, leave the keys in the vehicle. You and your friends are coming with us."

We were each cuffed with nylon ties, a first for Em and me, and pushed into the back of a cruiser.

The dashboard looked like some major control panel with a mounted computer, GPS, and other assorted technical stuff I was not familiar with.

"Can you please tell me what we're being arrested for?" Em had an edge to her voice.

"We're going to take you to the station until we get this sorted out."

James was strangely silent, staring straight ahead.

"What time is it?" I couldn't very well check my cell phone.

The officer checked his watch. "Three twenty-five."

"Humor us for five or six minutes."

"This is not exactly a laughing matter." He started his car.

"Officer, all I'm asking is that you drive by the vacant lot down by the Ocean Air Suites."

"I'm sorry, we're headed to the station. If everything checks out, you'll be free to go in the morning."

"Officer, we could make you a hero."

He was silent as the cruiser pulled away. James and Em both gave me strange looks.

"Listen, you said that somebody who works for Dr. Malhotra is using a truck to shuttle illegal aliens up to Miami, am I right?"

"That's what I said."

"I think there's a good chance I can show you where those illegal aliens are coming ashore. About two blocks from here."

"Skip, oh my God, it makes sense." James's eyes were big and wide.

"The vacant lot?"

"The vacant lot at three thirty a.m. I think the fishing tournament is still going on."

"Lines up at three o'clock," Em said. "Skip, you're right on the money." She bumped me with her shoulder. "What we saw those people smuggling was," she paused, "those people. I'll bet that the people we saw were being smuggled in from Cuba."

The officer pulled over to the curb, pulled out his radio, and called someone.

"This is Jakes. I'm going to need backup at the Ocean Air Suites."

There was a brief pause, then, "Ten-four. How many units would you estimate?"

He looked back at me.

"There will be two attack dogs and thirty-some people."

"Better send three or four cars."

"Three or four?"

"It's about the illegals. I've got some persons of interest who seem to think we're going to catch the smugglers in the act."

"Ten-four, John. They'll be there in a couple of minutes."

"Oh, and bring about forty Tuff-Ties."

"Forty? You've got forty people to cuff?"

"If my information is correct, we could have up to forty. That's a ten-four."

Officer Jakes turned and stared at me. "How do you know about this?"

"We stumbled onto it, officer. We just never put it together until now."

"Step out of the car."

We worked our way out and he walked behind us, cutting the nylon cuffs with a knife.

"I want you three to remain in the car at all times. Do you understand?"

"Yeah." James grabbed my arm and squeezed. "Damn, Skip. You've got to be dead on."

"The property is totally fenced in, so unless you want to jump the fence, the best place to observe and catch them is the beach down at the Ocean Air."

Jakes started up the car, getting back on the mike. "All cars, park on the street in front of the vacant property next to—"

He reached over and punched in something on his mounted computer. I could see the screen as Google Earth came into view.

"—next to eighty-two-eight hundred Old Highway."

He pulled up and parked. "Oh, and Joan, get a search warrant for that property and the adjoining properties."

"It may take a while."

"Wake somebody up. We need it now."

We were looking at each other, wondering if we should have gotten involved. We'd already had our excitement for the night and now—

"You three have jumped this fence?"

"Oh, no, officer. We just were walking the beach one night and—"

"Jumping the fence, that would be trespassing."

"Yes, sir."

He stepped out of the car and popped the trunk. We heard it close and he walked around the side of the car and up to the heavy metal fence. In the faint streetlight we saw him with what appeared to be a big pair of metal cutters.

Working the thick, rubber-coated handles, he brought the blades together and sliced that steel like butter.

"Are they allowed to do that?" James asked.

"James," Em gave him a puzzled look, "when did you ever worry about what you were allowed to do?"

"But he's a cop and all."

Within minutes he'd opened a hole wide enough to squeeze through. After putting the cutters back in the trunk, he leaned his head in the window.

"I checked that fence. There's an opening that somebody must have cut. I'm going to walk in and have a look around. For security purposes. You three—"

"We know," I said. "Stay in the car."

He worked his way through the narrow hole, fighting the trees and brush, and was lost from sight.

"I'm not staying in the car."

"No door handles." I had just realized.

James climbed over the driver's seat and opened Jakes's door. We followed.

"Now what?"

"Our usual spot?"

We walked over to the south side, kneeling down and looking through the opening in the foliage. There was Jakes, walking down by the boat dock and, almost immediately, I spotted a light just off to the east. It appeared that the boat would make an appearance this morning.

"He's going to be right in their headlight." Em pointed.

"Don't worry. He seems to be pretty sharp."

"How sharp can he be, amigo? He listened to you."

We heard the other cars pull up, the soft purr of the engines and the silence when they turned them off.

The boat was closer and now there was no sign of Officer Jakes. He'd disappeared. The west gate opened and we could hear the two dogs, their high-pitched whining now etched in my mind.

"Watch the gate by Ocean Air."

The north gate opened and I could make out the Indian doctor as he strode through. Nodding at the man who held the dogs on a leash, he moved down to the dock. The throbbing engine sound became louder and louder as the watercraft approached.

There was a gentle thump as the fiberglass boat bumped the wooden dock and then they were tossing ropes and tying up the vessel.

As before, the passengers paraded off the deck, onto the dock and dry land. The dogs sat on their haunches, whimpering, waiting to attack someone. Anyone.

Malhotra was pointing the way to the north gate, and that's when the lights came on.

A sudden burst of spotlights, some were from the squad cars on Old Highway, some were beams from heavy-duty Maglites carried by the officers. The field lit up like a firecracker and for a brief instant everyone seemed to freeze.

"¡Vámonos!" Somebody was shouting, and the Cubans started running. Some for the gate as two officers ran in, guns drawn.

There was mad scramble as the immigrants looked for an escape, and within seconds saw their only hope was to find another gate or vault the fence. Suitcases were dropped and bags were thrown at deputies as the boat passengers darted this way and that.

The dogs were yipping, growling, and roaring as if someone had let them off the leash and they had free will to maul whomever they wanted. Just as suddenly as they unleashed their fury, they were silent.

"Tranquilizer gun. Jakes called in that there were dogs. I'd bet on it," James said.

Two bodies dropped from the fence five feet from us and took off running. We backed off, crossing the street in front of the block houses.

Three more immigrants hit the sidewalk, picked themselves up, and jogged toward the highway, having no idea where they were going.

"Damn. This is a circus." James watched the action passing us by.

"We started it."

We could hear commands from inside the fence. "*Alto. Policia.*"

It seemed to have little effect. The scramble continued, and we could see shadows of people running up the street just yards away from us.

We eased along the sidewalk, back toward the police cars.

"Want to get back in?" Em asked. "It seems like the safest place to be."

"You know, our truck is just a couple of blocks away." James looked at me. "You got the extra key?"

I did.

"Let's go. I think these guys have their hands full."

"Thanks to you." The voice was cold, chilling.

He stepped out from the shadows, a pistol held firmly in his hand.

"Should have gotten rid of all three of you when we had the chance."

Dr. James O'Neill stood there, staring at us.

"I think maybe we should just walk back to my office and think things through." He wrapped his free arm around Em's throat and shoved the gun in her ribs. "I would hate to see this young woman get hurt."

We didn't argue and followed him to the office. The craziness behind us didn't seem to subside at all.

CHAPTER SIXTY-ONE

We sat in an examination room, Em on a table, James and I on chairs. The doctor stood in the doorway, the gun hanging by his side.

"The last time we met, I think you got the better of me." He smiled. "Didn't happen this time, did it?"

"The last time we met, we didn't know what a sleaze you were." James had obviously had enough of being pushed around tonight.

"I'm a businessman. An entrepreneur. And, might I add, a very successful one." His cell phone chirped and he answered.

"Praveen, I've got the three kids who are responsible. Where are you?"

He listened, nodded, then hung up.

"My friend is dodging some of the problems you caused, but he'll be here shortly."

That didn't sound promising. We'd blown their smuggling scheme and now they were going to decide our fate.

"You're bringing in Cubans using the same route that the

pineapple shippers did back in the thirties." Em was still working through it.

"It's worked up till now."

"Why? Humanitarianism? What's in it for you?"

O'Neill looked at him and smiled. "Are you kidding? You dumb, stupid child. These aren't indigent people from Cuba who are ready to beg on the streets of Miami. They're sponsored by wealthy families that live here. Families that are willing to pay for each of them."

"So you're making some pretty good money off this venture?" Even when we were in trouble, James was looking for the next business venture.

With a smug look on his face, he turned to James. "Oh, you could say that. Ten thousand a head."

"What?"

"We're averaging about three hundred thousand per boatload. We pick them up from a Cuban boat about halfway, time it so that we're part of a nighttime fishing tournament, and put them up at the Ocean Air. Then we bus, truck, or car them up to Miami. But you already figured that out, didn't you?"

"Ten thousand dollars a head?" James hadn't heard anything else.

"Until you showed up. Now, the whole business is busted."

Swinging the pistol back and forth he leaned against the door frame. "Who are you anyway? Why did you decide to mess with us?"

"Honestly, this had nothing to do with you. We're here looking for gold that was buried back in nineteen thirty-five."

He looked confused. "Then why did you—"

"Some of the information we needed happened to be buried on the vacant lot. And while we were retrieving it, your boat showed up."

"Bad luck, that."

"Maybe for all of us."

He nodded. "For you, for sure."

The outside door opened, closed and everything was silent.

"Hello, my friend." Malhotra walked up behind O'Neill.

"I assume the Cubans have scattered?"

"Some. I would estimate the cops rounded up fifteen or so."

"These three, they've pretty much destroyed any chance of our starting over."

"Thank you, kids. Because of you, we've got to get out of Dodge."

Malhotra walked over to me and swung hard, the back of his hand hitting my chin as my chair tipped over and I landed with a thud on the floor. Walking to James, he smiled.

"You're probably the brains behind everything, am I right? You look like a bright fellow." He stroked his short gray beard and studied James for a moment. "Ah, no matter." He backhanded him even harder than he'd hit me, rocking James back against the wall.

"You, missy, we'll have a special place for you when we get to Miami."

"We're going to Miami?" I asked from the floor.

"In your truck, my friend." The truck we'd left at the post office with the keys still in it. "And guess who gets to ride in the back?"

CHAPTER SIXTY-TWO

The truck rumbled and the ride was rough. All three of us were quiet, not sure if the two doctors could hear us in the cab. They'd left their fancy sports cars back at their office. They'd left everything, including our cell phones. Bits and pieces of conversation led us to believe that they had offshore accounts they could access, but it appeared to me that their days of living large in Islamorada were over. Their livelihood of smuggling for a living was over. Their lives as they knew them were over. I assumed they'd have to leave the country.

"Skip," Em whispered loudly, over the roar of the road beneath us. "I've still got my purse."

"Nail file isn't going to get us out of this jam, Emily," James said.

"No file, James. I've got the gun."

I'd forgotten all about that.

"I could shoot through the wall. We'd either hit one of them or give them a huge scare."

"I don't think we want to kill anyone."

"Pard, don't you think they plan on killing us?"

He was probably right.

"Let's think it through. We haven't been gone that long. Maybe ten minutes. Don't you think the cops are looking for us by now? Or the truck? Or Malhotra and O'Neill?" I was trying to be positive.

"I think the authorities have got their hands full trying to track down all the runaway Cubans." We knew it was utter chaos back there.

"We get much farther up the road, our lives aren't worth squat, Skip. They can pull over at any of those scenic views at this time of the morning, shoot us point blank, then toss our bodies into the ocean. Before anyone finds our remains we'll have been shark bait."

"Pray for a miracle, boys."

With that, the truck jolted to a stop. There was a loud grinding sound, a screeching noise, and we could smell smoke.

"What the hell. Did he burn the brakes?" Even in the pitch-black I knew James was on his feet pacing.

"Em's prayer was just answered, James."

There was a long moment of silence. Grumbling from the cab, both doors slamming and then we could hear them opening the back of our truck. Early morning light crept into our black cavern and there stood the two smugglers below us, frowns on their faces.

"What the hell caused this truck to stop?"

They were looking up at James and me. Em was farther back.

"Well?"

"Oh, shit." James looked at me. "We can say goodbye to the engine. No oil. It bound up."

I motioned to James. Looking down we saw no gun in O'Neill's hand.

I leaped headfirst into James O'Neill, driving him to the

ground and heard my partner hit Praveen Malhotra as he jumped on him.

I'm not a fighter, but during the last several days I'd punched a couple of people and come out on top. Straddling O'Neill, I hit him with a left, then a right, and he was out cold. At this point, I was with Em. I could have killed him and it wouldn't have bothered me.

James was struggling with the wiry Malhotra, and the Indian doctor was about to get the upper hand. He rolled James, coming out on top with his hands around my best friend's throat. I struggled to my feet, grabbed the guy by the neck of his Henley shirt, and hit him once on his chin. His eyes rolled back and he slumped back to the ground. Paybacks were hell.

"So you didn't need me at all."

Em stood on the edge of the truck bed, her gun by her side.

"I was hoping I could save you both. Then you'd owe me."

CHAPTER SIXTY-THREE

We met in Mary Trueblood's suite at one o'clock in the afternoon. I'd never seen her this angry.

"You didn't have the courtesy to call me, not once, and let me know what was going on? I can't believe that—"

"Mrs. Trueblood," I tried to calm her down. "It's not like ten things weren't happening at the same time."

"Damn, boy, you don't know how worried I've been. I hear a gunshot on the phone, you tell me not to worry, and I don't hear from you until an hour ago." She was pacing the floor, back and forth. "Damn."

"Mary," James said it almost seductively, "we're sorry. We haven't had any sleep."

"I didn't get any either. Worried about you two and—"

"We're fine."

"And Em."

Worried about her forty-four mill.

"So there is no gold?"

"We don't know that." I took the lead. "We opened two cases

and there are three more to go. We'll open those, but it's pretty clear that they will contain rocks and rusty iron. Plus, if you want to dig up the others, be our guest. It is our assumption that they are all filled with ballast. This friend of Bernie Blattner's, Jackie Logan—the one who bought a plantation in South America— we're pretty sure he went back to where he buried the boxes and stole that gold seventy-five years ago. We believe it is all gone, and we don't want to risk lifting the remaining crates at Cheeca Lodge."

"So you will go no further with this investigation?"

"There is nowhere else to go."

She let out a long sigh, eased herself down on the edge of her bed, and buried her head in her hands.

Finally she looked up.

"The sheriff's office is done interrogating you?"

I laughed. "We're 'on call.'"

"For the moment," Em said, "they are done with their inter-rogation."

"We were so close."

No one said anything. A minute went by. Another minute. I heard kids down at the pool, laughing, screaming, splashing. Bobbie was probably at the bar, chatting up some couple from North Dakota, talking about how cold it was back home.

"We were," James said, "so damned close."

"I think you boys, and you, Em, I think you did a fine job."

"Thank you."

"And no one except Maria Sanko knows anything about the gold?"

"What the sheriff's department knows is that Stiffle was killed by his twin brother because of a feud. No one is quite sure why it happened in our room."

She let out a long sigh. "It's not funny, but it is."

"They do know that Markim tried to kill me in my room with a handgun. He apparently thought that I knew about Weezle killing Stiffle."

"It just gets stranger, doesn't it?" Mrs. T. kept shaking her head.

"What sheriff's department knows," I continued, "is that O'Neill and Malhotra were smuggling in Cubans with wealthy relatives and being paid a boatload of money in the process. And that wasn't even on our schedule of events."

"What they know is that James and I duct taped the PI dudes when they tried to kill us."

"Weezle and Markim," she said. "Those two know all about the gold."

"And those two are going to keep their mouths shut." I'd thought it through.

"Because no one is certain that there isn't gold in the other eight boxes." When they finally talk their way out of the trouble they're in, if they ever do, they want to be able to come back here and dig up the remaining five crates."

"There's no gold left, is there?"

"No." James and Em said it together.

"And we finally made it clear to the authorities that it was purely by accident that we stumbled on Malhotra and O'Neill's smuggling operation."

It was all out in the open. Some of it distorted, massaged, and spun like fine silk, but there was a grain of truth in everything we told the cops. It's just that we never mentioned the gold. If Mrs. T. wanted to keep looking for her treasure, more power to her. We'd pretty much made up our minds that there was no future in our search for Kriegel's gold.

"I'm going to write you three a check for three thousand dollars. That should cover things."

We'd thought the party was over.

"The engine on my truck, that's going to be right around eleven hundred bucks, rebuilt."

She sighed. "Okay, James. I'm writing a check for four thousand dollars. Although technically, those two doctors were not my concern. Go buy yourself an engine."

I looked at Em and James. Three thousand dollars for the gold coins, four thousand dollars from Mrs. T., and a rebuilt engine for James. For James and me, not bad.

"Maria Sanko did do a lot of work."

Mary Trueblood gave me a dirty look. "Don't press your luck, boys."

"One last drink at the bar? Maybe a dip in the pool? This could be our last stay at a resort for a long time." I hated to think about it.

"You guys go ahead," James said. "I'm going to walk over to Rumrunners and see if Amy is there. There's something I needed to know."

He left and Em and I walked hand in hand to the pool bar.

"So you made some money."

"We made some money. But I am going to talk James into parting with a couple hundred bucks for Maria."

"We've been through a lot in our young lives," she said.

"We have."

"There's no one else I'd rather go through stuff with."

I hesitated before I spoke.

"You're not saying what I think you're saying?"

She laughed. "Heavens no. I'm just saying that—"

She kissed me.

I don't know where we're going, but there's never a dull moment.

AUTHOR'S NOTE

In 2012, Florida, the East Coast, and The United States of America will celebrate the centennial of Henry Flagler's historic railway. Nineteen twelve was the year that Flagler connected mainland Florida to Key West. The railroad pioneer lived to see the completion of his dream project, then died the same year. In 1935, a hurricane and twenty-foot tidal wave in Islamorada, Florida, destroyed the town and the railroad, killing over five hundred people.

Ninety-five percent of the historic information about Flagler's railroad and the 1935 hurricane described in *Too Much Stuff* is true. Firsthand accounts of the horrific details are documented in a number of journals, and I was able to talk to several historians who painted a graphic picture of what life was like after the storm. Through a letter and an interview with a fictional hurricane survivor, I believe that I have captured an accurate portrayal of the aftermath of the catastrophic destruction.

By the time this book releases, the value of the lost gold may be even more than the presumed value of forty-some million dollars. That should make it even more attractive for the treasure hunters. Skip, James, and Emily exist only in my mind (don't tell them that) and I am always flattered by the review from *Booklist*, comparing Skip's storytelling to the narrative style of Mark Twain's Huck Finn.

Oh, the 5 percent of the historical information that is fictional? You'll have to figure that out for yourself.

DATE			